Mea Culpa

Mea Culpa

Catherine R. Seeley

Library of Congress Number:		2002095366
ISBN:	Hardcover	1-4010-7947-4
	Softcover	1-4010-7946-6

DISCLAIMER

This is a work of fiction. The characters, incidents and conversations are products of the author's imagination and are not to be construed as real. Any resemblance to actual events or persons, living or dead, is entirely coincidental.

This book was printed in the United States of America.

To order additional copies of this book, contact:
Xlibris Corporation
1-888-795-4274
www.Xlibris.com
Orders@Xlibris.com

16855-SEEL

Acknowledgements

The first thank-you must be to Mary T. O'Neill for her great belief in "can," which magically afforded me the conviction and time with which to write. To author, Mary Higgins Clark, the deepest of thanks for her kindness and encouragement. Thanks to other dream catchers Mary O'Hora, faithful muse; Jackie Penney, artist/sage of Cutchogue; Moe Carey, pathfinder artist; Rosemary McCauley, gate keeper and "psychic;" graphics genie, Kas Carey of Carey Graphics.

Some of the best lines were inspired by Tuesday Night Dinner Club friends Maureen Ryan, Gert McGovern, Kathy Thomas, Peggy O'Neill, Suzanne Muccio, and Casey Lee. Jack McGovern and Jim McGovern, New York's Finest; Chief Tommy McKavanagh, New York's Bravest and dear wife, Mary Ann, all helped with technical details. Bridie Lane and Gertrude McGovern, Sr. have been my Celtic pray-ers throughout this project.

The keyboard kept clicking thanks to encouragement from siblings Ann Seeley; Mary Seeley Klair and husband, Jim Klair, my legal eagles. Hugs to niece, M.Courtenay Barranco and to nephews, Jeff C. Barranco; Greg, wife Allison, & baby, Luke Porter Barranco; David O. Barranco; loyal cousin, Judy Reitz Muhl and husband, Bob; and everyone's favorite aunt, Wonita Kelly. Dear parents, Catherine Ann Kelly Seeley and Roy Crofford Seeley, are remembered and thanked for all as regularly as is the One with whom they now reside.

Chapter 1

Winter / 1966

No sooner had Tommy Brogan glanced up at the picture of his daughter in her postulant's outfit on the day she entered the convent, than the scratchy squawk of the dispatcher's box popped on snapping him out of his fantasy about how she'd look much better in a wedding gown. He sighed "oh well," and grabbed his pen to jot down the location of the fire being called in on the board. The phone rang in perfect synchronicity to the alarm; no doubt another report of the same event. Eyes and descriptions are always better than buzzers and lights, he mused to himself.

"Tommy?"

"Yeah. Who's this? Can you hold on?"

"No I can't and don't cut me off! It's Ford. I'm on my way home from Mackie's card game and there's an all alarmer, fully engaged at the Marafield campus!"

"Marafield! My God, my daughter's there! What the hell are you talking about, Chief?"

"I can't tell which building it is yet, but the flames are shooting above all the houses on Talbot Street so it's not a trash can, that's for sure. I'm heading north on Talbot looking straight at it. The sky's one big ball of orange. You're going to need every piece of equipment from anywhere you can get it and pronto! Don't wait for me to call back; get on it now!"

"Chief, what's your exact location ?"

"I'm just entering the southwest gate of the campus and, Jesus Christ, Tommy! It's the nuns' building, the Motherhouse! Get Ryan to relieve you and jump on the truck with the others; you'll be useless there worrying about your daughter. I'm in the house wagon. You, Mills, and Driscoll report to me as soon as your feet touch the campus. I'm at the campus post office at the side gate and will command from here. You hear me, Brogan? Keep your head on straight when you get here and see me first. Ten-four."

Chapter 2

Half a mile away, at the bottom of a run on the northeast slope of the campus, a gang of about eleven seniors and juniors huddled around the last licks of a steel drum fire. The sweet cedar embers and the pinecones, tossed in for glow's effect, walled them in their own world, sweetly separating them from any consciousness of the rest of the campus. From way down here it was just stars and woods.

For this small Catholic women's college, this benign Courier and Ives scene represented life on the edge according to the handful of nun rules that were being broken by these "brazen hussies."

Rule: under no condition were cafeteria trays to be removed from the cafeteria. None of those starched dames could possibly know what outrageous sleds these trays made on "Penguin Hill" after a good New England snow storm.

Rule: on weeknights, all students must be back in their dorms by 11:00pm since the library closed at 10:30, the only legitimate excuse for true students to be out after dark. Right.

Rule: absolutely no open fires were to be set anywhere on the 300 acre campus. Footpaths winding throughout the ravine were conveniently dotted with perfect campfire settings: rings of substantial rocks encircled the remains of years of previous fires and logs had been arranged around the perimeter for comfortable gatherings. Some good scouts even left a tidy pile of wood for the next visitors. Try and let the nuns find them.

Gert McGedney, dorm prefect; Maureen King; Suzanne Hartsdale, and Peggy Kielty, all senior class officers, were the first ones to start heading back up the hill toward the dorms. With graduation only a few months away they couldn't afford to be caught with such disregard for the rules they were expected to uphold and, for that matter, help enforce. They were in their final season of "last time" sentiments and choices were governed more by "the last time we'll get to do this" than by fealty to rules.

It was so quiet crunching through the drifted snow, and so beautiful with the moonlight's trading of barren birch for licorice sticks strewn throughout the icy blue woods, that none of the girls spoke above a whisper. Puffs of steamy exhalations curled and wafted around the hoods of their parkas as they hiked back toward the dorms.

Over half a mile away now, the staccato hoots and yells of the remaining others slit the velvet aura in which these first prodigal daughters all sensed they had been surrounded. Coming from somewhere beyond them, the contra tenor plainsong of fire engines could be heard weaving a warning of danger not so far away.

Subtly and gradually, the midnight blue cast upon the snow began slipping into other hues. Those who've stood on shores at sunset and noted the pastel scarves of blue and gray, then gold and orange and pink being draped over the horizon by day's end will understand the awareness to which the girls began to awaken.

"Are my eyes going, or is it getting a little pink out here?" Suzanne asked at random.

"Hey, yeah," agreed the others.

It was when they climbed up the final bank that leveled off onto the side yard of the nuns' Motherhouse that they dropped their cafeteria trays and instinctively grabbed onto each other's sleeves. Carefree seniors no more, they were freeze framed in disbelief at what boiled before them.

The entire four story building that housed the "Junior Sisters" and college professor nuns blistered with flames slathering and rolling around and over every surface. From where these errant five stood, they actually began to feel a cloak of comforting warmth press against their fronts, while the polarity of terror and shock made them shiver with confusion at what to do next.

Fires and oceans emanate the same sound from their massive bodies, a roar that makes it almost impossible to hear human voices. So the blood-chilling screams of the fire's victims became muted in the undulating sea of fire and the weakening pleas of those critically injured by it were, mercilessly, rendered inaudible. Miraculously, the wind curled back toward the seniors and delivered into their consciousness a final ragged chorus of screams, launching them out of their stupor and into action.

"Keep coming, keep coming! Go to your left, your left! Please hurry! There're a lot of us and some are unconscious. Come on! Hurry up! For God's sake, hurry up!"

"We're trying!" Peggy shouted back in the direction from which she thought the voice was coming. "We can't see where you are though! Keep yelling; we'll find you!"

It was pitch black. All of the arriving fire trucks were lined up on the west side of the building. Kleg lights, thrown onto the four story brick structure from that side, steeped the east side of the building in contrasting darkness, blinding the girls as they trudged into the beams following the calls for help. The freshly fallen four feet of snow considerably handicapped how close to the building and how far around it the trucks could get.

Peggy panted, "This is crazy! There's not one fire truck over here!" Turning to Gert she said, "Let me run over and tell those guys there are people hurt over here. The rest of you keep looking for the nuns."

One of the young Sisters, who had jumped from the fourth floor and landed in a snow drift that nearly buried her broken body, watched with horror as Peggy's shadowed outline took off in the opposite direction from where all the injured lay. Heaving herself up on her knees, she screamed at her, "Where are you going? Don't leave us! We'll die! Please don't leave us!"

That energy of desperation was the radar on the map. "There they are!" exploded Gert and, as she ran toward the kneeling figure, the young nun doubled over at Gert's approach and sobbed into the snow a mixture of tears and blood.

Chapter 3

High above where Gert found the first of the wounded nuns, were three dorms on this side of the fourth floor of the building. Two small dorms housed sixteen Junior Sisters who had returned at the end of December after a semester away from campus "student teaching." These nuns were seniors at the college who would graduate in May and then be sent "on mission." The other larger dorm on the fourth floor housed forty younger sisters who were in their junior year in college. All the dorms were long open spaces with fifteen foot ceilings, impossible to heat in winter and sweltering in summer.

Running the full length of the dorm above the center aisle were three separate light bulbs –just the bulbs– dangling from solitary black cords with pull chains for "off" and "on," the only lighting available in the dorms. From the ceiling was suspended a maze of iron piping that also ran the length of each dorm about seven feet above the floor. Each wall had a series of additional pipes anchored into it that went from the wall out to the aisle piping and connected to it with elbow joints. From this piping hung as many white canvas curtains as there were "cells" in each dorm.

These curtains surrounded the entire cubicle that comprised a sister's private "room" of single bed, a straight back wooden chair, and an upright single-door metal locker in which habits were hung and all other personal things were kept. During the day, all curtains were to be pushed completely back against the walls, displaying the perfection of made beds and the stark unadornment of cells. No dorm was carpeted. All floors were wooden and the walls were wainscotted from the floor up to approximately four feet. Decades of weekly dusting and waxing kept the wood in its rich color and luster and, now, cruelly served to fuel the fire.

By all accounts of those who were asleep in those dorms the night of the fire, what woke them up was either the screams of their dorm mates or the bright crimson flames and intense heat they saw and felt from the curtains burning around their beds. It was too fast to assess. Dozens woke from sound sleep and instantaneously leapt through a curtain of fire without knowing what they were running into on the other side. Once there, it got no better. The fire knocked out all electricity and in the bedlam of this mounting disaster, enveloping smoke and growing flames created disorientation. "Where are the doors?" "Where are the stairs?" "We can't see the windows!" "How do we get out?"

Voices yelled back answers that the doorways and staircases were gone, totally engulfed. "Get to the windows! We have to go out the windows!" someone directed and a few others echoed the escape route in shouts up and down the dorms. No one thought she would survive jumping from the window sill of the fourth floor as she stepped up to it, terrified, trembling, hesitant. It simply was the only option.

Some souls, either brave or numbed by shock, climbed up onto the sill and sprang off as if the height were that of a curb. Others had to be coaxed, helped and even forced. Sister Maura, the former Siobhan Greene, commandeered a window in one of the smaller dorms and helped her dorm mates up onto the ledge, giving quick instructions of how best to jump to minimize injury. Keeping an eye on the fire that was closing in on them, she snapped orders and forced people up onto the ledge and then off into God knew what fate, but it was the only way.

The last sister to get to the window was the worst. She would not go; she couldn't. She was paralyzed with fear. Sister Maura grabbed her by both shoulders and screamed at her, "Move! Move! I'm not leaving you here! If you don't jump and jump right now we'll both die, do you understand me? We'll both die! I'm not leaving you! Now get your rear up on that ledge! We'll go together. Come on, dammit: NOW!"

With that, she heaved and pulled Sister Jane DeChantal up onto the ledge, counted to three, and then pushed her from behind before the woman could change her mind. Sister Maura framed herself in the center of the window and, for a second, envisioned her jump the way she used to do on her high school diving team. Then, aiming herself toward a clear patch of snow and away from those scattered below her, she took the biggest leap of faith in her life.

Chapter 4

In the largest dorm on the fourth floor, a similar scenario was nearing completion. Two windows, one at the north end and one in the center of the dorm, were being used as the only remaining escapes out of the inferno that trapped them all. Sister Ciarin grabbed Sister Hildegarde from the cell next to hers and drafted her into helping herd the other thirty-eight toward the only two available exit windows. "There's no other way out, Hildie! Go to the next window and make everyone climb up and jump whether they want to or not! I'll cover this window. You cover that one. We have about sixty seconds to get everybody out of here or we're dead. Okay, Hildie? Be brave! We can do this; we HAVE to do this! God bless you, Hildie! God be with us all! Now get going!"

Sister Hildegarde's legs could barely support her as she ran to her assigned post. The curtains on the other side of the dorm were all ablaze and now the curtains on the windowed escape side were beginning to ignite at the end of the dorm, finally claiming the entire dorm inch by inch. With each "whoomph" that could be heard as a new curtain caught on fire, the two escaping clusters of nuns pressed in closer to the windows, trying to help each other up onto the sill for the jump that would either kill them or save their lives.

Hildie parroted the orders she heard Ciarin shouting at her station and tried to sound as brave and confidant, but she knew her own was a false bravado and she fought fainting as each new person stepped up to the window sill to jump, looking to her for strength.

Finally the last sister had made the dreadful climb onto the window sill and leapt. The relief that swept through Hildie because those in her charge had gotten out, allowed her to now feel all the terror she had masked so heroically for the sake of the others. Feeling her legs buckle, she held onto the window sill and half sank to her knees. She tried to muster whatever courage remained, but sadly realized it had all been spent. From far below she could hear Sister Ciarin calling her name, crying her name in pain riddled anguish, over and over and over, getting fainter and fainter.

Hildie grew dizzier and dizzier as her lungs filled with the thick white hot smoke that swirled around and past her, billowing out the windows. She gave one last superhuman effort to raise herself to a standing position, and leaned out the window to try and breathe so she could climb up onto the ledge and force herself to jump. The ice cold air swathed her face and her hands as they clutched the exterior ledge of the sill. For a fleeting second or two she became aware of the contrasting temperature of the furnace that roared at her back. Suspended in the confusing slow motion enjoyment of the comforting sub zero temperature that cooled her, she somehow became removed from the scene as victim and surreally lapsed into becoming observer.

Within her, a convergence of images and words, perhaps hallucinations, met in these final flashing seconds: her certainty that she would never be found; her grief laden family; her dorm mates who would suffer the inevitable "survivor guilt"; the sound of the Christmas hymn, "See Amid the Winter's Snow," that filled the chapel just weeks ago; her grandmother and younger brother, both deceased, whom she sensed with certainty standing on both sides of her; the books she had borrowed from the library; her favorite passages from scripture that now came to mind; the letter to her sister that would remain unfinished; prayers from vespers that came unbidden; the complete dissolution of the marrow-deep terror she felt; the surprising calm that now, mysteriously, overtook her.

Thick white smoke peppered with millions of sparks raged around and over and past her body and out the window. Hildie could hear her own voice softly, calmly recite,

" 'Some say the world will end in fire, some say in ice' . . . Frost or Sandburg? I know, I remember: Frost . . . Frost . . . Hail Mary, full of grace, the Lord is with thee . . . Dear God, please be with my mother this night; help her and my family in the days to come . . ."

The white knuckles that gripped the window ledge involuntarily began to lose their hold, and her overly strained body slowly slumped back down the inside of the ledge and against the wall. Her arms still stretched across the wide sill holding her in an upright kneeling position. "Holy Mary, Mother of God, pray for us sinners now and at the hour of our death . . ." She could feel consciousness ebbing from her, so she rested her head on the window sill. Struggling to lift her head in order to take a last glimpse of the temporal world, her sight line caught snatches of the white covered hills of the Marafield campus in between the full drafts of smoke that rolled through the window.

As if answering the desperate calls she could still hear from four stories below, she spoke into her arms that now cushioned her forehead. "I hear you dear Ciarin . . . I almost made it . . . don't worry, be well . . . O God come to their assistance." Her eyes widened in new found wonder and she said, "look at all the snow . . . when did it snow? . . . it's so beautiful . . . O Lord . . . let my prayer rise like incense before thee . . ." At twelve forty three on Monday morning, the first day of February, the soul and prayer of twenty year old Sister Hildegarde Noonan did exactly that.

Chapter 5

On the west side of the building, the fire drills that each dorm conducted twice a year were kicking in with the precision you'd expect from this no nonsense college. Double lines of college students, armed with two blankets each, snaked along the campus down to the only available exit from this enormous "motherhouse" that housed one hundred and fifty nuns.

The back porch door had not become engaged yet by the fire that wrapped itself around every inch of this landmark building. So through it came scores of sisters in all manner of nightdress. The students closest to the back porch would go up in groups of four to the escaping nuns, place blankets around their shoulders and escort them to the farthest dorm. Then the next four girls would step up and repeat the exercise innumerable times in ten degree weather. Every dorm on the campus had out performed anyone's wildest imaginings under such shocking circumstances at 12:45 in the freezing, snow blanketed morning.

The sisters who emerged first from the burning building were the older sisters and those who were professors at the college. Had it all not been so fierce and terrifying, there were countless opportunities for screaming laughing at some of the "get-ups" worn by these otherwise dignified women.

Some were toothless, some wig-less, all bra-less and massively drooping and flapping in those nun night gowns that were, of course, white or pastel yellow or "our Lady's" pale blue. Most managed to yank something out of somewhere and put it on their heads as a make shift veil.

The best combo was when some came out in nightgown, bonnet and veil with the long fifteen decade rosary, usually worn around the waist cincture, tossed around the neck like an Isadora Duncan scarf. In weeks to come, when the shock of this night would finally wear off, these women would eventually look into the eyes of every student and recall with horror the knock that convent "mystique" took that night.

It seemed that only one sister managed to have either the presence of mind or the speed of her much more youthful age with which to be completely dressed in full habit, including shoes and stockings. Her crucifix and rosary must have been out of reach though, in the total darkness that enveloped the building and were the only parts missing.

Since the young sisters in the building were actual classmates of the college girls, the sight of this younger, fully dressed nun hurrying out with the others lifted the girls' spirits that their classmates were, thank God, safe and about to soon emerge. All eyes were on that back door waiting, searching for the familiar peer to emerge.

Suddenly, the right back quadrant of the building fiercely groaned like Godzilla and, in what seemed to be slow motion, heaved to the left and began toppling over floor by floor, spewing sparks and flames like hot lava in a downward arch. That's when the crying and screaming began to tear through this silent movie of disciplined efficiency. Everyone on campus knew that what had just fallen into disintegrated rubble was the section of the motherhouse where all the young "Junior Sisters" lived. It would be a full day before the firemen would make their horrible discovery.

Seconds before that collapse, the final few nuns had just cleared the porch and were whisked away to safety. No one else followed; the line of evacuees had stopped. The portion of building that had fallen caved in the far end of the back porch and now the porch was becoming fully engaged, the fire seeping its way toward the only escape door.

The firemen started screaming for the girls to move back to their dorms but no one moved. Everyone was still fixed on that door and to move now would be to give up hope. Where were they? Where were all those beautiful, young shining faces? While the nuns were emerging from that doorway just minutes ago, you could look down the long corridor and see all the bobbing heads making their way to safety. Now, however, there was no visibility, only a dense white mist that looked like steam floating ethereally. No one came down the corridor to disturb the thickening smoke.

Campus maintenance men, neighbors and students with cafeteria trays frantically had shoveled a clearing in the back of the building to make the delivery entrance to the Motherhouse accessible. At last, fire trucks backed into the area right off the back porch and men raced to find hydrants buried in snow.

One truck aimed its contained water canon at the last remaining part of unscorched wood and was about to open the valve when the crowd started yelling at the top of their lungs, "No! No! Wait! Here they come! Here they come! Wait!"

With that, three firemen jumped up on the porch yelling and waving their arms at the aimed canon, "Hold it! Hold it! Hold it!" While one stayed to make sure the men on the truck understood, the other two firemen headed into the building, whipping the thick cotton into wild swirls that billowed out the door behind them.

In seconds, two gasping, charred women in pajamas that were completely blackened with smoke and soot, burst out the door gasping for air with the two men that went in after them. Only the whites of the eyes and teeth of the junior Sisters Mary Shannon and Brigid Marie, could be seen by the onlookers, along with the sheets of white paper each clutched to her chest.

Those papers well could have cost them their lives. It was in the midst of the chaos and the "running for their lives" of scores of women, that these two had the simultaneous realization that there would be no way to account for all the junior sisters without a list of some sort. They knew that three of the dorms were complete furnaces.

Both desperately had tried to get through to their friends in those engulfed dorms but were turned back by floor to ceiling walls of flame. The shock of knowing their friends were on the other side of that inferno nearly paralyzed them both till Mimi, suddenly aware of their own peril, screamed at Kate and pulled her out of her frozen horror.

That is when they knew having a list was imperative. The two, Sister Mary Shannon, the former Kate Fitzmaurice, and Sister Brigid Marie, known in secular life as Mimi Aroho, ran toward the Directress of Junior Sisters' office and, of course, found the door locked. Dragging a chair from the library across the hall, they helped each other lift and heave it through the frosted glass of the door. Once inside, they grabbed the first complete listing of names they could find in the smoky pitch dark and bolted.

As they raced from the office on the third floor down the long polished corridor, the walls and woodwork sweated, blistered, and then popped into flame almost in synchronicity with each step they took. Each staircase they encountered, every corner they turned roared hot red flames in front of them.

Their options finally were narrowed to just two possible escape exits: the chapel or the kitchen. They were now beginning to encounter more smoke than their lungs could handle much longer and fear within was rising. Somehow Kate instinctively knew to avoid the area above the chapel with its wide opened space and jet wind drafts so she yelled, "This way, Meem! We won't get through any other way!" It was the longest possible way out of the building but the only one left to them now.

Finally, they reached the back staircase leading to the kitchen area and the coolness of the banister offered the relief that they could get out this way. At the same time that Mimi and Kate's bare feet landed on the freezing cold marble of the ground floor, they heard the commotion of the firemen yelling for the college students to go to their dorms. They were okay now; the back porch door was at the end of the corridor and they ran toward it not by sight but by rote, and surely with the grace of God.

Chapter 6

Winter / 2000

Kate Fitzmaurice's last appointment of the day had been a doozy and a glass of wine with her shoes off at her home in Cape Porpoise, Maine, was just a mile away. A middle aged nun had come for her first counseling session and it had been exhausting. Kate had been troubled at the edgy impatience she kept monitoring in herself throughout the entire session.

The nun's affect was all off: smiling her way through her sad account of her brother's death and her very refined rendition of "dealing with it." This woman may have presented herself for grief counseling, but her sibling's death was only one among the many issues Kate assessed simmering beneath the more "appropriate" emotion of sorrow.

As an ex-nun, Kate could read a "lid," as she jokingly referred to nuns, the way radiologists read x-rays. Her twenty-four years in the convent gave her distinct insight into that lifestyle and a reputation as a good referral for nuns and clergy, though they did not dominate her busy practice. Nowadays she fit them in as a professional "courtesy." She had done quite a lot of homework of her own before and after leaving the convent and, for all her flippant referral to them as "lids," she was always soft to help one of them work toward greater freedom, whatever its guise.

She was a strong believer in the axiom, "the quality of one's life is in direct proportion to the quality of the questions one is willing to ask oneself." She had great respect and endless patience for people in those vulnerable times of honest investigation. Conversely, she had no tolerance for "phony baloney" and thought nothing of naming it on the spot, telling the client to come back when she or he was ready to deal honestly with issues.

She was willing to continue seeing this last appointment of the day, and directed her to see Rosemary, the secretary, on the way out to make an appointment for the next week. A routine soon would follow: Rosemary would see the woman out, come back to Kate's office, lean against the doorway and the games would begin.

"Another 'live' one, huh?" Rosemary teased. "I've gotten so good at this! Not only can I spot a nun a hundred yards away no matter HOW hard they try to look 'with it,' I can even tell in ten words or less when I've got one on the phone! They do that 'precision-speak' thing, y' know? And they all swear to be your 'long lost friend from Killala!' You give too many talks; everybody wants an appointment after they hear you. You better start cutting back a little; there's a lot of room for improvement in that department, if you ask me." One never needed to.

Kate called Rosemary the "pit bull receptionist." Absolutely no one got past her to just "drop in for a second" to Kate's office, and for that Kate was grateful that you actually could take the woman out of New York, but you couldn't take the 'New York' out of this woman! Transplanted from The Rockaways to this rocky coast city of Portland, some folks were even intimidated by Rosemary's brusqueness which, back in New York, was considered cheery efficiency.

Kate shook her head in mock disbelief at Rosemary's latest assessment. She did enjoy her instant "takes" on people that often proved uncannily accurate, and both women shared an understanding and respect for how close to the line of confidentiality they could play. It was no secret between them of Kate's "other life" as she referred to her many years in religious life. Which is why Rosemary loved to go into her "I Spy a Nun" routine for her.

Chapter 7

Second generation Irish American, Kate Fitzmaurice looked pretty much like half of the middle aged women you might see at Dunne's Pub, where she did enjoy a decent pint of Murphy's Amber. She had fair complexion, rosy cheeks, blue eyes and, thanks to L'Oreal #9a, mid-length light ash blonde hair that looked pretty darn natural. None of the Fitzmaurice "girls" had a chance in that category, since their mother's hair was cotton white by the time she turned thirty. If one of the daughters caved in now and went "natural" the cover would be blown for the others.

Kate was tall, ever longing for the preferred shape of yesteryear but too sedentary and overbooked to repossess it. She had two styles of clothes: tailored, Talbots or Brownstone Studio, and casual: khaki, denim, oxford, mock turtle necks, Aran knits, fleece vests, loafers or Timberlands.

Whatever she showed up in at work told you her schedule in a glance faster than a day-planner. Suits meant meetings, lectures, consultations or "glad handling the martini crowd for some money for the facility." Casual indicated persons were returning for appointments or she was catching up on paper work. She had a little fuddy-duddy rule that first-time appointments would not be met in casual clothes. She felt it established for the client that this time and this person would be taken seriously by her.

Kate Fitzmaurice was one of the funniest people you could ever imagine to be a therapist. Yet she was excellent, nearly clairvoyant. She could deftly and accurately sort out the circumlocutions of the most distraught or tortured soul sitting in front of her. She never took notes, but had this technique of envisioning a little flag driven into a word, phrase or sentence just spoken by a client to which she intended to return at the right moment. She always returned.

It amazed persons spilling out their sagas that someone had been so attentive to their every word and nuance. It baffled them that, from week to week, she precisely remembered the content and tone of every single previous session and steered them along contiguously. And, it was with sheer incredulity that clients heard themselves having good belly laughs with a therapist they had initially dreaded meeting.

Something about her manner with everyone, whether dirt poor, filthy rich, well educated and articulate, or lacking opportunities and bumping along, presented Kate as a "companion" to them through their travail rather than as some "grand guru of psycho-dynamic therapy." Savvy about the old superior/subject, dominant/subordinate models of the past, she was careful and deliberate in her model of mutuality and respect in any arena in which she participated.

Also, she understood that essentially all humans are experience-rich but vocabulary-poor in times of crisis, and that her job was to help people put expression on experience. Otherwise, when things are left unexpressed, they inevitably turn into behavior. So about twenty-five years ago, Kate Fitzmaurice elected to help make peace on earth by assisting one troubled person at a time.

It seemed more than ironic, then, on this particular nun-laced evening, that when she got home and played back her voice mail, Kate had heard from three different women with whom she had been in the novitiate over thirty years ago. All, like Kate, were long out of the convent and lived in different parts of the country.

One of the callers, Mimi Aroho, had remained a constant friend and Kate and she spoke on a fairly regular basis. The second caller, Siobhan Greene, was also perennial though with longer stretches between calls and get-togethers. The big surprise caller was Annie Silo, who had not been heard from nor seen since the sixties when they were all together as young Sisters at Marafield in Dunhill, Massachusetts.

Kate stopped dead in her tracks when she heard her message. "'Fitzie?' This is a blast from your past! Give up? Well, it's Annie Silo calling from Denver! Can you believe it? So how the hell are you? Still pumping the beads?" Her laugh, tumbling out between every sentence, was proof positive of her identity even after all these years.

You could tell that Annie was calling on a cell phone from some highway. She continued, "Look, I'll call you tomorrow night when I can talk more, but for now I just want to give you a heads up on something. Be sure to watch 'Crime Line' tonight. Someone we both know from our long ago pasts is going to be the feature story, so be sure to watch it. Make sure you watch it, Fitzie; I think some old bones are about to be dug up and they could do a pretty good tap dance if the music's right. Take care, Fitz! Gotta go!"

Before she could find the "replay" button on the answering machine to absorb all that had just been said without the surprise factor, the next message began. "Kate? Hi there! It's Siobhan . . . Siobhan Greene. How are you? I've got a rather strange message I'm passing on to you; I hope you get it in time. Do you remember Annie Silo? Well, she left a message on my machine telling me to watch "Crime Line" tonight and that I should pass the same message on to you if I could track you down before nine!"

Siobhan had a little giggle going on as she continued, "I have no idea what the show is about or why we're supposed to watch it. She just said that someone we all know from our novitiate days is going to be on and that everyone in our group should see it. I feel like I'm in 'Murder She Wrote' with Jessica Fletcher! Wonder what's going on? I'm definitely going to watch. I hope you get this in time! Will you give me a call after the show? Bye, Kate. Talk to you soon!"

Chapter 8

Kate went into the living room shaking her head in amused disbelief, turned on a light, picked up the Portland News and paged through to the t.v. listings searching for Crime Line's air time. Twenty minutes to go. Moving to the kitchen, she poured herself a glass of cabernet sauvignon, took two slow appreciative sips, heated some soup and went down to the bedroom to change her clothes and put on jeans, turtleneck and sweatshirt. She noticed a little tinge of excitement coursing through her as she slipped into her boiled wool clogs and headed back to the kitchen to get her chowder and go into the den in time for "Crime Line."

"What is this all about?" she asked the air in the den as she pushed the power button on the remote. "'Someone from the novitiate' . . . and on 'Crime Line'! I can't even begin to imagine." With that, anchorwoman Jane Early introduced the show with a pre-commercial promo, "Tonight a female teacher tells her story of being stalked for months by another female teacher in her very own school. Join us when we come back for 'The Stalked Teacher' on this evening's edition of 'Crime Line.'"

Kate worked on her soup while the commercials ran and looked up when the show resumed. The host of "Crime Line" began the segment with a "brief" about the rise in reported stalking incidents over the past few years and about the psychological toll it takes on its victims. As she talked, she moved away from the backdrop graphics that supported her words.

Crossing the set toward a woman seated in one of two club chairs to the right of the screen she continued, "With us tonight is a teacher who has been living this nightmare for nearly two years." Perfectly timed, Jane Early reached her chair and sat across from her guest as she said, "Josephine Quarters, welcome to 'Crime Line' and thank you for being here." The name didn't ring a bell at all. It was the close-up that did it.

The woman addressed by Jane Early sat stiffly with ankles crossed just off to the left of the chair's center, hands resting on top of one another on her lap. She leaned forward just enough to keep her back from resting on the chair's cushion. She wore an uninteresting steel blue dress with a cowl neckline and push up sleeves. Her hair was a brittle looking mousy brown that swept down to her eyes and was shoulder length; a kind of Loretta Lynn look, but not as successful in the color selection or style. Her complexion had a sallow cast that was either a bad make-up job at the studio or anxiety draining her of color. This one had all the tension of a pre-op patient waiting in the holding room.

Kate Fitzmaurice felt her bowels clench and her body go cold as she looked into the technicolor face of Josephine Ahearn Quarters, the former Sister St. John of the Cross. With quiet, even intensity barely audible to even herself, Kate said to the t.v., "well, well, well, Josephine; what are you up to now on national television?"

Chapter 9

For the entire hour long show, viewers were threaded in and out of Josephine's labyrinthine stalking drama. Another female teacher was "jealous" of her and wrote over forty threatening letters that evolved into sicker and sleazier diatribes against Josephine. One morning, Josephine arrived in her classroom before school and found human feces all over the front of the room and around her desk.

She recounted that she had been followed in her car by the alleged stalker a number of times and that attempts to run her off the road had been made on more than one night time occasion. Clusters of double–edged razors had been taped under the door handle of her car and also under the middle drawer of her classroom desk.

Even a package had been mailed to her home. Josephine's voice quivered as she described how she carefully unwrapped the package and found a Barbie doll loaded with huge sewing needles sticking out of its head, the rest of it loaded with razor blades dug into the body and protruding at all angles. Barbie even had been painstakingly dressed in an outfit similar to one from Josephine's school wardrobe.

Kate's soup had gone cold and untouched throughout the entire segment. When the show went to commercial, she hurried to the kitchen, dumped her soup into the sink and grabbed the wine bottle along with a handful of pretzels. She scooted back to the den, braked, slid back into the kitchen to take the phone off the hook, intent on not missing a dot of this intriguing show. She settled into the chair closest to the t.v., poured a new glass of wine and put the bottle down just as the show resumed.

Jane Early reminded viewers, "before we went to commercial, you heard Josephine's harrowing account of what it's like to be a victim of stalking. Now we'll hear from the accused stalker, a mother of three who was named 'Teacher of the Year' three times over a ten year period. Our correspondent, Lee Kelly, visited with Judy Mazola in her home just three days ago." The camera switched to a monitor that took the audience to Lee Kelly sitting with Judy Mazola in her immaculate, modest home in Asquith, Massachusetts.

Judy Mazola looked like a raccoon in a suit. The shadows under her extraordinarily sad eyes were so dark and large that you barely noticed any other facial features. Her body posture betrayed the creative, energetic "Teacher of the Year" image one had before "Crime Line" went to commercial preceding this segment. It was instead a petite-gone-wiry frame that appeared saturated with world-weariness. When Lee Kelly asked her if she was, indeed, Josephine Quarters' stalker, Judy Mazola spoke with a calm, measured cadence that hinted not only at the effort of restraint but at some medication residuals.

"I am not, nor have I ever been, a stalker. I am not Josephine Quarters' stalker, if there even is such a stalker."

Lee Kelly fielded that one right away. "What do you mean, 'if there even is'?"

"I have been a teacher in the same school for fourteen years. I know the faculty very well. We're a very small school and we have all thought of ourselves as friends. We go to each other's families' weddings and funerals; we have showers for births. No one at our school would stalk Josephine Quarters. No one at our school has ever stalked that woman."

"How is it, then, that you were specifically named by Josephine as the person stalking her all these months with frightening letters, vile acts and attempts on her life with an automobile?"

"That's exactly what I'm desperate to know. That's what my husband would like to know. Even worse, that's what my humiliated and confused children would like to know . . . and my elderly, infirm parents. We have lived a very happy, nice life up till now. We're not rich people. I'm a teacher, for crying out loud; my husband drives a bus!"

Judy reached for a Kleenex from the box on the end table next to the sofa on which she alone sat. She went on, "Now I've lost my job until this ridiculous mess is settled. We've had to hire attorneys. We've hired a private investigator. We're in the most serious debt we've ever been in because of having to defend me for no reason on God's earth! Our savings are all gone at this point and we'll probably have to file for bankruptcy by the end of this month. So no, Miss Kelly, I don't know why this has happened to me! In my heart I believe this is the evil, destructive work of a very sick woman."

Chapter 10

"So . . . you're saying that you think Josephine Quarters is a sick woman, perhaps delusional?"

"Yes, I am saying that . . . to you and to everyone watching this show. I am the person you hear joked about who takes bugs and flies outside and releases them rather than see them hurt or killed. Here I am, unable to kill a spider or swat a fly, and I'm being made out to be this warped, violent predator!"

Suddenly remembering something else, her energy picked up. "And the letters! Why, some of the contents of those letters she allegedly received –which I have been accused of writing– have language that I NEVER use! I'm almost embarrassed to admit this, but I had to ask my husband if he knew what certain words meant. He could barely tell me what they meant. That's the kind of people we are: good, decent people."

"Tell me, Judy, how you were made aware of the allegations against you?"

"It was 10:30am. I was in class. A knock on the door interrupted a quiz I was giving. The principal asked me to step into the hall. Behind him were two policemen. The principal said he would take my class and that I was to go to his office with the officers."

"Weren't you startled to see policemen at your classroom door?"

"Of course I was startled. I just shook from head to foot thinking that someone in my family had been killed and here we all were, suspended in this incomprehensible moment in a school corridor. As soon as I found my voice I did ask, 'has someone died?' They said everyone was fine and would I please go with them."

"That was it? Just . . . go with them?"

"Yes! We walked down to the principal's office and as soon as we got there, the younger of the two officers, whose child I taught four years ago, told me that I was under arrest! I actually thought that this was some very elaborate joke someone was playing on me. Then he started listing all the things I was being arrested for: stalking; destruction of property; menacing and endangering a life with an automobile and writing threatening letters to a fellow teacher. While he was saying these things the other officer took out handcuffs, put my hands behind my back, and put them on me. I really thought I was going to pass out at that point."

"You were handcuffed in school?"

"Yes I was! Then I was led out of the building and past the lunch moms and the playground moms and what felt like a million people all staring at me like I was suddenly an axe murderer. And that's how I'm looked at every day I dare to go into town for groceries or something else we need."

Chapter 11

Lee Kelly asked another question. "Judy, I'm curious about the last thing you just said. What has life been like for you since these allegations have been made against you by Josephine Quarters?"

Judy Mazola took a deep breath and closed her eyes for a second or two; it appeared she was struggling for control. Naturally, this was a cameraperson's dream moment so there was an extreme close-up. There were no tears though. What brewed under the show's make-up and non-sheen powder was an aura of defeat tamped down with real, pulsing anger.

"I'll tell you what life is like. All the awards, all the achievements, all the respect I had gained, which were the results of how I conducted myself professionally and personally throughout my entire life, are gone. Forgotten. I'm avoided by people I thought were my friends. I can go nowhere without fingers pointing at me, heads turning, people whispering . . ."

Her voice trembled as any mother's would when she added, "my children have come home in tears because of cruel things other children have said to them. Some kids they used to play with aren't allowed to play with them any more.–Just in case it is true that I am some kind of pervert. I understand it some days: it's a crazy world and, unfortunately, such things do occur. But on most days, I go from feeling crushed and confused to feeling enraged that one person can do this to another innocent person and drag others down as well, like my family."

Lee Kelly wondered aloud for the audience, "I can't imagine what I'd be like in your shoes! What do you plan to do with all of this?"

The "Teacher of the Year" was no fool. "I have met with attorneys; I've met with the private investigator we've hired and they all tell me this will be a tedious process but that, in the end, justice will prevail and I will be completely exonerated."

"Then I have one last question for you, Judy. Who do you think would do these things? Who do you think the real stalker is?"

"You know, Miss Kelly, I cannot think of one single person in this whole community who would do such a thing. I'm not being a little Pollyanna here; I honest-to-God cannot fathom that anyone in this little town could do these things. Our crimes are more related to driving too fast on the back roads or breaking the noise ordnance after eleven at night in the summer! As I said, I've hired a private investigator to help answer that question, and he's coming up with some very interesting leads already."

"Can you share any of his findings with us tonight?"

"Oh no. No way! I don't want anything to interfere with his work. I don't want to compromise the pleasure it will give me to see justice served."

The camera pans back into the studio to Jane Early, who is now standing next to a desk and resting one arm on it. "When we return, some startling findings from the DNA tests conducted during this investigation."

Kate Fitzmaurice could feel that her face was hot and flushed. She wasn't so sure it was the wine or the show. Something in her gut was kicking about wildly and she was feeling like a restless tigress prowling, prowling back and forth, back and forth within the walls of her psyche. A line from one of her old professors suddenly occurred to her that had a little of the "aha" to it: "The mind constantly tries to erase, but the body carries the memory."

What had her mind successfully erased, she wondered amid the din of three "dot.com" type commercials in a row? What was it her body was beginning to remember in its own visceral way? She poured the last of the wine bottle into her glass and stared at the ceiling, searching for a clue to the questions that rose within her. The theme for "Crime Line" didn't let her get too far in that reverie.

Jane Early started the segment. "Welcome back. So far tonight we've heard from Josephine Quarters, who has been a victim of stalking and we've also heard from Judy Mazola, the woman Josephine has accused of being the stalker. Both women taught at the same school in the little town of Mt. Hussey, Massachusetts, which was part of the Barata School District where, as in many small towns, mischief is more usual than crime. So for something so sophisticated as DNA testing to be introduced into this case at the insistence of Mrs. Mazola's attorneys, all eyes were on the results."

A zoom-in to the screen behind Jane Early took us to what looked like a hotel room with its generic furniture. Seated across from one another, in different clothes than both wore for tonight's pre-recorded broadcast, were Josephine Quarters and Jane Early. Jane had the mandatory clipboard in hand as she began in a lower, more tentative voice. "Josephine, I know you are aware that DNA tests were performed on some of the saliva samples scraped from the stamps and envelopes of the threatening letters you received over the past two years." The camera pans to Josephine, who was nodding in agreement. "Have you personally seen the results of those tests?"

On this close-up shot of Josephine you could actually watch the beginning of a blush fan around her otherwise sallow cheeks. "No, I have not seen them myself and I knew you were going to do this and I have an . . ."

The anchorwoman rolled right over Josephine's sentence, "Well, before you go on, I think it's important for our viewers to know the results of the DNA testing. This testing, by the way, is almost one hundred percent foolproof. The DNA samples taken from those letters actually identified the DNA as yours! How on earth could that be? Miss Quarters, how could your DNA be on the stamps and envelopes that were mailed to your home as threats against you?"

Josephine didn't flinch. She didn't cower. She didn't blink. She got her back up. Leaning forward into Jane Early's space, she poked the air with her finger as she hissed out, "I KNEW you people would do this! I KNEW you'd try to paint the picture this way and I'm ready for you. I'll tell you exactly how my DNA got on those letters!"

She had both hands palm up, one on top of the other on her knee, slapping the top right hand onto the open palm of the resting left hand every other phrase or so. "The police confiscated all those letters to hold as evidence at the police station. I hadn't had access to them in quite a while. I wanted to look at a few of them to find something I was looking for in them that I might need to bring out in the hearing."

"You mean you went to the police station and asked to read the letters?"

"Yes I did."

"And the police let you read through them when you went there?"

"Yes, of course. They're my property, after all. They had no problem with that. They knew what I had been through and they've been really great with me."

"So you were at the police station reading the letters . . ."

"Yes. I started putting them all in a neat stack to put the rubber band back around them," she used her hands to demonstrate how she ordered the pile. "So I tapped the whole bunch on the desk about three or four times to make a neat stack so the rubber band would fit back around them all. When I lifted up the pack to put on the rubber band, some stamps had fallen off some of the letters and were on the table. I thought I'd die! I thought, 'Oh my God! Oh my God! Now they'll think I've tampered with the evidence!'"

Chapter 12

Jane Early earned her salary tonight; she followed up immediately, "So, Ms. Quarters, you're saying that some stamps fell off the envelopes at that time and onto the desk. I don't think I'm following this . . ." she nicely feigned.

"Yes! Stamps from the envelopes fell onto the table. I knew it would look pretty suspicious if the letters were returned in different condition than how I received them. So I took the stamps and re-licked them and put them back onto the envelopes."

"I understand that you did that, but I'm curious about the remarkable precision with which you were able to replace the stamps. It's my understanding that the ink lines from the cancellation stamps were perfectly aligned as if they had never been moved."

"And DON'T think I wasn't aware of the kind of twisted interpretation that would be put on a very innocent action that you're trying to insinuate other things about now! What I've told you is exactly what happened. Exactly. Don't try to do what happens all too frequently in this country. Don't try to make the victim a victim again!" Her face was hard set and quite red as the camera faded to the "Crime Line" logo and went to commercial.

It wasn't the wine that did it. It was pure fury that prompted Kate's tirade at the television screen, drowning out the new batch of commercials. "You bitch! You little bitch! You're at it again! I can't believe it! That poor lady; that poor family! You little jerk! You won't stop till you kill somebody, will you!" She got up, ran to the laundry room and wildly pitched the towels lying in a heap on the floor into the washing machine, all the while muttering to herself "God! This makes me so sick! I'm so upset! I can't believe this!" She hurried through putting in the detergent, setting the wash cycle dials, slammed down the lid and dashed off to the den when she heard the theme music begin.

Jane Early was standing alone in the studio in front of a bookcase as she delivered her wrap-up. "Tonight's story is a troubling one. A life is threatened. Two careers are jeopardized. A close knit community now eyes one another with suspicion. For sure, the evidence is there: 'The Stalker' does exist. Who it really is, though, remains to be discovered."

Turning for another camera to get a full length angle on her she continued, "Crime Line' learned just this morning that there will be a hearing conducted by the Barata District School board, with the School Chancellor presiding, to determine the status of these two employees. From there, it could move to our judicial system where outcomes are not about status, but about sentencing. We'll keep you posted as these events progress."

The camera lens came in for a final tight shot. "Thank you for joining us tonight on "Crime Line." Be sure to join us next week for our investigation into the highway E-Z Pass scam that you may be helping to finance! See you then. Good night."

Kate turned off the t.v., and numbly sat staring at the blank screen till the crinkling and pop of electricity and static faded. She could feel the polarities of inertia and energy pressing in on each other within her, making her feel at once nauseous and wired. Finally, she got up, put on her fleece vest and Timberlands, and went outside for a walk in the crisp night air.

Outside, she inhaled long drafts of the blended fragrances of juniper, balsam, and brine threaded with the merest hints of burning oak and cedar wafting from the fireplaces of some nearby homes. For a few minutes, Kate stood perfectly still, listening and feeling the holy unction of silence slip into her soul, cleansing it somewhat from the destructive, twisted tale just heard. She turned her head upward and searched the broad night sky. She needed to see lights in darkness tonight. She needed clarity. She searched the star dotted sky and was not disappointed in the celestial proxy she found above her.

Chapter 13

By the time Kate made it to her two mile marker on the neighborhood walk she took this night, her heart finally had stopped racing and her shallow tight panting of aggravation stretched into longer, deeper breaths. "Thank God I can breathe again," she thought to herself. "Wouldn't that just be great: a 'Crime Line' coronary just as I step onto memory lane!"

The return walk back to the house betrayed the frosty temperature that would have had most people stepping in double time. She noted the slow meditative footfall of her trek back up hill, a ponderous pace set by the sheer weight of all that was loading onto her screen of the self. In the moonlight that beamed down on all creatures this night, she wondered if any of her old novitiate classmates were looking up at the same overarching luminescent companion, while finding themselves sinking into a similar funk.

Home again, Kate could hear the phone ringing in the hallway as she reached the front porch, kicking the toe of her boots on the bottom step to dislodge snow and ice from the treads. It stopped ringing before she opened the storm door. When she pushed open the old hunting lodge front door that was a distinguishing feature of the house, the ringing picked up again and this time she answered.

"Hello?"

"Hey, Kate! It's Mimi. Did you get my message about 'Crime Line?'"

Mimi Aroho, the former Sr. Mary Brigid who ran through the burning Motherhouse thirty years ago looking for an escape exit with Kate, the former Sr. Mary Shannon, had faithfully stayed in touch over the years. A short, dark haired, "determined" (code word for "stubborn Irish") woman with a great and generous heart, Mimi was a mix of Mother Earth, Dorothy Day, and Bette Midler.

Mimi's house, a gutted old funeral home, was now a three story eye-popper with an indoor swimming pool and guest apartment on the third floor. Since she had elected to stay in the little village of Glendarff, just thirty miles from Marafield and five towns away from her parents and some of her siblings, "Claddaugh House" had become the site of many reunions and gatherings of friends from the old convent days.

Kate caught her breath, "Yeah, Meem! I got a couple of messages about 'Crime Line.' Did you see it?"

"Of course I saw it! Did you?"

"I sure did."

"So, what do you think? Can you believe it!"

"I don't know if I can tell you what I think yet, but I sure can tell you what I'm feeling! I sat there with my jaw on my toenails for a whole damn hour. All I kept saying was 'she's at it again!' Mimi, this is just unbelievable!"

"I know! I'm like a raving lunatic and I'm the only one home. I had to call you right away. If it took all night I knew I had to connect with someone from our group or I'd explode! No way I'm going to sleep tonight, I'm so wound up. And Poor Siobhan: I just got off the phone with her. She called you but there was no answer, so she called me.

She's in buckets; she's so upset! You remember the deal with Siobhan and Josephine, don't you?"

"Definitely! Josephine accused Siobhan of stalking her in the novitiate! How wacky was that? There we were, a bunch of altruistic 18 and 19 year olds in the convent, full of zeal and Jesus, and suddenly living in the fear that one of our fifty-five 'good little sisters' had some kind of stalking thing going on! Who could forget that! And of all the people to accuse: Siobhan! You couldn't find a gentler, kinder soul on this earth than dear Siobhan Greene!"

"You've got that right! But don't forget, Fitz, Josephine accused about five different people back then. All at the same time; all of the same thing. The whole time I'm looking at this poor Judy Mazola on television tonight I'm having flashbacks to that ridiculous stalking fiasco back in the novitiate. Do you remember all that sick nonsense? My God! Hey, Fitz, hold on; I've got another call. Give me a second . . ."

Kate was reminded of how she hated call waiting and renewed her resolution to never succumb to its lure of not missing a call. Certain amenities simply needed safeguarding.

"Okay, I'm back." Mimi's voice was charged with even more excitement than when she first called Kate. "Guess who that was? Annie Silo! Can you believe it! I haven't spoken to her since I left the convent, have you? We're talking a lot of years here, you know?"

"Of course I know! I haven't spoken with her yet. That's who left one of the messages about the show on my machine today! I felt like I was in a time warp when I heard her voice. It's been over twenty-five years since I've spoken with her, but I got her voice immediately . . . you know how she always punctuated her sentences with little chuckles in between phrases. She still does."

"Yeah, you're right! Well, I'm to call her back after I finish with you. She said she'd called your line, then mine, and figured we had to be talking to each other. She also said she couldn't believe you didn't have call waiting. I told her it was a Quixote thing for you but that at least you had a computer!"

"I yield having one conversation at a time to no one, thank you very much! Anyhoo, Meme, call me back after you speak to Annie. Oh, and find out how in the world she knew about the show in the first place. I'll try and give Siobhan a call. Or do you think it's too late for me to call her; the 11 o'clock news is just starting?"

"Are you serious? Who could sleep? I think this is going to be an all nighter for a lot of us. Call her. Look, I don't know if this will be a long or short call to Silo; want me to call you back tomorrow if it gets to be too late?"

"Absolutely not! I'll probably just paint the house, hook a rug for the living room, or strip and pickle all the floors tonight!" Switching into a light brogue, she added, "The sleep is off me tonight, darlin', so don't be worryin' yerself about the hour now, sure ye won't!"

Not missing a beat of an old routine, Mimi, whose parents really talked like that answered, "Then, grand, ye little pet! I'll be after ringin' ye up once I've spoken with yer one! Talk to you later, Kate.!"

"Talk to you later, Meem! Ta!"

Chapter 14

Kate went into the kitchen and turned on the burner beneath the kettle to make a pot of tea before she called Siobhan. While she waited for the water to boil, she stepped out onto the porch and brought in some firewood. Might as well be comfy. She had just finished laying the fire when the phone rang. She lit the starter under the kindling, saw it catch, and sprinted over to the phone by the third ring. The answering machine kicked on and then off when she picked up the receiver.

"Hello?"

"Kate?"

"Yes . . ." That wonderful voice of an old friend was unmistakable. "Siobhan?"

"Yes! Oh, I'm so happy you got my voice right away! How are you, Kate?"

Kate felt the warmth in Siobhan's voice floating north from Thistle, Connecticut through the magic of fiberoptics. The inordinate lapses in time between seeing or talking to each other were confounded once again by the gift both had in their ability to pick right up from wherever it was they last left off with each other. It was like that with Mimi too.

All three of them owed it to the fire they were in together at

Marafield. "As gold is tested in fire, with the dross burned off and the pure remaining . . ." was a phrase from one of the psalms that they thought underscored the quality of their friendship over these many years. Having escaped with their lives that terrifying night, the "junk" really did fall away and what remained for them as friends was true gold.

"Well, Siobhan, generally speaking, I'm great! But, speaking for tonight, I'm having a few very serious Heinz Fifty Seven moments . . . all kinds of things are starting to brew! How 'bout you, Siobhan? Mimi told me you saw 'Crime Line' tonight and that it hit you pretty hard. A little too close to the bone, wasn't it?"

Siobhan's voice sounded like she had allergies, a cold, or was tucking in this phone call between bouts of tears. "I'm a mess! I'm so angry! . . . And sad! I'm even shaking all over! I just can't stop crying, which I know doesn't surprise you or Mimi since you two labeled me the 'designated crier' a long time ago! But, my God! Here is that woman, all these years later, still hurting people and getting away with it! Am I over-reacting or did seeing Josephine tonight upset you too?"

"What, are you kidding? I could bubble the paint off the walls! Looking at that rehearsed 'poor me' face of hers, complete with those weeping willow eyebrows and that jaw clenched in defiance when her veracity was questioned: jumpin' Jesus! It's a bloody miracle I don't have lacerations from going through the t.v. fifty times tonight!" Kate could hear Siobhan laugh at her expressions and relax into the conversation a little more.

"Hey, Siobhan, how the heck did you know she was going to be the feature story on 'Crime Line' tonight?" As the answer came, Kate poured a little boiling water into the tea pot to heat it, swirled it around a bit, dumped it into the sink, dropped two Barry's tea bags into the pot, and filled it again with boiling water. She took down her favorite Tara mug and repeated the same hot water ritual with it.

"Well, that's the really weird part! I had a message on my machine from Annie Silo. I mean: Annie Silo? First of all, when has she EVER called me? Second of all, how did she even know where to find me? Third of all, how did she know about the show? I mean, doesn't she live out in Denver or some place like that? Isn't she a vice president for some big publishing house? Anyway, that's who called me and told me to watch the show because someone from our novitiate was going to be on. So, naturally, I called you and Mimi right away."

Kate may have been off duty, but she had embedded skills. "You sound like you're calming down a little, Siobhan; how are you feeling now?" Kate poured herself a cup of dark tea, plain, and sipped it on her way into the living room. She settled into the winged back chair closest to the fireplace and draped one leg over the arm as she listened to the answer and watched the flames.

"Calmer, but still sad . . . still angry. I just needed to talk to people with the same history. I don't know why I always second guess my own feelings about things. After what she put me through –put us ALL through–it's perfectly legitimate for me to be in the state I'm in after watching that disgusting charade."

"You bet!" Kate recollected, "I wasn't even one of the ones Josephine accused back then, but I so resented the Gestapo-like state we lived in because of her! That's what's flared up for me, so I can only imagine what you and a few others are reliving."

"Yeah," Siobhan agreed, "I know I'm going to be visited by old and new nightmares tonight because of this. God, this certainly has been some night for all us old ex's, hasn't it, Kate? Maybe we should get together in the not-too-distant-future to sit down and "debrief" from this . . . we probably all have some form of post traumatic stress disorder kicking around inside us from those so called 'good ol' days'!"

"Oh, I'm sure we do! However, pinning the tail on WHICH trauma could be the tricky part!" They both laughed at the awful absurdity and truthfulness of the line. "Okay, dear Siobhan, one more cup of tea for me and I'm going to try reading a little till I get drowsy. I'll call you before the week is over."

"Okay, Kate. Thanks a million. I know sleep will be tricky for me tonight, so I guess I'll stack up all my catalogues and page through them till the sun comes up. Charles Keath and Winterthur usually help me switch gears. Talbots' doesn't hurt much either . . ." Siobhan paused and heaved an almost mournful sigh before hanging up, musing half aloud and half for Kate to hear, "You know, we're good people. And at the tender ages of 18, 19, and 20, we were very good young women with aspiring hearts full of noble things. How in the name of God could a group of such genuinely nice people be treated the way we were treated?"

"The simple answer would be that the people in charge back then were poorly informed and woefully misguided. Too damn proud to admit the former; too damn blind to recognize the latter," Kate said wearily. "Now with that pithy, entirely subjective summation, Siobhan, I bid you a peaceful goodnight!"

"Goodnight, Katie Fitzmaurice . . . talk to you soon."

Chapter 15

Around 4:00am Kate woke on the sofa in one of those winter weather dilemmas: she was cold enough to need a blanket, but too cold to make herself move around to get one. Instead, she tried raising the book that had slipped from her hands back up to her chest and pulled her sweatshirt sleeves down over her fingers, bunching the cuffs in her palms to form make-shift mittens. She desperately needed, she muttered to herself, "at least two flippin' hours of sleep" before the alarm went off, so she was staying put. Staying put, however, did not guarantee somnolence.

"Oh, for hell's sake!" she growled at 4:45 am. Pitching the book to the floor, she grudgingly declared the day begun and much too early. She started the kettle for tea and went down to the computer in the den to fiddle around with it at least till the sun came up. She was suddenly convinced that the way she felt right now was the whole reason why the word "Oy" got coined. Okay, maybe she was Irish, but it worked for her and she used it almost mantra-like with every little movement in the cold, oy, creaking, oy, house: Oy!

When Kate opened her e-mail, the little truck zoomed into the upper left corner of the screen while some perky little cyber voice announced, "mail call!" She had three messages: one from another long lost novice classmate, Eily McVetty; one from a mutual friend of Mimi,

Siobhan and hers, Carrie McCall, who quite amazingly was still "in" and principal of a school in New Jersey. The third message was from a Robert R. Young, who she didn't know from a hole in the wall. She started with the most familiar, Carrie's.

> "Talked to Mimi late last night. Saw 'Crime Line.' Ugh! Please give me a call asap. Don't call the convent; call me at my office. Hope all's well. Love, Carrie."

Good ol' Carrie: always right on the ball. Kate wondered if the hint of mystery she detected in her e-mail was really there or was it just some low level transference going on. She filed the note in the "in" basket and scrolled down to the next message highlighted in blue, which was from Eily McVetty. The world had Kate's e-mail so she didn't puzzle too much over how Eily found her address.

> "Surprise!" it began. Kate noted that it also had been forwarded to Siobhan, Mimi and Annie Silo. "I hope I've found all of you; that everyone's in good form; that life is being good to you and that you're all 'following your bliss'!"

"Oh, God," thought Kate, "I hear crystals and smell incense . . ." She continued reading.

> "Please let me know if any of you saw 'Crime Line' last night. I am WILD after watching it! Josephine Quarters was on for the whole hour show! She was 'featured' because she claimed that she had been STALKED by another female teacher for over a year. Any bells ringing in any ears, girls? Well, ladies, I'm GONGING AWAY! Any of you remember that I was one of 'THE GANG OF 5' accused of the same thing by her 'way back in the novitiate? Siobhan, you should remember; she screwed you too! I'd love to get together with you east coast types to have a GROUP PURGE about all this. See what you think and we'll figure out place and dates. Give me three options; I travel a lot. Hope I hear from you. Sick as this all is, it could end up being fun!
>
> Ciao.
>
> Eily McVetty / a.k.a Sr. Moira Ann"

Kate thought, "well, it's universal: that show really did 'get' to everybody!" She also thought that Eily was on to something: maybe it would be helpful getting together with the old "gang" somewhere . . . have a kind of "Big Chill" weekend. A cast of ex-nuns probably wouldn't be as saucy, but it definitely would be fun. She filed Eily's note away and scrolled down to the last one from Robert Young.

> "My name is Robert R. Young. I am a private investigator hired by the Mazola family. Mrs. (Judy) Mazola has had serious allegations leveled against her by a teacher named Josephine Quarters. These allegations have gained notoriety in the region in which both women live and work and have been covered in the press and on local t.v.. Most recently, 'Crime Line' aired a full length program on which both Josephine and my client appeared separately. Ms. Fitzmaurice, your name, as well as other classmates of yours from Marafield, has been given to me to aid in my investigation on behalf of Mrs. Mazola. I will be contacting you by phone either at home or at your place of employment and I appeal to you for your cooperation in this very serious matter. An innocent person has been wrongfully accused. If you would be willing to answer a few questions for me, you would be helping to right a wrong and thus see to it that justice is served. I will call you next week. Thank you in advance for your consideration of this very weighty matter.
> Very truly yours,
> Robert R. Young, P.I."

Kate read the e-mail again and then again, filed it, and did what she knew she had to do. She ran to the bathroom in the dawn's early light.

Chapter 16

Unlike the restless Kate Fitzmaurice in Maine, Robert Young had enjoyed the luxury of a deep sleep. He had been up till about two in the morning, taping the "Crime Line" special that featured his newest client, Judy Mazola, and her accuser, Josephine Quarters. While it aired, he wolfed down pizza and played with several drafts of the emails he would send right after the show. He wanted to be the first to greet his potential witnesses as soon as they booted up the next morning. He also placed a call to his client immediately after the show. It took him an entire hour of busy signals before he finally reached her.

She was appreciative of his call, sounding understandably distraught at having witnessed yet another way that her here-to-fore private life was stripped from her and tossed into public domain. They both settled on the dramatic ending that cinched the interview with the DNA results and he could feel a few drams of vindication tip through her angst. He noticed in himself a genuine empathy for her plight tonight and felt a little assuaged that the "it's her dime" attitude that prompted the call in the first place was giving over to something a little less calculating.

To him, this case initially looked like a small town cat fight seen through the big lens of hysteria and he was reluctant to take it on. The need for money soon scraped the scales of preferential case selection from his eyes and he agreed to meet with Judy Mazola and her husband, Ray, for the first time about eight months ago. Since that meeting he had collected enough information to sway him to take the case. He figured that in such a small town a stalking story would eventually hit the paper, but he never considered it to have the stuff of prime time national television appeal. That was eight months ago.

Now he was convinced, more than anyone yet knew, that he had stumbled onto a case that would reach back in time and break open some closets that had been locked, sealed and barricaded. If he was right and kept his ambition checked, he'd have a future that spelled a steady cash flow of m-o-o-l-a-h. Mark Furman had not cornered the New England market on investigation by arriving in Connecticut for the unsolved Moxley murder case.

Robert R. Young was in his late forties with a decent head of light sandy brown hair that nicely blended in the gray that had begun to feather through, especially on the sides. A retired state trooper, he still maintained a meticulous appearance and trim body. His taste in clothes ran more to the sporty than the business side. You wouldn't find a single suit in his clothes closet. He'd spent too many years in "Statie" matching shirt, pants, and hat to go that route. What you would find would be a serious indulgence in good looking sports jackets: Donnegal tweeds, herringbone, cashmere, wool blends. He had loosened up a little since leaving the force and was bent on not having that razor sharp military look that always seemed to scream "cop" no matter how hard some guys tried. Rob, as he liked to be called, thought the guys on the Fox news network had wardrobe just right: relaxed, but smart.

Chapter 17

Rob's office was in an old shipping warehouse in downtown Boston that had been converted to a multi-purpose corporate and residential facility about twenty years ago. "Penny Lane," an indoor mall and food court, was on the ground floor; "The Buff Zone," a fitness center, was on the lower level; "The Enclave" was on the second floor where offices and conference rooms were leased. The remaining four floors above were divided into pricey condominiums with fabulous views of the waterfront.

The only way Rob could manage to have an office there was by sharing an office and its expenses with an old friend of his, a licensed social worker with a private practice on the side. On the solid wood door to the office were two brass name plates. On the top plate was "James G. Carey, C.S.W."; below that was "Robert R. Young, P.I." The arrangement, though alphabetical, was purely financial in Rob's mind, and fair.

James G. Carey had gone to elementary and high school with Rob. For the entire four years of high school, both had been on the football team in winter and the swim/diving team in summer and were so much alike that there was little effort put into being friends. They just were. Their differences were assigned more than assumed: Jim was from a fiercely Irish Catholic family and Rob was from strictly observant Protestant parents. Neither ever attended church with the other, successfully conditioned to that taboo as they had been.

At the end of summer in senior year of high school, sitting on the side of the club pool on a hot but brilliantly blue August morning, Jim casually announced to Rob that he was leaving for New York in two weeks to enter the priesthood. Though a foreign concept to Rob, it was a disappointing one. It felt mysterious and exilic. Jim was too athletic, too easy with the girls and too full of fun to do such an extreme thing.

"This seems to be the day for big announcements," Rob said, staring at the swirls in the water he was making with his feet that dangled over the side of the pool.

"Why?" Jim asked, not taking his eyes off the boats bobbing in the cove at the end of the pool property. "What do you know?"

"I got drafted. Letter came yesterday. I leave next week."

"Oh my God . . . are you going?" Jim's shock ran deep.

"Of course I'm going!" he snapped. "Like I have a choice . . ." With that Rob curled his body in one quick, sweeping liquid motion and cut into the pool swimming hard. Jim stayed locked in place. Without moving a muscle, he felt that he and his friend had just been hurled into a much darker side of life on this sunny summer day.

Rob had remained a faithful friend over the years, attending Jim's ordination in Rome with the rest of the Carey clan. Three years later, "Fr. Jim" stood beside the first woman pastor of St. Paul's Episcopal Church and joined in blessing the marriage of Rob and Linda Young, risking a reprimand from the Catholic Bishop for doing so. He attended the baptismal services of Rob's two infant daughters, Kerry and Linda. Rob, the "dirty black Protestant," as he was always affectionately heralded upon entering the Carey home, was a reader at the Masses of Christian Burial for both Jim's sweet mother and towering, wild father. From his pew he wondered how a grieving priest could conduct such funeral services for his own family members.

Years later, when daughters Kerry and Linda entered junior and senior years at their respective colleges, Jim consoled Rob over a few beers at Rory Dolan's when Rob's marriage to Linda broke up irrevocably. Jim wondered between sips of Guinness how many marriages of cops are claimed by the gradual shutting down of emotions at the horrors witnessed with unrelenting regularity.

It was Rob that Jim called just two years ago when he returned east from a ten year teaching stint in Berkley that had a weekend parish commitment attached to it. He loved teaching. He loved ministry. He was gifted in both and loved by many. But the split he was experiencing in himself between the lived realities of daily life and the imposed authority of the endless disheartening declarations from Rome left him, finally, spiritually pained, ideologically compromised, and physically exhausted. The collision of his post-modernity vision against Roman medieval mindsets, at last, had taken its toll. At the end of the Spring semester, James G. Carey relinquished both titles of professor and "Father" and headed back to New England to begin again.

Having had no family of his own to support all those years of his priesthood, in addition to the money he had inherited from his parents, Jim was able to purchase a modest beach house in Marble Head, Massachusetts. He easily landed a job teaching in the Social Work program at the University campus in Boston and, with an eye to developing a growing private practice after hours, he honed in on "The Enclave" as his office location. He did not care about the forty minute commute from Marble Head to the campus or office. He wanted to be able to jog, walk the beach or socialize without bumping into his students at every turn.

Jim's move into the Marble Head house had coincided with Rob's retirement from the State Troopers and the launching of a new solo career into private investigation. While helping to paint the wrap around porch of the weather worn beach house with his old pal, Rob was completely caught off guard by Jim's generous proposal that he consider sharing Jim's newly leased office space at "The Enclave." It was an offer Rob couldn't refuse.

Chapter 18

The office at "The Enclave" was spacious enough to accommodate their two large desks in front of the window at opposite sides of the room with two chairs for clients in front of each desk. As you entered the office, to the left was a sitting area with a navy blue and white striped sofa, end tables and lamps, and two blond wood club chairs with navy blue seat cushions dotted with tiny red, white and yellow nautical flags. Across from that area and to the right was a round table with four chairs, all of the same blond oak.

Lining both walls were filing systems that included a credenza on each side, one with a standard corn leaf plant and the other, with a copier and fax machine shared by both men. Notes, books, binders and files could be neatly hidden from view in these cream colored matching metal sets. In the corner just behind the door were a Poland Spring water bubbler and a cabinet that housed the Braun coffee maker and its essentials. It was great space and both men hoped to hold onto it as long as possible.

Rob's desk was the one on the left of the room as you faced the window from the doorway. From it, he could swivel his chair around while he was on the phone and watch the boats coming in and out of the harbor. He had a better view at work than he did at home. His desk was completely covered with organized columns of newspaper clippings, copies of articles and lists of names and phone numbers. Apparently, he had worked late the night before chronologically assembling these puzzle pieces. It was mapping out something, but what that something was, for now, laid there waiting to be discovered.

Beginning on the left side of the private investigator's desk was a column of papers related to the current Alpine School District stalking allegations. Blue index cards, written on with thick black magic marker, headed each column. Topping the first column was one printed, "CURRENT / ALPINE." The papers assembled below it contained data about Josephine Quarters' to-date place of employment, clippings from district, community and local papers about the stalking allegations, and notes that outlined all items covered in the "Crime Line" interview.

The index card heading the top of the second column read, "BARATA," the name of the school district Josephine Quarters worked in prior to Alpine. Faxed and xeroxed copies of anything to do with files on or records of Quarters from the Barata School District were fanned down the row. Neon orange sticky notes dotted the row, marking complaints personally filed by Josephine Quarters either with her principal or with the district office. The complaints lodged had the general theme that she was a victim of someone's dislike.

"QUEENSMONT," the place of her very first teaching job in Clarke, Massachusetts, began the third row. On the "QUEENSMONT" card was a large question-mark, representing the unknown cause of her abrupt departure from that first teaching position in mid semester. The nuns who ran the place back then were all dead now. There had been three other "lay faculty" along with Josephine. One had since died; another had been stricken with a debilitating stroke that left her aphasic and apractic. The third, the school's sole social worker, was now living somewhere in New Mexico according to the notes Rob had scribbled while he spoke by phone to her estranged brother.

Chapter 19

On the far right side of the desk was the final column labeled "MARAFIELD." Josephine Quarters' curriculum vitae led Rob to Marafield College and he only had begun to collect the data from that far back. The top papers were copies of Marafield's alumnae, Class of '66 and Class of '68. From the list of '68 graduates one name was highlighted in neon yellow, Josephine Ahearn Quarters. According to Josephine's age, Rob figured she should have been in the Class of '66 and wondered about the discrepancy. He called the Director of Alumnae Relations and inquired about it as a possible mistake.

The woman with whom he spoke, Sr. Patricia Spillane, was semi-retired and helping out part time in the office. This was just the kind of thing she was in charge of: updating, correcting, and also deleting any names of the deceased from the active file. Since she said she'd need a few hours to look up the name in question, Rob asked if he could stop by the following day to speak with her and she obliged. He took the next morning and drove out to the Marafield campus in Dunhill and found his way to the alumnae relations office. Sr. Patricia was in the reception area when he asked for her and a slightly younger version of the actress, Maggie Smith, turned to him when she heard her name. She went right over with hand outstretched to shake hands.

"I'm Sister Patricia. Are you Mr. Young?"

"Yes, M'am . . . Sister." He winced at the gaffe and gave an endearing shake of the head acknowledging his unfamiliarity on this turf.

"Well come right in! You're very welcome! Is this your first time here?"

"Yes, M'am. Sister. Oh boy. I'll try to get it right before I leave. You should know you're the first nun I've ever spoken to or met."

"Really, Mr. Young! How on earth did you manage to be such an artful dodger all these years?" She had a great little wink that flashed so quickly as she spoke it barely punctuated her jest, but he got it nonetheless.

"Well, I guess you could say I'm sheep from another fold than yours. I was raised Episcopalian and went to public school all my life. So, Sister, I'm afraid you're 'it!' Feeling pressured?" He could do the friendly tease thing too.

"Tremendously! Will we talk conversion if I find what you're looking for, Mr. Young?" She gave him a level look to see if he was shocked or enjoying the banter. He didn't miss a beat.

"Conversion? Hell, I might have to marry you!" They both burst into laughter, having successfully sized each other up as pretty sharp.

Chapter 20

She led him into a small rectangular room that housed a conference table and chairs. At one end of the table were giant binders with the last two digits of the years printed four inches high on the spines of each. She pulled out the chair in front of the two binders that were open and indicated to her visitor to have a seat.

"Mr. Young, you were quite right about the discrepancy in graduating classes for Josephine Ahearn Quarters. I think the mystery is solved, however" she said with a little relish. "You see, Mr. Young, Josephine Quarters actually should have been listed with the Class of '66 but, because she left the community before the end of her senior year, she did not graduate with her class, finishing, instead, two years later. Hence, the Class of' '68."

"Sister, what do you mean she 'left the community'? She moved away?"

This time it was Sister Patricia who shook her head in a self deprecating way. "I'm sorry, Mr. Young, that is 'nun-speak,' if you will; I didn't even hear myself! 'She left the community' is usually what we say when someone leaves the convent." Seeming to compensate, she enunciated those last three words as if he were deaf. He heard them alright; he just couldn't believe his ears.

"So Josephine Quarters was a nun . . . actually in the convent back in the sixties . . . well, how 'bout that. So how would a poor Protestant fellow like me get information about her time in the nunhood?"

"Mr. Young, I'm very happy to have helped you sort out her class affiliation. Now may I ask you a question?" She tilted her head ever so slightly in his direction.

The private investigator shrugged his shoulders and said lightly, "Go for it, Sister."

"Why are you so interested in Josephine Ahearn Quarters? I could be getting myself 'in dutch' for helping you this much. Answer that sufficiently for me and I'll have a second question for you."

Rob leaned in, indicating implicit confidentiality, "Sister, I represent an elderly uncle of hers that I've known for years. I've handled all of his legal matters ever since I got out of law school. Anyway, he moved to Nova Scotia about thirty years ago after he retired. His wife died back in 1958, they had no children and he never remarried. Josephine Quarters is his niece and his only living relative. He was never in touch with her or her family again once he moved to Canada. Well, Sister, sadly, Mr. Ahearn died last week and his entire estate, including a house and several hundred acres in Nova Scotia, have been left to Ms. Quarters. It's my duty to find her now and have her sign some papers and make some decisions."

She was a lovely old gal, he had decided half way through his lie, and for a nano second he felt a tinge of guilt looking and sounding so convincing. He watched her closely as he spoke, trying to detect if any antennae went up on her, but she seemed to believe him.

She offered, "well, I'd say that's one alumna who'll be in for quite a shock when she hears all this! God bless her and God bless her poor uncle." Briefly bowing her head she added, "May the soul of Mr. Ahearn rest in peace."

"Amen," came out of Rob's mouth right on cue, surprising even him. He shifted in his chair to change the conversation from this fabricated topic back to Josephine. Crossing his legs, he said "Sister, is there any way I could get my hands on a picture of her from, say, an old year book or something like that?"

"We do have yearbooks, but they're over in the library, I believe. I know that we keep only the last ten years here in this office. You can see we're pretty limited with space. Why don't you take a walk across campus to the library? I'd be happy to give you a guest pass; I'm afraid you won't get past 'Officer Krupki' otherwise."

"You're very kind, Sister, and you've been extremely helpful. I will take you up on that offer of a guest pass. Oh, and purely out of curiosity, are the nuns who were in classes back then included in the yearbooks?"

"Never! Picture taking wasn't allowed back then . . . vanity and all that nonsense. No, you won't find any of the young student sisters in the yearbooks. You will, on the other hand, see some of the sisters who were professors . . . or rather you will see their profiles which are artfully obscured by the 'headgear' worn then."

"So there are no pictures of the young sisters . . . Ms. Quarters and her nun-mates . . . around? Not even for archives kept somewhere? This is my own Protestant curiosity speaking here now."

"We do have Community archives . . . I know that each sister was given a formal black and white photo of her whole crowd on Reception Day –when a young woman is received into the novitiate and, in the old days, 'took the veil,' as they used to say. Another picture was taken on Profession Day, the day when the novices 'graduated,' so to speak, and professed their vows, receiving the black veil. Both pictures were to be given to the families on visiting days."

He could see that she was lost for a second or two in that reminiscence. Then suddenly, with a burst of energy, she got up from the table walked out into the office and over to the wall opposite the reception desk. Those who worked there dubbed that wall "Memory Lane" and on it were all black and white photos of Marafield in the old days. Sr. Patricia flipped off a group shot of nuns in the old habit, fully aware of being watched by the receptionist. "I'm borrowing this for a few minutes," she called over her shoulder and walked back to the Conference room.

"Here you go, Mr. Young. This is what we all looked like back then. You can see why the college girls named one of the hills they used for sledding 'Penguin Hill,' can't you!"

He shook his head and chuckled at her comments as he examined the picture. "How on earth did you ladies put all that on every day? You get a general sense that there's youth looking out at you, but everyone looks so much the same all covered up like that it's hard to tell. It's a great photo though. Thanks for showing me."

"You're very welcome. You know, in recent years we've only had about three of four girls for these formal group photos . . . a far cry from the fifty or sixty as in this one! We're in different times now and opportunities for women abound." She turned the picture over and pointed to a faded label on the bottom of the frame's backing. "Here's one thing that has remained the same for as long as I remember: would you believe that the same photo company still does the group picture? They've done it since 1940, gratis, of course. It's 'The Guild Studio.' A father of a nun owned the business and it's remained in the family ever since. The granddaughter owns and runs it now. She's on our board."

Robert, the investigator, filed "The Guild Studio" away and would stop there before he headed back home.

He stood and thanked Sister Patricia for her assistance and shook hands with her.

"Sister, it's been such a pleasure meeting you. You've actually made me feel sorry for never having attended Catholic school!"

"Well, now, don't go overboard, Mr. Young," she quipped. "I'm sure you've done as well for yourself as any Protestant possibly can! And, as the daughter of a very Protestant father, I say that with very 'cheeky' humor!"

"Before I go, Sister, you had a second question for me that we never got to; do you remember what it was?"

"Indeed! How is it that a good Irish Donnegal tweed jacket is worn by a fine Protestant like yourself, Mr. Young?"

"Good eye, Sister! It's a plot. All my best friends are Irish. When I wear it, it tricks them into buying me a beer!"

"In that case, may you wear it till it's threadbare!" Having had the last word, Sister Patricia walked him to the door and watched him walk in the direction of the library.

As he made his way across campus, he was aware of two things tossing about in his gut. To his complete amazement, Josephine Quarters had been in the convent! To his consternation, he now wondered about the veracity of Judy Mazola.

Chapter 21

Rob finally had traced Josephine Quarters back to the first group other than her family with whom she had a history. A copy of a black and white glossy of fifty-five young nuns in white veils, all with garlands of flowers attached to the top of each nun's "bonnet," was now in his possession, thanks to The Guild Studio in Dunhill. The nuns in it were arranged on front steps leading up to the grand entrance of an old ornate building. Two sisters in black veils were on the top steps in the center of this sea of white veils.

One, on the cusp of being elderly, wore wire rimmed glasses and looked straight at the camera without any trace of affect. Hers was the only hand visible in the picture and it rested in a practiced and fixed pose at the base of the large crucifix she and the others wore around their necks. It would be no leap at all to designate her the "high llama" of the outfit. The other black veiled woman barely looked older than the young ones who flanked her. She had a shy sort-of smile that reached up through the eyes of her slightly bowed head. She was in charge in some way, but definitely trumped by the authority that silently asserted itself next to her.

The original 8x10 picture from The Guild Studio files had been under an ivory mat. A little window beneath the picture was cut out of the mat and a calligraphy caption was inserted: "Fifty-five Received

Into Novitiate, June 1963." Rob jotted that info down on an index card he had in his jacket pocket. On the back of the photo were the names of everyone in the picture listed row by row. Rob asked the young clerk in the shop if she would please make a copy of the photo and names on the back and she cheerily agreed.

Back in his office in Boston that night, Rob carefully poured over the copy of the names in the picture. Next to that list, he lined up the Class of '66 alumnae list. Then he searched for the corresponding names on both. He highlighted certain names with neon yellow marker. When he was satisfied with this matching name and face exercise, he took a red, water-soluble "Vis-à-vis" overhead projector pen and made circles directly onto the picture around the faces of two nuns. The faces encircled with red were those of the younger black veiled nun on the top row along with the skinny, pale novice standing next to her. On various steps below them, five more faces were circled with a green marker.

When he finished, Robert Young took his newly collated pages and typed out a legend that decoded in corresponding ink who was circled in red and who, in green. At first glance, the top half of the paper was in green and the bottom half in red. In green ink the targeted identities in the photo began:

"1) Sr. Brigid Marie. Aka: Mary Aroho / Glendarff, Massachusetts
2) Sr. Mary Shannon. Aka: Kathleen Fitzmaurice. Portland, Maine
3) Sr. Maura Kathleen. Aka: Siobhan Greene. Thistle, Connecticut.
4) Sr. Moira Ann. Aka: Eileen McVetty. California.
5) Sr. Elizabeth Ann. Aka: Anne Silo. Denver, Colorado."

Several spaces down and continued in red ink were the remaining names:

"1) Sr. Dolorosa Feeney (black veil). Directress of Novices. Aka: same. Location:?
2) Sr. St. John of the Cross. A.k.a.: Josephine Ahearn Quarters. Sparrows Point, Mass."

Tired and satisfied with his discoveries of the day, he lined up his final column, "Marafield." Tomorrow he would begin making contact with the people circled in green.

Chapter 22

It took several rounds of emails and phone calls among the old Marafield gang to arrange for the "Crime Line" post mortem reunion that Mimi Aroho offered to host at "Claddagh House," her place in Glendarff, Massachusetts. Because three weeks had gone by since the show, they were now in the trickiest month for snow, February. They decided to meet on Presidents' weekend since it gave a long weekend for travel for Eily McVetty, Annie Silo and Carrie McCall, who would be flying into Boston's Logan Airport. The others would be driving. Siobhan Greene had just gotten a brand new black "bug" and wanted to take it on its first long run out of Connecticut. Kate Fitzmaurice was only two and a half hours away and didn't mind the drive.

Annie, Eily and Carrie had agreed on waiting for one another's arrivals at Logan and getting a car service together out to Glendarff, which was in the middle of the state. Annie was the first to arrive and, with thirty minutes to wait for Carrie's arrival, she worked her cell phone and laptop nonstop from the Starbuck's table she had taken over facing the busy walkway. When it was approaching the time that Carrie's flight from Newark was due to land, Annie gathered up her "office" and headed for the United arrivals area. As she approached, she could see a stream of newly arrived passengers bobbing their way down the corridor toward the baggage area.

Annie spotted Carrie immediately and registered that Carrie was not recognizing her yet from that distance. No wonder. Annie Silo did not look the way Carrie had remembered the last time she saw her some thirty years ago. Sporting a stylishly cut spiky blond and black coif that topped off her petite frame, Annie wore a butter-soft black leather jacket with collar up, a dark charcoal gray cashmere mock turtle neck, matching black leather pants and sunglasses. Shoes and shoulder bag were Prado. Both wrists were circled with bracelets and a Longine watch set off her left wrist.

Her fingers flashed three rings: a sizeable diamond; a signet ring; and a thick gold dome ring with lapis sunken into the center. There was certain glamour about Annie Silo, that was undeniable, but too many years of smoking had created "smoker's lines" around her mouth and eyes. Annie always had a furrowed look as a young sister, and now her forehead bore its long term effects. Carrie didn't know what she was expecting, but she was a little surprised at this version of Annie and how reliant she was on her practiced use of good make-up.

Carrie, on the other hand, was so physically unchanged by the years that if you knew her thirty years ago you wouldn't have to look at pictures to see what she looked like then. She still looked like she was in college: face, figure, bearing and energy –all remarkably young in appearance. She had on khakis, red turtle neck and navy blue argyle pullover, a long Stewart red plaid scarf around her neck, and tassel loafers. She carried over her arm a dark navy blue long coat from Talbots and dragged behind her a monogrammed dark green LL Bean carry on bag with wheels, last year's Christmas gift from the faculty.

"If I thought that staying in the convent would have preserved me the way it's preserved you, I might have reconsidered leaving!" Annie Silo bubbled as she stepped up to Carrie and both embraced.

"My God, Annie, hi! Ohhh yeah! I'm just the picture of youth! Who are you kidding?" Carrie stepped back from the hug nearly squealing, "Look at how thin you are! I'll tell you, it took me a few seconds to register who this rich looking 'Mrs. Got-Rocks' is that I'm looking at! How ARE you?" Carrie held Annie's hand for a minute just to stay connected in the hello.

"Good, Carrie, really good . . . and exhausted, and thirsty, and a nervous wreck. But look at you! You have one stinking little crinkle around the eyes and that's it! My God, you look absolutely the same! Please tell me you dye your hair and that this isn't your real color . . . and also maybe that you were sucked up by an alien ship and freeze dried in a stress free vacuum tube for thirty years somewhere!"

"Stress free tube . . . that's me! You got it! No, no: look right here on the top. See? I have a few grays starting to come through." Carrie patted the top right side of her head at the spot where at least four silver strands could be picked out against the thick suit of chestnut.

"That's it? God! I think I'm all salt and pepper by now, but damn if anyone'll know! C'mon, let's go have a drink while we wait for Eily. Her plane's due in at 4:30 at American; that gives us a good forty-five minutes."

Chapter 23

Annie located the closest "Premier Club" and steered Carrie to it. Annie belonged to the clubs of every major airline because she positively hated the over crowded waiting areas. The "Premier Club" was quiet and civilized. They headed for two cushioned club chairs by the window overlooking the runways. As soon as they sat down, a waiter came over to take their drink orders.

"Good afternoon, ladies, welcome to the Premier Club. May I get you something from the bar?" Annie ordered an extra crisp Absolut vodka Gibson. Carrie asked for a Coke.

The waiter then instructed them that at the end of the lounge was an hors d'oeuvres table with cheese board and finger foods and that they should help themselves if they'd like; he'd be right back with their drinks.

"Carrie, don't you drink?" Annie was curious.

"No, Annie. I think drinking is morally wrong and I really don't approve of it." She said this while arranging her coat on top of her carry on and not looking at her.

"Are you serious?" Annie nearly whispered in a low voice of complete shock.

"Of course I'm not serious!" she laughed. "You haven't been to one of Mimi's little reunions, have you? I'll have something there, so I'm just going to go with the Coke for now."

"Well, I need a little pop in the here and now! You might not believe this, Carrie, but I'm pretty nervous about seeing everybody. I mean, I'm excited to see what everybody looks like and to hear what everyone's been up to and all that. But I am a little anxious, which is perfectly par for the course for me."

She took out her lipstick and compact, applied a new coat, checked herself in the tiny mirror and continued, laughing, "Hell, I've paid for two therapists' vacations, beach houses and children's college education, just trying to deal with anxiety issues alone!" As she talked the waiter quietly set their drinks down in front of them and left. Annie picked hers up and toasted, "Here's to a good weekend and here's to Marafield, font of my neurosis!"

Carrie reached across and lightly clinked her glass of Coke on the martini glass saying, "Cheers!" As she sipped her Coke, Carrie did a flash inventory of what was going on inside her body and noted that she felt a little awkward, being the shyer of the two and having to spend this time with, actually, a stranger. She breathed a quick prayer that Eily's plane would not be delayed. "How 'bout some hors d'oeuvres? I didn't even get the six airplane peanuts you get for a four hundred and eighty five dollar ticket. I need to nosh on something."

"You go ahead. I'll stay with our stuff and go up when you come back." Annie flipped out her cell phone and made a quick call while Carrie went to get some food. When she came back, Annie took her turn. Carrie waited politely till Annie returned before she started in on her plate of cheese, buffalo wings, celery and carrot sticks and blue cheese dressing. By contrast, Annie had two cubes of Swiss cheese, half a breadstick and two rounds of cantaloupe. Noticing the difference in portions, Carrie joked, "Did I mention that my flight from Newark took twelve hours?"

"Don't be silly! I came first class and had filet mignon and a complete 'Wolfgang Puck Gourmet Dinner' only about two hours ago. Pointing to the cantaloupe and to the three little white onions in her Gibson she said, "I'm just forcing myself to get my quota of fruits and vegetables," and they chuckled together.

Chapter 24

"So, Annie, everyone wants to know how in the world you found out about the 'Crime Line' show. I mean, you're all the way out in Denver and all the rest of us are on the East Coast except for Eily, of course." Carrie took a sip of her Coke and waited for Annie to dab the corners of her mouth with her napkin before answering.

"Well, this guy, Robert Young, is a private investigator hired by the woman that Josephine Ahearn accused of stalking her. Somehow, he found out that Josephine had been in the convent with all of us back in the sixties. So one day I'm on the road and my office calls me in my car and says I have an important personal phone call. They put it through and the next thing I know I'm being grilled by this guy from Boston about my being in the convent with Josephine Ahearn, for crying out loud!" Her voiced peaked and fell every three or four words, underscoring her surprise at all of this. "I had to pull off the road! I couldn't believe I was having this conversation. In fact, I thought some of the guys in the office found out I had been in the convent and were playing a joke on me!"

"How did he get your name, though . . . and everyone else's?"

Annie took a swig of her drink and said "This guy told me that a priest gave him my name! Can you believe it! He said the priest knew a lot of the young nuns from Marafield because he was a seminarian at that same time and worked one summer in that horrible camp we were all forced to help out in. Remember that hell hole?"

"You're kidding! I was at the camp! We called it 'Camp Horrendous,' remember?" Carrie looked out the window for a few seconds trying to retrieve a name or face from all those years ago. "The only seminarian I remember from then is Tish O'Grady's brother, John, but that's it. I don't remember any of the others."

"Well, according to Robert Young, this priest, whoever the hell he is, remembered my name because I was in charge of getting all the little gerbils on and off the buses everyday at the camp. And that's the whole flippin' connection! So he told Dick Tracy that the only one he remembered from the Marafield novitiate days was me and didn't the guy hit pay dirt!"

"So he tracked you down out in Colorado?"

"You bet!" She finished her drink and speared one of the onions with a toothpick. "I don't think it was all that hard. I've been pretty generous to the alumnae association over the years . . . corporate matching funds and all that. I'm easily traceable."

"Okay. So Robert Young found you. Now: how did he put together a list of all the others?" Carrie was a definite "sensing type" on the Meyers-Briggs Personality Type Indicator and her strong suite was detail and facts. She watched Annie turn in her chair looking around rather urgently for the waiter and suddenly Carrie sensed a kind of confessional feeling starting to creep in.

"Well, I uh, heh," Annie was doing the nervous laugh-between-words thing she was famous for and continued, "Awww, jeez, I'll just say it! I gave the guy some names. Accidentally."

Carrie's eyes widened over the rim of her Coke. Pulling the glass away from her lips in mid sip she sputtered, "YOU gave the names? Oh my God! And what do you mean you 'accidentally' gave the names? Oh my God!"

"No! No! It's not as bad as it sounds and I'm not the imbecile I'm making myself out to be! What happened was this: he started hammering me about being in the novitiate with Josephine and said he just wanted me to verify some other names he had. I was curious, so I said 'go ahead.' He must've had a class list in front of him 'cause he started rattling off names like a litany. I said, 'you've got it, Sherlock; that's the class.' To which he said 'thank you, I needed to verify that I was in the right ball park.' Then he said he was going to be in Denver that Friday for a meeting and did I think we could meet? I figured, what the hell, he had a great voice and he already knew somebody who knew me, how bad could it be?"

"So you've actually SEEN this guy, Robert Young?" Carrie asked with unmasked incredulity.

"Hey! YOU should see this guy: easy on the eyes, let me tell you! Anyway, he came to my office. I wasn't about to meet him alone or without seeing some credentials. Next thing I know, it got to be lunchtime. He offered to buy me lunch, we left and, four hours later, I finally stopped yapping about 'Life in the Convent' at Marafield!"

Carrie just shook her head, smiling. "That's when you gave him everybody's names?"

"Well, I didn't actually GIVE him the names. I told a few stories here and there and mentioned a few names as part of the stories and, by God, he remembered every bloody name!" Annie looked at her watch, straightened up in her chair abruptly and said "Hey! Eily's plane's been in for ten minutes; we've got to get going!" With that, she put a bill under the martini glass, put on one more round of lipstick and hurried the two of them to the American Airlines arrival area.

As they sprinted through the airport pulling their luggage behind them, their conversation turned to the task at hand which was finding from which gate the "Left Coasters" were disembarking. Carrie now could understand a little of Annie's anxiety about meeting the others and was glad she was already primed for the more than interesting night that awaited them all. She was sorry she ordered Coke.

Chapter 25

Eily McVetty was tossing a bright red ruana around her shoulders when Carrie spotted her. "I see her!" Carrie waved till Eily noticed them approaching. Eily McVetty was a little taller than Carrie and Annie and, from that distance, bore a striking resemblance to Joan Baez. Her hair was the salt and pepper that Annie denied having. She wore a black turtleneck and chimney style black corduroys with a black leather woven belt that had a silver buckle and tip, complementing her silver jewelry. Tucked onto her belt was a beeper that she wore over her back pocket.

"Don't you guys ever give me that 'laid back Californian' line; I've been patiently waiting here for you two for twenty minutes!" She gave a toothy smile. "Hi, girls, how are ya?" The three reunited friends wove in and out of an impromptu choreography of hugs and kisses and marvels at how great each other looked. Eily hooked her arms through Carrie's and Annie's and said with warm sincerity, "Hey, thanks both of you, for hanging out here till I got in. It's so nice to be met at these big ol' airports." Picking up her shoulder bag, she announced, "Now, girls, the car's on me and that's that. There should be some guy at the baggage area holding a sign with my name on it, so keep a look out when we get there."

"The baggage area? Oh Gawd. Why didn't you just bring a carry-on, it's only a weekend." Annie's general disdain for airports was surfacing from too much down time in this one.

"I have to fly down to Atlanta Sunday night to give some talks at a conference there next week, so I brought the good threads with me." As they began walking through the terminal, Annie, who had been out of the loop for so many years, asked Eily how she ended up in California.

"I think it's my blood, Annie. I could never get warm enough in winter living in the northeast. Then one day I put my snow boots on one damn time too many and said 'okay, I'm outta here!' I spent that weekend searching for MD openings in gerontology anywhere in the country it was warm and, bingo! I found this opening at The Crofford Institute in Southern California and applied. That was nineteen years ago. I'll never move back east, girls. I'm freezing already and we haven't even gone outside yet!"

Carrie filled Annie in that Eily was now the head of Gerontology at Crofford and had been awarded the prestigious Theodore Blaine Woodson chair at the University.

"That is fantastic, Eily!" Annie enthused. "My God, 'who'da thunk' we little plebes from Marafield would turn out so well? That's just marvelous, Eily; I'm really happy for you."

"Ah, don't be too impressed, sweetheart." Eily graciously interjected. "Carrie's doing what I KNOW I could never do; she's principal of 'young America,' God help her! Give me alzheimer's patients any day; just don't give me a bunch of smart ass kids."

"So Annie, you're in Denver now, is that right?" It was Eily's turn to quiz as they breezed along the walkway.

"Right. I'm with Henderson Publishing House. I was with Waterbank for about ten years, then this opportunity for Vice President of Acquisitions came up with Henderson and I took it. A case of perfect timing. A relationship I had been in went south and I was pretty miserable at the time. Colorado seemed just fine all around."

"Has it been?" Eily asked as they rounded the corner to the baggage area.

"Yeah, I love it. I'm there five years now, have a townhouse and a nice circle of friends and, you might remember, I love to ski, so it's a great location for me."

A phalanx of car service drivers, mostly in black coats or suits and holding signs with names written on them, lined the cordoned exit area of the baggage claim section of the terminal watching for their prospective passengers to notice their own names and pair off with the correct driver. Eily spotted her name before she went to claim her baggage and went over to identify herself to the driver. He smiled, nodded, broke rank to fetch a baggage cart and went to Eily's side, loading onto the cart the one large and one medium suitcase that she attempted to wrestle off the conveyor and that he, in chivalrous fashion, intercepted.

When they reached Carrie and Annie who waited outside the cordoned off area, he relieved them of their bags too and piled them onto the cart saying, "Ladies, if you'll follow me, your car is right outside. I'll just ask you to step a few feet to the right when we go out and wait at the curb. I'll load and pull right up there before you even realize how cold it is here today!" Eily turned grandly to the other two, arched her eyebrow in a contradictory "oh really!" look and whipped her red ruana around her throat and chin, signing beautifully in merino wool, "too late, pal."

Chapter 26

If it hadn't been for a fender bender that tied traffic up in Sumner tunnel heading out of the airport, the trip would have taken ninety minutes instead of two hours. With small talk nearly depleted and the sights of the city well behind them, the three passengers lapsed into silences and mini naps, resurfacing to apologize, make another stab at conversation and then drift off again in the darkness of the countryside. Carrie sat contentedly in the quiet, not as tired from her trip as the others were from theirs. As the car turned off the highway and crested a hill, Carrie could see the little village of Glendarff ahead in the distance. It was just eight o'clock.

"Girrrrls . . . we're almost theeeere . . ." Carrie softly announced in sing-song to her companions. A bugle couldn't have produced such snap to attention. Reading lights went on, purses opened, make-up mirrors flashed. Once the "freshening up" routine was over, the Lincoln Town Car turned on to the top of Locknell Way, where Mimi's house was on the corner just five more blocks ahead. The homes were massive and old and perfectly maintained. Mature gardens, century old trees and, silhouetted against the sky, tall evergreens sculpted the road and homes on both sides. There was an old neighborhood feel to the place, in spite of the historical assignations given to most of the properties.

Carrie offered, "It's such a beautiful town. You might be interested in a little walking tour tomorrow. All I'm good for is telling you which ones I like! Mimi's the restoration architect; she usually parades us around giving little architectural didactics about the houses! It's not unusual to see students with cameras and sketchbooks walking around. I think she said this street has one of the densest clusters of famous architecture around."

"Hoo! This one's nice! Looks a little like Hammersmith Farm in Newport." Eily had her "second wind" and was eyeing the homes appreciatively.

"What did you say Mimi does?" Annie asked as she craned around trying to catch another view of the house Eily had just pointed out.

"She's a restoration architect, " Carrie repeated. "Her specialty is restoring or replicating historical homes. She bought her house about twenty four years ago. It used to be an old funeral home." All three caught the driver's eyes in the rear view mirror on that one.

"You have GOT to be kidding me!" Annie gasped. "Honest to God! Leave it to Mimi to set up camp in a funeral home!"

"Yeah, but wait'll you see it; I don't think you'll mind staying here for a couple of days," Carrie reassured Annie.

Carrie leaned forward and told the driver, "Sir, the corner house on the right at the end of the next block is our stop. You can just pull into the driveway. It'll circle around and point you back onto the street." No sooner had the nose of the car turned into the driveway when the front door opened and out onto the porch stepped Mimi, Shiobhan and Kate, all smiles and waves.

"Howdy doody, girls! How was the trip?" Mimi asked as she hugged each guest in order of emergence from the car. "Long!" "Great!" "Where the hell are we?" were the crisscrossed responses. While the driver put the luggage on the porch by the front door, Siobhan and Kate worked their ways around the car greeting and hugging the others. Mimi joined again in the melee and got in line for Siobhan to hug, which she did automatically before realizing it wasn't a newcomer but the hostess she had been with for three hours. They all laughed and, as if rehearsed, started hugging each other again goofing off in Mimi fashion. The driver stood patiently at the trunk of the car.

Eily saw him and slipped over to where he stood as the others finally headed up the steps. "What, are you ladies all related? Is this a reunion of some kind?" He asked while Eily opened her wallet. "Yes, it's a reunion. We all went to college together . . . we're just sorry our good friend Eleanor Roosevelt always has to miss these." Blank. No glint of recognition at what had just been said.

Eily knew then that the guy was calculating the tip in his head and peeking to see if she was thumbing through enough bills. She had already paid for the service by card but handed him the tip in cash. He nearly made out with her on the spot. "Thank you, Miss! Any time you need a ride in Boston . . . anywhere in Massachusetts . . . you call me. My pleasure!" He shook her hand, he bowed, he walked her to the steps. When he got back to the driver's door he shouted over the roof, "You ladies have a great reunion!"

"Brrrrrrrrr!" she shuddered as she waved him off and opened the door, stepping into the warmth of "Claddagh House."

Chapter 27

"Jumpin' Jesus, Mimi! This place is unbelievable!" Annie put her carry-on down and moved slowly through the house in a dazed state of wonder.

Eily moved around pointing to things that were redone or new since her last visit, "Was this always here?" she asked, pointing to the large slate and bronze waterfall nestled into the cove of the winding staircase. Mimi delighted in people's reaction to her home and quietly chuckled as she nodded an affirmative.

Siobhan urged Annie to continue on past the kitchen to the end of the room walled with French doors. "Annie, go over there and flip on the lights on the right side." Annie crossed the room, found the light panel, pressed two buttons and screamed. Lights came up on the other side of the paneled glass revealing a large filled indoor swimming pool, a bar, loads of patio furniture and a table for dining poolside. The entrance into the pool was a semicircle of extra wide steps that also served as a Jacuzzi since they were outfitted with jets that hit you at every possible angle when you sat near or stretched out around them.

The whole gang followed Annie to the pool area. Kate instructed Annie to take off her shoes, which she did. "Holy cow! This floor is heated! This feels great; I might sleep here tonight! How the hell did you heat the floor?"

"Copper tubing. Hot water runs through it and it heats the brick. Not bad, huh?" Mimi was so low key about it all by now she almost missed the "wow" factor her renovating genius inspired in others. But this, she was definitely enjoying since everyone razzed her for staying so close to her point of origin all these years and not moving "far and wee" as had the others.

Mimi gave a clap of her hands as she said, "Okay. Let me show you to your rooms. Get comfortable, come back down and we'll have a drink or two or ten. Dinner's just light fare tonight: chowder and some wraps. I've got lobster, chicken, or veggie wraps . . . okay with everybody?" Mimi asked.

"Yummy!" they all yelled. "Mimi," Kate called after her as she started up the stairs with the three latecomers, "want me to put some logs on?"

"Pleeeeeeeeeeaze!" Eily dramatically whined from the landing. "Load those log puppies on and have them roaring down here when I get back."

"Hey, Siobhan," called Annie, "load a vodka Gibson in a glass for me and have THAT roaring when I get back!" "Three onions. Extra crisp and thank you very much!"

Kate smiled at Siobhan on her way to the back porch to bring in some logs, "Let the games begin!"

Chapter 28

Annie was the first one down and had changed into jeans and a sweatshirt over her turtleneck and had put on socks and a pair of leather fleece lined moccasins. She pulled out a stool from under the breakfast bar and leaned on the counter facing the kitchen where Siobhan carefully poured the Gibson that Annie requested into a martini glass and placed it on a cocktail napkin in front of her. "There you go, Annie Silo. Slainte!"

"Slainte!" She took a taste and raised her eyebrows with dreamy approval. "Siobhan, this is perfect; thanks. So fill me in a little: you're in Connecticut now, right?"

"Thistle, Connecticut; that's right. I have a little house there and a cat that's in her little cat-condo right now up in my room. Mimi hates cats but lets me bring her as long as she doesn't roam around the house. You're not allergic or anything are you?"

"No, not at all. I'm not a big time animal person, but your cat won't bother me. The last I heard, you were doing something in early childhood education, weren't you . . . I thought with Carrie at one point?"

"Whoa . . . you're really dating yourself! That was when I was still "in!" Oh my gosh, when was that, '77, '79? I don't remember. Anyway, yes, Carrie and I did work together for a few years."

"Right!" Annie was remembering now, "You guys set up an early childhood Ed Center together out on the Cape. Didn't it get all kinds of awards and press?"

"Boy, you're good!" Siobhan, uneasy with too much hooplah about her accomplishments, said this as she kept busy by setting out glasses and freshening up the pretzel bowl and dip. She continued as she filled the ice bucket, "After I left, I was offered a job as an early childhood education consultant down in Connecticut. It's in conjunction with "The Master Teacher Program" some of the colleges have there. It's the best of all worlds for me. I don't loose my contact with kids and I get to mentor student teachers and other teachers who want to hone their skills in early childhood learning."

Kate finished lighting the logs in the living room fireplace and came into the kitchen to wash the black off her hands from opening the flue. Annie included her, "Fitzie, you're still doing the same thing up in Maine?"

"I am . . . The Big Ear." Kate mocked.

"Don't you get sick of listening to everybody's crap all the time?" Annie winced.

"Sometimes it gets to me. Most times it feels like work that makes a difference. When I need a break I know this nice funeral home with a swimming pool . . ." She heard Mimi and the others coming into the room and timed her remark just right.

"Who's a dimwit fool?" Eily joked as she pulled up a stool, "or did you say 'swimming pool'?"

"And lay off the funeral home thing, will you?" Mimi teased, "You're going to 'skeeve' everybody out! C'mon, girls, bring your drinks in by the fire and relax. By the way, the coffee table is right where they used to prepare the bodies . . . kidding, girls, just kidding!"

They all settled in the comfy sofas and chairs while Mimi put a bunch of cds on the Bose in the corner and lit a few candles around the room and on the mantle. Before she sat down, she raised her glass and said, "Now this is what makes "Claddagh House" Claddagh House. Here's to us, friends always!"

Six glasses met rim to rim as their bearers offered "Here, here!" "Thank God!" "Cheers!" "Thank God again . . ." "Here's to you, Mim!"

Chapter 29

Cocktail hour was spent decompressing from the day's trips and doing a status quo of what each was "up to" at the moment. Finally, Mimi, in response to the reviews of the house and coaxed a little by Carrie, gave a little history of the house.

"Well, this little gem was built in 1877 and is a classic nineteenth century 'Shingle Style' which accounts for all the beautiful interior wood, the complex shapes, and the taut skin of shingles on the outside. The part that makes other architects drool is that it was actually built by Henry Hobson Richardson, an important residential architect in America." Mimi was on automatic pilot. "In fact, if you take a walk around the neighborhood tomorrow, you'll see two more Richardsonians, one at the top of the street and one two blocks down, turn right and it's in the middle of the block."

"It's so aesthetically engaging," Eily commented as she looked around from her cocoon in the corner of the sofa. "Would this have been built around the same time as Marafield? There's something vaguely reminiscent going on for me . . ."

There was a group groan protesting her comparison of Claddagh House to Marafield.

Mimi put her hand up to quell the clamor and said, "Hold on girls. Eily's more right than you realize! Over the years I've learned that

Marafield had been built by the architectural firm of Mead, White and Levy. And guess what? Follen Mead and Stanford White had been students of the very guy who built this house, H.H. Robinson.!"

"Ahhhhhh," they all said with new found appreciation.

"Richardson also influenced Frank Lloyd Wright and his Prairie School Movement with the use of wide open spaces instead of little tiny rooms. This area has homes by Wright, Frank Furness, Charles and Henry Greene. You must walk around tomorrow or I change the locks!"

"I hate to bring this unsavory topic up but, Mimi, how do you fire proof a place like this?" Annie asked with great seriousness. "I mean, I'm looking around at all the timber it took to build this place and I can't help but think of our own little 'Bonfire of the Vanities' back in '66. That motherhouse went up like a torch and nobody had a chance."

Mimi walked over to one wooden pilaster pillar after another, pressed a panel, and a little door swung open revealing a red fire extinguisher tucked inside the pillar. She then pointed out that the ceiling was discreetly dotted with barely noticeable nozzles. "And, Annie, in all the bedrooms, there are fire extinguishers behind each door. Check the ceilings up there too; you'll feel better. Hey, most of the people who stay here were hurt in that fire. I want to make sure everybody feels safe . . . right, Siobhan?"

Siobhan spoke up, "Oh I feel very safe here, Annie. Mimi has more flashlights, nightlights, and fire extinguishers than Home Depot! And if anything ever happened, God forbid, I'm jumping in the pool this time!"

Annie quickly added, "Sorry, girls; I didn't mean to get so serious about fire safety on you! Mimi, I hope I didn't offend you. Your house is fantastic and I really do feel very safe here. Eily spooked me when she compared it to Marafield!" Eily swatted Annie with the end of the throw she had over her legs and feet.

"Well, now that we've finally said the 'M' word," Kate interjected, "let's put dinner out, sit at the table and settle in for this weekend's hot topic, our now famous Marafield classmate and t.v. celebrity, Josephine Ahearn Quarters! Okay, all together: one, two, three . . ." And with that the entire group gave a wild full throated scream, merely hinting at the ferocity of the discussion ahead.

Chapter 30

When dessert was finally served, a platter of cut fresh pears, cubed angel food cake and whole fresh strawberries, arranged around a bowl of hot semi-sweet dark chocolate for dipping the skewered morsels, was placed on the table. It was then that "Crime Line" got put on the table too.

Kate, at ease with facilitating group discussions, served up the topic as the others took their turns selecting, piercing, dipping and putting dessert on their plates. "Okay, let's get to it! Everyone saw 'Crime Line,' right?" Nods all around as the group worked their plates.

Siobhan was the first to offer her impressions, since the others were caught by the question in mid bite. She took a sip of tea before answering. "I've already told Kate most of this on the phone a couple of weeks ago, but I couldn't believe my eyes that, after all these years, I turn on the t.v. and there's Josephine Ahearn! I actually was yelling at the t.v. during some of it!"

"Why?" Eily was curious.

"I got angrier and more upset as the show went on. All I kept thinking through Josephine's recitation of all that had happened to her while she 'ALLEGEDLY' was being stalked was 'she's lying; that other teacher didn't stalk her!'"

Eily made slow circles with her spoon in her cup of tea as she responded, "Siobhan, that's very similar to my reaction. I had something short of fury trigger off in me as I watched that show. Initially, though, I was quite neutral . . . just sort of doing an intake of the complaints she had, much like I do every day with patients. Then WHAM! all of a sudden it wasn't so neutral any more. I had this flashback of my having been in a stalking psycho drama with Josephine Ahearn not terribly unlike this one!" She looked at each of her table mates to see if they were registering what she was alluding to.

"Yes!" Siobhan slammed her hand down on the table, "Exactly! I'm so glad to hear you say that. Exactly!"

Kate sized up that Carrie was struggling to decode the reference they were making.

"Carrie, you know what they're referring to?"

"I'm not sure . . . don't forget I was a year ahead of all of you and missed a lot of the 'fun and games' your group went through," Carrie explained. "Tell me a little more."

Mimi joined in now, "Back in the novitiate, Josephine claimed that a diary of hers had been 'taken'." She leaned on the last word, pressing unmistakable implication into it.

"Ha!" snapped Siobhan, 'taken,' my foot! She accused five different people of STEALING it! I'm one; Eily's another!"

"Count me in!" laughed Annie, "I was grilled about it too!"

"Fitzie, were you involved in any of that?" Eily asked Kate.

"No. Not directly as one of the accused; just indirectly as one among the one hundred and some intimidated, frightened eighteen and nineteen year olds who lived under the increasingly large cloud of suspicion," she recalled grimly. "Will you ever forget what that little 'psycho drama,' as you so aptly dubbed it, Eily, did to the quality of life for the rest of our time in the novitiate?"

"Well that's just it: apparently, I can't!" Eily admitted.

Carrie timidly queried, "well, wait a minute: is that all there is to it: Josephine thought someone took her diary and then thought a group did it? I know I'm a bit of an outsider to this, but I have to tell you this doesn't sound too much like stalking."

Mimi got up and went to the kitchen saying, "I'll put a kettle on for tea." On her way back to the table, she broadly rhymed "Now listen carefully, Carrie, my dear; the story of 'The Diary' you're about to hear . . ."

Chapter 31

Mimi sat down at the table and continued, "allllrightie, then: I'm going to be 'Madam Interlocutor,' helping connect all the dots in the diary story. I'll start. One morning after morning prayer, Mass, and breakfast, Mother Dolorosa floated into the refectory and said, in her usual Morticia-from-The-Munsters delivery," Mimi cracked everyone up with her pained, pinched look and slow, sonorous imitation, " 'Sisters, immediately after grace and when kitchen and pantry duties are finished, every sister is to report to the conference room.'

"Dolorosa knew she hit a home run in the anxiety department and that we were all dying to know what was going on. So she turned up the laser beams in her beady little eyes, withering everyone upon whom they fell, and said, 'Anyone who breaks silence will be dealt with severely.' Then a puff of smoke went up and she disappeared!" Mimi's guests thoroughly enjoyed her rendition.

"McVee, you sat at the table right in front of her in the conference room; pick it up from there, if you will."

Eily sat up a little straighter in her chair and leaned on the table with her elbows, fingers threaded through each other and clasped just under her chin which rested on them. "I'll try to do justice to your opening! Let's see . . . I think I have it now," she had briefly closed her eyes to retrieve an old picture. "Every chair in the conference room was filled, except for one. We were sitting in silence, of course. Oh! There was a conference table at the front of the room with chairs facing us. The door opened and, to our complete shock, in walked the 'triumvirate': Mother Dolorosa, Directress of Novices; Mother Kevina, V.P., and the Grand Pubah herself, Reverend Mother Majella. I remember Rosie Atleigh bursting into tears before we even sat down, she was so nervous, the poor thing. We knew it had to be something big to have all the brass on deck.

"Then Mother Majella held onto her cross and announced 'My dear Sisters, it behooves me to inform you that evil has made its way into this sacred place.'" Eily had bowed her head and hunched her shoulders just a tad in the overly burdened manner of Majella's demeanor as she delivered this speech. "'The devil himself prowls these sacred corridors and stealthily . . . '" Eily slowly, gravely looks around the table in imitated intensity, "'fiendishly . . . walks among you. I have been informed by Mother Dolorosa that a diary has been taken. It is the diary of one of your sisters, Sr. St. John of the Cross' . . . which explained the one empty chair." Eily continued, "'I pray that whoever has done this despicable deed will return it to Mother Dolorosa's office before retiring for this evening.'"

Annie shuddered, "I think I'm having a Maalox moment . . . you're giving me the creeps! I feel like I'm right back in that room. Ugh!"

Mimi picked it up from there. "Well done, Eily! To continue: night follows day, day follows night and no one coughs up the diary. Three days later we're herded back into the conference room with the same three grand gurus, only now they have a priest in tow, 'Monsignor Ghoul' or whatever his name was, I don't remember. Anyway, Mother Majella tells us that no one has returned the diary and that evil has become . . . what was that line? 'stronger than the graces necessary for courage and integrity,' something like that. The good Monsignor was going to pray over all of us and then he and the three of them were going to go around and bless each dorm and room in the building. Remember that?"

Various versions of "Oh my God, yes!" we're signaling all the memories being quickened by the original participants in these recollections.

"That scared the crap out of me," Annie admitted. "You know, for about a month I slept with my rosary in one hand and the wooden cross from my cell in the other. I had nightmares about demons and devils; it was awful! I was just a kid. What the hell did I know about that stuff?"

"Oh boy, me too! I think I just cried my way through the rest of the novitiate," Siobhan joined in. "I was so terrified by what they had said! I was afraid to go anywhere by myself. I never made a visit to the chapel after dark if there wasn't someone else there. Isn't that pathetic? I used to love to sit in the quiet of the chapel any ol' time at all. Not after that, though. I was terrified! You're right, Annie, we were just kids. That kind of talk to innocent young girls was just awful!"

Kate interjected, "Yeah, and in case you weren't afraid of the 'devil prowling about,' you could just be afraid of living in close quarters with someone who didn't have both oars in the water!"

Chapter 32

Eily leaned back in her chair and ran her fingers through her hair, musing aloud to the others, "You know, this is the first time I'm hearing all the parts of this saga."

"Same here," responded Kate and, similarly, the others. "Anyone not in the convent back then couldn't begin to understand what you just said, Eily! I mean, how could it be possible for all the players in a story not to know all the parts?"

"That's the way it was then," Mimi added. "If you were told not to discuss something, that you were 'placed under silence' about it –as we all were– it was a sign of strength of character not to discuss it. So, it didn't get discussed. Period."

"Okay, so the difference between saints and lemmings is what, exactly?" Eily playfully mused as she looked at the ceiling. She continued, "Look, I know we sit here with the privilege of history on our sides, knowing so much more than we did then and understanding now how wacky a lot of it was, but . . . oh never mind! We can wax philosophical later. So what happened after the 'God squad' de-bugged Beelzebub from the dorms and all?"

"Well, apparently, it didn't 'take' cause things got worse," Mimi recalled.

Kate picked it up from there. "I remember that about a week later, at around two in the morning, a fully dressed novice whisked into our dorm ruffling all the cell curtains as she tiptoed by. I heard her knock on the wooden partition of your cell, Siobhan, and heard her call your name . . ."

"Ugh! Yes! I'll never forget it." Siobhan had taken over the account now. "'Sr. Maura, Mother Dolorosa has sent me for you. You're to get dressed in full habit and report to her office immediately. I have been instructed to remind you to keep the Grand Silence.'" "God, I thought someone in my family had died! I said, 'What? What! Did someone die? Did someone in my family die?' I threw my habit on, ran all the way down the back stairs, through the building and down the hall to her office. And there you were, Eily, leaving her office! I couldn't believe it! Then, when I finally came out of her office from being accused and grilled by Dolorosa, you were there too, Annie, waiting to go in!"

"But WHY?" Carrie wanted to know, "what happened that couldn't wait till a decent hour, for crying out loud?"

Siobhan narrated further, "Well, Josephine had augmented her stolen diary story. Now she was claiming that her diary had been set on fire! She told Dolorosa that little pieces of burnt pages were 'planted' in her prayer book, her pew, her locker, her cell closet, her bathrobe pocket, her bible, her desk . . . you name it. There were little snatches of burnt pages, all with just enough of her handwriting showing on each of them, to help make her claim seem believable to Dolorosa and the rest. Apparently, she knocked on Dolorosa's door sometime after ten the night of the 'inquisition,' clutching the burnt pages and pieces in her hand. She was in hysterics –crying, sobbing, wailing, fainting from fear for her life–at least, that's what Dolorosa told me when she called me to her office.

"Josephine told Dolorosa that when she returned to her cell from taking a shower that night, she found that a burnt page somehow had been slipped –now get this– into her robe pocket presumably while she was in the shower! There also was one on her pillow when she returned to her cell. She claimed that she just 'fell apart' with terror and felt she was living in fear that her life was now being threatened and she just couldn't take it anymore.' When Dolorosa asked Josephine who might want to frighten her, she named ME!"

With that, Eily glibly raised her hand and said, "and me!" Across the table Annie raised her hand and also said, "and me!"

"The other two who had been accused lived in the cells to either side of Josephine's cell and were briefly considered 'likely' candidates but only by proximity, and to appear 'fair.' They were 'off the hook' early on in this charade." Kate remembered.

Annie added, "Yeah, it didn't hurt either that one's father was president of the 'Fathers of Sisters Fund Raising Committee' and the other one was the niece of the college president! No special treatment there at all, of course . . ." Groans all around the table seconded the sentiment.

Siobhan looked over to Kate and said, "what I never 'got' about this whole thing was why Josephine singled out us three." She moved her hands to indicate the other two at the table. "It is absolutely implausible that I or Eily or Annie would do such a thing. It's implausible that anyone in our class was up to such a nasty premeditated prank."

Kate said, "Oh, I think each of you was 'just right' for Josephine's warped idea of who must be 'punished.'" Kate pointed first to Siobhan, then to Eileen, then to Annie and assigned to each the crime they had been found guilty of by Josephine Ahearn: "Pretty. Smart. Popular."

Chapter 33

"Oh, come ON!" Siobhan protested. "Josephine and I were in charge of the altar and of setting up for Mass and prayer times. That's the extent of my relationship with her. We talked about whether or not we needed to order more candles or incense or altar wine. Really! We didn't speak outside of those instances. So why would she 'have it in' for me? I was always nice to her, always polite."

"I think you're right, Kate," Eily said thoughtfully. She gave a side look to Siobhan and said, "Siobhan, face it: you were the picture perfect nun, a movie version 'beauty' who rivaled Audrey Hepburn in 'The Nun's Story.' Annie, you had the bubbly personality and center stage charisma that Josephine could never hope to acquire. She practically disappeared into the woodwork by her ordinariness. Very unlike you!"

Annie added her own appraisal of Eily back then. "Eily, I don't know whether you know this or not but I think you intimidated a lot of people in our class with your smarts. Maybe you intimidated her."

"I can't pretend I'm not aware of that in some way, but I surely never meant to intimidate anyone," Eily recalled. "I vaguely remember helping Gail Winters write her metaphysics paper in the back of the novitiate library one Saturday afternoon. 'St. John,' or Josephine, sat at another table facing us the whole time and I was half aware of her watching every now and then. When she got up to leave, she came over and actually reprimanded Gail for the 'dishonesty' of not doing the term paper on her own. She never looked at me, though, just glared at Gail."

"Hey Kate! How is it that you escaped being named one of Josephine's 'stalkers' like us?" Siobhan teased.

Mimi jumped right in. "What are you crazy? Josephine would never mess with Kate. She wouldn't get away with it. Same goes for me too. We both decided to let Dolorosa know what we thought about all the bullshit that was going on. Kate got away with it because she was majoring in psych at the time and put the right spin on everything. Though it didn't make a dot of difference. They thought Josephine Ahearn was a saint!"

"I, on the other hand, gave Dolorosa the non-textbook, unedited-from-the-spleen version of what I thought was going on and she took offense. Big time. I was made to repeat it all the next day to Mother Majella. Dolorosa thought I would demur, but I didn't. I was put on silence for a month. I also had to eat all meals alone; couldn't go to recreation, couldn't go outside; you know, the whole McGillicuddy. It helped me to know I wouldn't last much longer with that crowd." Mimi got up and conducted with her hand a nonverbal inquiry as to whether or not anyone wanted a refill of tea. They all nodded 'yes' and Mimi headed quietly to the kitchen to put on the kettle, listening to the conversation that continued.

Kate added her own reminiscence. "You know they really did think Josephine was a saint or some kind of mystic. In the second year of the novitiate, she went through this sickly phase. We all had to take turns delivering trays to her, remember? She was 'too weak' to leave her bed and had to have her meals brought to her cell. The trays went back untouched and well noticed by the little nun who ran the kitchen , who reported it to Dolorosa. The word was that she 'no longer desired earthly food' or some line like that."

"My God, I almost had forgotten that!" Annie said. "I had to take afternoon tea to her every flippin' day for weeks and weeks. She actually had Dolorosa convinced that she was the new St. Therese of Lisieux . . . including some stigmata thing she faked!"

"Get outta town!" Eily yelled.

Mimi, waiting in the kitchen for the kettle to boil, leaned across the breakfast bar to face the crowd at the dining room table and yelled over, "True, Eily! True, true, true!"

Annie was on a roll. "No, really! You know how Dolorosa loved that stuff! Josephine had totally duped Dolorosa into believing she was some sickly mystic. Dolorosa even had little groups of the first year candidates go up and say the rosary with her, naively suggesting to them that she was some kind of mystic. In the meantime, Josephine was spotted more than once scurrying out of the professed sisters' pantry with a sandwich or package of cookies."

"What about the stigmata deal?" Eily asked.

Annie filled in. "I must be having one of those combat flashbacks; I can't believe how vivid this is! One day I was bringing her tea a little earlier than usual because I had to drive one of the older nuns to the dentist later that afternoon. As I was rounding the corner to her dorm I heard glass break. When I got to her cell she was sitting on the side of the bed holding her hand which was dripping with blood. There were shards of mirror on the floor. You know me: I saw the blood and nearly fainted."

Eily tried to follow. "So she simply cut her hand accidentally?"

"Noooo . . ." Annie intoned to indicate "not quite." "I had a very strong sense then that something was 'not right' in that room. Josephine was acting really weird and not like someone who had accidentally cut herself," Annie recounted. "I ran to get bandages and yelled for someone to come help me. Little Hildie –remember poor Hildie, God help her, she was studying nursing–well, luckily, she was stocking the first aid closet at the time and came to help."

"Hildie asked Josephine what happened and Josephine did this far away trance-like monotone rendition," Annie imitated Josephine now in a robotic flat voice as she slowly raised her hand, "of how, when she reached in her closet for her mirror, she raised her hand and the palm of her hand began dripping blood . . ." With a trance like stare, Annie held her hand aloft just to spook the others.

"Oh, for crying out loud!" Siobhan exhaled with some disgust.

Annie stopped playing at "channeling" Josephine and resumed in her own voice. "Josephine told us her hand just started to 'spontaneously' bleed. She said the shock of it so startled her that she jumped and accidentally knocked the mirror to the floor. All Hildie did was flash me this deadpan look and I knew she was buying this crap about as much as I was."

Eily was completely fascinated. "Where exactly was the wound, do you remember?"

"Right in the center of the palm." Annie indicated on her own hand. Everyone looked at their own palms. "Hildie figured that the location alone would make it difficult to heal just because of ordinary hand movement. She was pretty sure that Josephine irritated it to bleeding point to keep up the stigmata ruse. However, Dolorosa and 'The Brass' got the 'Padre Pio' version of the sickly mystic from the sickly mystic herself. Most of her classmates, on the other hand, had concluded their own versions of Sister Mary Wackadoo of the Bleeding Paw."

Kate was listening intently and joined in now. "And that's when she 'fell out of grace' with the majority of her peers, isn't it?"

Annie said, "Yeah, I suppose so. After a few months of this routine and being more and more convinced that she was screwing around with everyone's good nature, people started to avoid having to deal with her. I felt bad for her. It was almost like the attention she was seeking was backfiring and making her even more isolated . . ."

"An interesting progression," Kate concluded, "losing her appetite; becoming bedridden; having a 'stigmata,' and, with that not working out as well as she thought it might, her diary gets stolen, set on fire, and then burnt remnants of it are 'planted' to frighten her . . . what a troubled novitiate."

"Yeah," Siobhan ruefully said, "all around . . ."

The doorbell could not have rung at a more unguarded moment. Everyone jumped and then laughed at their reactions. Mimi guessed aloud that it was her sister, Kathy Gordon, stopping by to say hello to the 'old gang' on her way home from her son's hockey game. That's just who it was and everyone was delighted to see and greet her and to be snapped back into the present comfort of safe and enduring ties.

Chapter 34

Mimi's sister, Kathy Gordon, was an 'old shoe,' always comfortable to be with and everyone was genuinely glad to see her again. She was a graphic designer and "web master," having gone from being senior editor of the regional paper, *The Gull*, to her own cyberspace adventures and graphics design business.

"Have you women made pate of 'Crime Line' yet?" she asked as she took off her barn jacket and gloves, dropping them on the parson's bench in the foyer.

Carrie said, "Let's see . . . we've covered the show, the novitiate, the stigmata, the diary, the diary being set on fire, and little burnt pieces of the diary being planted around the novitiate. How's that for the first night!"

"And I had to show up late!" Kathy wrinkled her brow and asked, "What's the story about a diary being set on fire? I don't know that one, do I Mimi?"

"I don't think you do. I never talked much about that stuff," Mimi answered.

Turning to the others, Kathy said, "That's news, isn't it girls; Mim's not a talker!" They all laughed, including the target of her dig. Kathy went over and stood in front of the fireplace to warm up saying, "That's exactly why I'm here to see all of you. I want to get all the good dirt I've missed over the years!"

Carrie asked, "Kathy, would you like something to eat, drink?"

"Actually I would, Carrie, thanks; I'm starved! Michael went home with his dad and sister and I never got to eat tonight. Anyway, let's get back to where I came in: who's diary was set on fire? And please don't tell me it was Josephine Quarters!" She looked around at the faces of friends settling into the living room and said, "Oh, God! It was?"

Mimi shot Kathy a two-eyebrows-up look and nodded toward the others in a 'go ahead, tell them' way as she delivered a tray of mugs filled with Barry's tea, milk and sugar, and a plate of Walkers shortbread cookies.

"Wait a minute, I saw that little communiqué! What's going on, you two?" Eily wanted to know.

Carrie waited for Kathy to get settled in her chair then handed her a steaming crock of chowder and a glass of Chardonnay. Kathy spooned a tiny portion to taste and went "mmmmm" like everyone else had done earlier. Till it was cool enough to sip, she cupped the mug in her hands appreciating the warmth.

"Kathy was telling me last week that she got hold of some old news stories that Josephine's been in over the years." Mimi offered with a little glint in her eye as she set the tray down on the cocktail table. "Kath, tell them what you found out."

The chowder was just the right temperature now and Kathy was enjoying it. "Well, I watched Crime Line, same as all of you did. Mim called and told me to watch it. I knew about the stalking accusations because they were all over the local news here and in the paper months before 'Crime Line' got the story. Anyway, when the show was over, I called Mim back and, my God, my stalwart sibling here had completely flipped out! She said more to me in one phone call than she had in a full year!" Everyone laughed at Mimi's taciturn tendencies, including Mimi.

Kathy continued, "Anyway, the week after the show aired, there was a surprise shower at *The Gull* for my old secretary, Jen, and I went. Naturally, discussion eventually segued to the bizarre stalking story that made it to 'the big time' on national t.v. No one's figured out yet how 'Crime Line' picked up the scent on such a small town story as this."

"C'mon, will ya?" Mimi urged. "Tell them about the *old* news stories!"

Kathy rolled her eyes as she took another spoonful of chowder and then continued. "I asked David O., my old pal at the paper there, to see if he could run the name 'Quarters' through a check for any old articles in the archives that included her in any way. Next day I got a call from David telling me he had something for me he'd drop off in my mailbox on his way home from work. So I had this manila envelope sitting on my desk unopened for about a week and a half because I had a massive deadline for a new client that I had to meet. I only got to David's envelop last week. Inside were copies of three newspaper articles. Looks like your friend had an unfortunate history with fires . . ."

Chapter 35

"Fires? What?" Siobhan sat up in her cushioned chair with such attention that two throw pillows toppled off and onto the floor. "What do you mean she had a 'history' with fire . . . do you mean in addition to the Marafield inferno?"

Kathy nodded. "Apparently. All I know is what the articles reported. The first story was just a short report, one of those 'from the news blotter' kinds of thing. It seems that back in the seventies, her house caught on fire. Oh: it started in the sofa. Oops: her husband was asleep in it." Kathy slowly sipped her wine after lobbing that grenade.

Mayhem erupted. Siobhan, Kate, Eily and Carrie jumped to their feet or pounded the arms of the sofa and chairs while shouting versions of "What!" "Are you kidding me?" "Get out!" "I can't stand this!"

Kate asked, "what happened to the poor husband on the sofa?"

Mimi answered this time, "Not good. He nearly died . . . may well have, after all these years. He was in ICU at the hospital our niece used to work in, her unit. He was very badly burned, had a stroke either during or right after the fire, I forget. Anyway, he eventually ended up with substantial brain damage and partial paralysis and was in a nursing home somewhere last I heard and that was a long, long time ago."

"I didn't know Josephine had gotten married," said Eily.

Mimi nodded an affirmative and continued, "I think her house burned down around 1971 . . . she left in '66, right? So she must have gotten married somewhere within that time frame. Not an impressively long life of wedded bliss at any rate."

Kate was completely intrigued. "You know, I don't think I ever knew she left! It never entered my mind that she would ever leave the convent . . ."

Siobhan concurred. "Hey, I never knew it either! I was in the hospital till May after the Marafield fire, so I missed a lot. I don't remember anyone saying anything to me about her leaving when they visited me in the hospital all those days and weeks."

Eily added, "I was in a different hospital than you, Siobhan, dear. But I must say, I never knew it either. No one ever told me she left. And don't forget, when we were released from the hospital, we were shipped out to other convents and not back to the Marafield campus . . . their idea of protecting us from seeing and smelling the burnt rubble."

Kathy was dumbfounded. "Is this really true? Or are you just giving me the business? Don't tell me none of you knew that Josephine left the convent back then! I just don't get this secrecy nonsense! What was wrong with you people?"

"Well, it's true, sweetie pie," Eily toned in an easy sing-song voice. "I'm actually learning things here tonight I never heard before!"

Kate brought them back to the other two news stories. "I want to get back to Kathy's other news stories first, then I have a question about when Josephine left the convent."

Kathy picked up her cue. "Right! Here we go! The next story was about an abandoned car having been set on fire in a field in Clarkson township in, I think, '76. It turned out to be Josephine's car, which she had reported as stolen about two weeks before. The article mentioned sympathetically her earlier 'hardship' with losing her house and 'now this' . . . that kind of empathetic tone, you know."

Mimi took a turn. "There's one more clipping David found 'From the News Blotter.'"

Mimi's eyes locked onto each person in the room as she added the last of the retrieved news items involving Josephine Quarters. "In 1981 the apartment she rented in a private house caught on fire." Gasps all around. "The article said that the alert responses of the next door neighbor, who had gotten up in the middle of the night to take some medication, saved the house from being destroyed by the call she placed to the fire department just in the nick of time."

The room was stone quiet. Siobhan whispered in a tiny voice, "Another fire?"

"Yeah!" Kathy said with an implied "duh!" inflection. "I gotta tell you girls, that 'burnt diary' story you referred to when I arrived has my interest a little more than piqued, having read those three accounts of her life as a campfire girl!"

Kate was deep in thought but surfaced to ask, "Do they know how it started?"

Mimi picked up where she left off. "Paper said there was too much lint in the dryer in the basement. Josephine had put a load in and gone to bed. It was an old house, the paneling and rafters caught, then the kitchen above where the dryer was. Lucky for the landlady," Mimi said, "her bedroom was next to the kitchen; she could have been a 'goner.' Her neighbor was at her kitchen sink getting a drink of water when she heard the basement window on the house across her driveway explode. When she looked out, she saw flames shooting out of the basement and up the side of the house and called the fire department."

"Plausible cause," Carrie thought aloud. "They always tell you to empty the lint tray . . ."

"Or clever." Siobhan sourly grumbled.

Chapter 36

The silence in the room crackled with the energy of synapses at full tilt. For a minute or two everyone was lost in her own reactions to and thoughts about what had just been reported. Kathy, not a party to any of the group's convent history, observed their faces. Mimi, having had the advantage of reading the articles days before, watched too but soon broke the silence and turned to Kate.

"Kate, you had a question but I forget what it was."

"Oh, yeah . . . right . . . I think I 'zoned out' for a few minutes there," Kate said as she stretched to change her position. "I was off fighting the lesser angels of suspicion but I think I lost. Anyway, my question: When did Josephine leave the convent?"

"Josephine Ahearn, a.k.a. 'Sister St. John,' left the hallowed halls of Marafield the first week of April, 1966, at 11:00 o'clock at night, by taxi." Mimi announced.

There was a convergence of separate dawns rising on the horizon of each one's disbelief at what she had just learned.

"Mimi, how do you know that?" Carrie asked. "I mean, the fire only had happened the first week of February and you say she left in April."

Mimi took her feet off the edge of the coffee table and sat up straight. "I found out a couple of interesting things since 'Crime Line.' I found out that Josephine was sent home by Reverend Mother Majella and the big wigs. No warning, no clue: just bounced! You all remember the poor young gal they saddled with the job of Assistant Directress of Junior Sisters, don't you?"

"Sure: Sister Gloria Penney. She was so nice . . . afraid of her own shadow, but a nice person," Eily said. "Is she still 'in' or 'out'?"

"Oh, she's very much 'in,' Carrie volunteered. "I see her once a year at education meetings."

Mimi resumed, "I saw her at South Street Station the weekend after 'Crime Line' aired." It seemed that Mimi never went anywhere without running into someone who knew her. "She recognized me and came over to say hello. After we exchanged the usual pleasantries of 'where do you live, what do you do now,' I asked her if she saw the show; she hadn't. So I told her about it and then I asked her when Josephine left the convent.

"She said, 'Oh my goodness, that's such a long time ago, give me a minute.' Then it came back to her. She said, 'Indeed, I do remember when she left.'" Mimi spoke as if she still found the exchange incredible. "Gloria told me that, one night after she was sound asleep, Dolorosa knocked on her door and said that Mother Majella wanted to see her in her office right away.

"When Gloria got there, the whole Council was there, sitting in state. Mother Majella told Gloria that she was to go and waken 'Sister St. John,' tell her to pack her things, and that Gloria was to personally escort Josephine to the front 'receiving' parlor and wait with her until the taxi that had been ordered arrived."

"What?" Kate asked softly.

"Ahyup." Mimi continued, "Gloria told me that she told Majella and the brass that she could not possibly go wake a young woman out of her sleep and tell her to go home in the middle of the night. She also told them that, as one of Josephine's directors, she should be told why Josephine was being sent home."

Mimi wasn't finished. "Well we all know how receptive to 'input' those girls were so, of course, Mother Majella told Gloria 'do as you're told!'" Mimi's sister, Kathy, sat with her jaw dropped and the others winced with their familiarity with such rich conventual 'dialogue.'

"Well, Gloria said that, for the first time in her life, she really lost it. She laughed as she told me this, but she said she screamed at Mother Majella at the top of her lungs and said, 'I will NOT go tell ANY of my charges to leave here in the MIDDLE of the night! ESPECIALLY when I have no reason to DO so! You must tell me why! I am FED UP with all the secrecy around this place! I have a conscience too and I cannot do this to a young sister at eleven o'clock at night!'" Mimi was enjoying the vision this unlikely encounter conjured up in her mind as she relayed Gloria's account to the group.

Kathy Gordon was enrapt. Everyone was enrapt. Finally Kathy blurted, "Is this real? Did this stuff really happen or am I on a movie set?"

"Kath, it happened," Mimi deadpanned and then continued. "Poor Gloria was actually a little embarrassed telling the story, but you could see she was getting a kick out of her own feistiness back then. Anyway, Reverend Mother Majella stood up at her desk, glared at Gloria, and actually shouted back at her, 'UNDER THE VOW OF OBEDIENCE I COMMAND YOU TO DO AS YOU ARE TOLD!'

"That snapped poor Gloria out of her silly senses and she left, told Josephine to pack, escorted her to the front door and into the waiting taxi. No explanation. Gloria said that when she closed the front door after the cab pulled away, the hall door to the front parlor opened and Majella, Dolorosa, and the other three on the council silently stepped out and into the chapel. Gloria thought they had staked out the front parlor to make sure Josephine left as swiftly as directed."

"Oh my God . . ." Annie whispered.

"You don't think . . ." Siobhan couldn't even say aloud the stormy thought that was rising in her like a flashflood from which she could not escape.

"I do, Siobhan. I know what you're thinking and, God help me, I do," Mimi confessed.

It was difficult to distinguish whether the stultified mood of the group was travel fatigue, mellowness from the meal combined with the warmth of the fire, or private concatenations being conducted in each one's mind. The room had grown heavily quiet.

Kate finally offered, "I don't know about anybody else, but I need to shift gears before I even think of going to bed tonight. My brain hurts. Is a moratorium on discussing any more of this stuff reasonable until tomorrow?"

Eily eagerly agreed. "I think that's a good idea, Kate. I need to decompress a little."

Kate stood up and suggested, "I know it's midnight, but how 'bout a little walk by the 'light of the silvery moon'?"

Surprisingly, everyone agreed and went to get their winter gear on. Kathy said that she'd go with them and head home afterward. As they went out the front door and down the steps Kate said, "Hey! I almost forgot! Have any of you been contacted by a private investigator named Robert Young?"

"Oh my God, yes!" Eily yelled. "I meant to ask earlier! I got an email from him!"

"Who's he?" Mimi's sister wanted to know.

"He was hired by the gal that Josephine accused of stalking her," Kate said.

"Now girls, I thought we made a pact not to discuss anymore of this stuff tonight; we'll never get to sleep. In fact, I propose to the hostess that when we get back we all have a little Hennessey as a nightcap and then go off to our trundles," Annie bravely recommended.

Carrie, remembering Annie's nervousness at the airport over the prospects of the Robert Young discussion, came to Annie's aid. "I second that! Let's just enjoy this clear night, the bazillion stars, and the full moon."

"Agreed!" Eily declared. "Now if you turkeys could just pick up the trot a little I might get some body heat going and get this miserable walk over with faster! Come on, girls, move those glutes! Mr. Hennessey is waiting to take me to bed!"

Chapter 37

What Mimi didn't know about her exchange with Sister Gloria Penney at the train station in Boston was how disturbed Gloria had been by her account of the 'Crime Line' broadcast. The 'Silver Streak' Metroliner to Washington, D.C. had proven to be one long ride on the uneven tracks of stream of consciousness for Gloria. The paperback she had taken with her to help pass the time was barely started. Torrents of episodes from the time when she had been Assistant Directress of Junior Sisters kept sweeping through her concentration, finally foiling all attempts to read.

She was going to the centennial celebration of one of the academies her community ran in a suburb just outside of D.C. All former faculty had been invited and she knew she would see many Sisters she hadn't seen in years. Since Dolorosa had been principal for a few years in the 80's, Gloria presumed she would see her there too. "I wonder if Dolorosa saw that show?" she mused to herself as she watched the sign for Stamford, Connecticut blur by. "I'll have to be sure and ask her about it. She was quite involved with Sister St. John in the novitiate as I recall. Quite protective of her I always thought . . ."

Gloria remembered the time that Dolorosa asked her for a meeting in Dolorosa's office. Even though Sister St. John, or Josephine, had been professed for over five months and was no longer under the direction of Dolorosa, it was Dolorosa in whom Josephine had continued to confide. Gloria closed her eyes as the train headed south and saw that meeting projected on the lids of her shut eyes.

"Sister Gloria, thank you for coming." Dolorosa indicated the two chairs in the corner of her office and sat down in one while Gloria followed and sat in the other.

"Not at all, Sister Dolorosa. What can I do for you?" the ever cordial Sister Gloria offered.

"It's not what you can do for me, Sister Gloria; it's what you can do for one of the Junior Sisters."

Gloria's face pinched in concern that one of her "charges" might be in some difficulty.

Dolorosa fiddled with freeing her veil from being caught between her back and the back of the chair and tugged it up toward her shoulders a bit as she spoke so she could move her head about easily.

"It has come to my attention that Sister St. John is not fairing very well at the Motherhouse. This is your first year as a member of our formation team. What you do not know is that Sister St. John underwent many trials and tribulations while she was a novice here. Personally, I believe she endured 'the dark night of the soul' we read about that only a very few saintly souls are privileged to experience."

"Sister Dolorosa, I've only known Sister St. John these five months. According to your recommendations after Sister St. John's profession, I was instructed by Mother Majella to assign Sr. St. John to one of the private rooms the college sisters have on the other side of the building. In the meantime, all the other Junior Sisters in her class are living in appalling conditions in dormitories that probably could and should be condemned. My experience of Sister St. John is that she is very limited socially.'

"'Limited socially'? This isn't a finishing school, Sister Gloria! We're grooming these young women for holiness, not the Cotillion! Sister St. John is a fragile soul and I'm afraid, being such, she invites misinterpretation," the Directress of Novices evenly said.

"Nonetheless, Sister Dolorosa, I find Sister St. John does little to socialize with her peers . . ."

Dolorosa cut Gloria off, "She's very shy, Sister, and given to very little frivolous conversation. She has an intense spirituality and is not as animated as others may be."

"My experience of Sister St. John is that she is intense, but not in a healthy way. The intensity I'm describing feels more disquieting than spiritual."

Dolorosa looked genuinely surprised and curious. "What do you mean?"

" At my probing, she has admitted to struggles with anger. When I press her about the source of the anger she only says 'Please forgive my pride in not being forthcoming with you, but I would like to leave the novitiate behind.'"

"Precisely," Sister Dolorosa said as she tapped her forefinger on the wooden arm of her chair. "I think Sister St. John is lonely. I believe she feels the other Junior Sisters in her class regard her as receiving preferential treatment by her not living in one of the dorms as they do. She feels they harbor ill feelings toward her and she intentionally excuses herself from their presence in a valiant effort to not tempt in them uncharitable thoughts or actions. What you perceive as anger, I perceive as genuine humility."

"Well, of course, any behavior on the part of anyone in the Juniorate that would smack of exclusion or deliberately isolating someone from the community must be addressed," the dutiful Sister Gloria acknowledged.

"I had hoped you would see it that way," Dolorosa victoriously countered. "We have just begun the first week of December; a little variation on this season's theme of 'no room at the inn' couldn't be more timely. It saddens me to think that Sister St. John has voiced intimations of loneliness, especially in this festive and joyous season. I trust, however, that you will use prudence in your meeting with the Junior Sisters and call the meeting when Sister St. John is not available. I also hope you will be delicate enough in your message to not make her the scapegoat for their necessary chastisement."

"I will spend a few days in prayer before I do anything. I honestly have no quarrel with the Junior Sisters; they are wonderful young women. However, in this season of peace and good will, I will take our conversation to heart and reflect on how to address the topic of inclusion with them. Please keep me in your prayer," Sister Gloria requested.

Standing up and putting her hands in her sleeves, Sister Dolorosa bowed slightly to Sister Gloria who returned the bow and quietly left.

"Princeton! Princeton, New Jersey!" cried the trainman as he walked through the car jarring Gloria out of her uncomfortable reminiscence. She stood up to stretch a little while the passengers got off at this stop. When she sat down she reached into her bag and pulled out a cheese sandwich and a bottle of Poland Spring. Maybe a little food would help the knot in her stomach.

Chapter 38

At eleven o'clock the following day, the centennial Mass for "The Academy" took place with great pageantry. Because it was being held on a Saturday, the auditorium had been transformed into a large church to accommodate the crowd. As Sister Gloria Penney entered the lobby outside the auditorium, she was approached by members of the student council who asked if she was a guest or a former faculty member. Once she identified herself as the latter, she was given a badge with her name on it and a corsage. A queue of people waiting to say hello to her formed while one of the students struggled with pinning on the corsage. She blew kisses, waved, winked and mouthed "how are you?" to the happy faces before her.

The roar of the lobby's capacity crowd and the squeals of excitement at meeting friends from the past were instantly hushed as a student stepped to the main door of the auditorium and rang a large bronze hand bell signaling that Mass was about to begin.

An orchestra was seated below the stage upon which an altar had been placed. As the first notes of the opening song were played, everyone stood.

An endless procession, led by student representatives carrying a cross, candles and banners, entered the auditorium and slowly made its way to the stage. Immediately after the students followed Sister Diane

Huntley, President of the Marafield Sisters, then the Regional Superiors of the Order. Behind them were members of the school board and present and past faculty members.

A deacon, the father of one of the students, came next. He walked alone and slowly waved an ornate golden incense burner that filled the assembly with an old familiar fragrance. Immediately behind him was Sister Dolorosa Feeney, flanked by two more deacons. She carried the book of scripture that was encased in an elaborate gold jacket. As liturgically prescribed, she carried it above shoulder height for all to see. Next came about fifty priests and finally two bishops who preceded the Cardinal of Washington.

Gloria was impressed with how little Sister Dolorosa had changed. No longer in veil but in a simple black suit, there was no mistaking that she was still a nun. The priests, bishops and cardinal all looked at the people gathered, nodding greetings to or recognition of those around them as they made their way down the aisle. Not Dolorosa, though. Neither looking left not right, hers was the very face of solemnity. "As usual," thought Gloria who waved back to one of the priests who spotted her in the crowd.

When the liturgy was at long last over, everyone was ushered into the new gym that had been set up like a catering hall. There were buffet tables set up around the perimeters and hors d'oeuvres stations were in the center of the floor. Gloria made her way to the hors d'oeuvres station with three of her cronies she had been on faculty with at the Academy. As she stepped away from the crudités a hand touched her elbow. It was Sister Dolorosa. Gloria's friends motioned that they'd save a place for her at their table and left.

"My goodness, long time no see, Sister Gloria," Dolorosa said trying to reach for ebullience. "It's so good to see you. How have you been?"

"Very well, thank you. I'm back in Boston now. I was in Florida for a while doing some ESL classes with the immigrant population there. How about you? What are you up to these days?" Gloria could feel the effort of this little exchange.

"I live here now," Dolorosa told Gloria. "I'm 'in residence,' as the saying goes. I work at the Cathedral and commute from here. I'm so pleased for the community with the turn out today," she said as she scanned the room. "It's nice seeing so many faces from the past."

"Speaking of faces from the past, something came to my attention yesterday. Did you happen to see 'Crime Line' a few weeks ago? There was a woman on who was in the novitiate when you and I were on the formation team." There was great relief in having a topic to discuss with this woman Gloria had always considered 'formidable.'

"No, I'm afraid I didn't," Dolorosa cocked her head in interest. "Who was the woman? Did you recognize her?"

"I haven't actually seen the show yet myself. I'm hoping someone somewhere taped it and I'll get to see it eventually. Anyway, the woman was Josephine Quarters."

Dolorosa was blank.

Gloria tried again. "Josephine Ahearn Quarters." A glimmer. "Sister St. John of the Cross. Remember? St. John . . ."

The glow of the reunion at hand faded from Dolorosa's face. "What on earth was she doing on 'Crime Line'?"

"She was on because she had accused a female teacher of stalking her for over a year. The show was entirely about all the stalking allegations . . . a whole hour's worth! The disturbing part was at the end of the show. The interviewer found out that Josephine's DNA had been discovered on some of the horrible letters she had received from the stalker. I only heard this yesterday, but I can't get her out of my mind. I wish I had seen the show."

Dolorosa was now oblivious to the tumult of festivity around her. "How did you say you found out about this?"

"I ran into one of her classmates at the train station yesterday; she told me about it." Gloria continued. "Apparently, since the show aired, she and dozens of others from Josephine's class are being contacted by a private investigator hired by the woman she accused of stalking her. God help the poor woman if she has been wrongfully accused. On the other hand, God help poor Josephine if it's all true and that teacher did do all those things to her: what a nightmare!"

"Good Lord!" Dolorosa gasped. "I wonder if our president is aware of this? Do you see Sister Diane Huntley anywhere?"

While both women looked around for Sister Diane, Gloria wanted to know, "why should Sister Diane know about this?"

"Gloria, don't you realize that the community could be dragged into this?" a hint of impatience could be detected in Dolorosa's delivery. "I mean, if a private investigator is contacting people who were in the novitiate with Josephine, the 'novitiate' is 'us'! We'd be foolish not to give Sister Diane and the administration a 'heads up' on this. Are you going to be here for a while? Let me go find Sister Diane before she slips away. I'll find you before you go." Dolorosa stood on her tiptoes to survey the room, spotted her target and made a straight line toward the president of the Marafield sisters who was chatting with a bishop.

Chapter 39

Sister Dolorosa worked her way behind the bishop to whom Sister Diane was speaking. When she caught her president's eye she discreetly motioned that she needed to speak with her. Sister Diane winked to let her know she got the message; the bishop nodded to let Sister Diane know he caught her wink and that he understood she was being summoned. After shaking hands with the bishop, Sister Diane went over to Sister Dolorosa.

"Hi Dolorosa. You looking for me?" the middle aged president asked. Before Dolorosa could answer Sister Diane said, "what a wonderful gathering you sisters and your committees put together. I'm sure everyone associated with this event is exhausted by now, but all your work has certainly paid off. Thank you so much for your time, your dedication and your own personal part as a former principal here in keeping The Academy 'on the map.'"

"You're very welcome, Sister Diana. We're very pleased with the turn out. And we're very grateful to you and all the members of the Provincial Team for taking time out of your busy schedules to come down here and celebrate with us."

Sister Diane offered, "Did you just want to catch me to say goodbye before I take off or did you need to speak with me about something?"

"I do need a minute with you. I think it's fairly important. Would you mind if we went down the hall to one of the classrooms?"

"Is everything alright? You haven't bad news about anyone have you?" Diana's face looked concerned.

"Oh no, it's nothing like that. I'm sorry if I alarmed you. Someone told me something a few minutes ago that I think you should know as president of the order, but we'll be interrupted a thousand times if I try to tell you here."

"THAT is for sure!" Sister Diana laughed as she received a kiss on the cheek from one of the guests who was leaving. "Let's duck out now. Where can we go?"

"This way, please," Dolorosa said as she escorted her president into the first classroom they came to and closed the door.

Dolorosa began, "By any chance did you happen to see 'Crime Line' recently . . . about a teacher who accused another female teacher of stalking her?"

"Yes! Yes, I did!" Sister Diana was very animated. "Throughout the whole show my heart went out to that teacher. But then at the end, the interviewer totally confused the viewers as to who did what. I'm not sure I ended up completely believing the victim."

"Are you aware that the stalking victim is a former nun of ours?"

"Really . . ." Diana dramatically exaggerated the length of the word. Then she giggled a little as she said, "and there I was, grateful to God she wasn't on faculty in any of our schools!"

"Well don't give a sigh of relief yet, Sister Diana," Dolorosa nervously warned.

"Why is this of such great concern for you, Dolorosa?" Diana sensed the tension in the nun in front of her and adjusted the lighthearted manner with which she was handling the encounter.

"I need to tell you a few things in greatest confidentiality. I and a few others made a solemn pledge to Reverend Mother Majella, God rest her soul, never to discuss any of what I'm about to tell you. I feel so conflicted. I gave her my word and I have been true to it all these years, but there are things you should know in case the community is ever questioned about this woman."

"Sister Dolorosa, perhaps you're worrying unnecessarily about this.

We often receive inquiries and background checks about people who once were associated with the community because of certain jobs they may be seeking. Tell me why you're so concerned."

"I was told that a private investigator is in the process of contacting people with whom this woman was in the convent." Dolorosa spoke in a hushed voice. "I was on the formation team when the woman on the show, Josephine Ahearn, was in the novitiate and when she was a Junior Professed Sister at the Motherhouse. There are things I think you should know lest this man contact you or any of our sisters."

With that, Sister Diane pulled two desks to face each other and sat down to hear a piece of Marafield history that neither she nor anyone would discover in the community's archives.

Chapter 40

There was a knock on the classroom door followed by the four members of the Provincial Team opening the door and playfully charging, "So there you are! We've been looking all over for you!" When they saw the gravity on the faces of both Sister Diana and Sister Dolorosa they instantly stopped and began backing out the door while one of them said, "I beg your pardon. Sorry for interrupting."

"No, wait, please; come in all of you and close the door," Diana directed. She turned to Sister Dolorosa and said "I will honor your request of confidentiality, Sister Dolorosa, but I think we need to bring this matter to the attention of the whole council. Since they're all here let's do it now. Is that okay with you?"

Dolorosa nodded agreement. Diane stood as she began speaking.

Turning to bring all of them into her crosshairs she said, "Sisters, Sister Dolorosa has just apprised me of a situation that I believe warrants legal counsel for the community. There was a show on television recently about a former member of the community. A private investigator has begun contacting several members of her class in the novitiate . . ."

"The novitiate! Who is it? When was she in?" one of the 'provincial leaders' asked. Another, "What show? What was it about?"

Diane answered all questions in one statement. "The woman's name is Josephine Ahearn Quuarters. She was at Marafield in the mid sixties. She was on a recent 'Crime Line' telling her story as the victim of a year long series of alleged stalking incidents."

Three of the 'leaders' chimed in excitedly that they had actually seen this particular show. However, none of them knew her.

"Why would the community need legal counsel for this?" one of the 'leaders' wanted to know. "We weren't mentioned in any way on the show were we?"

"No, we weren't. However, we should find out from our attorneys whether or not any of our sisters have to cooperate with this private investigator should he begin contacting any of them. Hopefully, this may be an unnecessary exercise on our parts. He may be contacting only those who left the community. At any rate, when we get back to Marafield tonight I will find out the exact year that this woman entered. I'd like to meet with all of you at 8:00 a.m. tomorrow in my office."

"What on earth could we possibly accomplish on a Sunday morning?" her first assistant asked, already tired at the prospects of the long trip that was ahead of them that afternoon.

"I want each of you to go over your membership lists of all sisters in your particular regions. Any sister who was in the convent with this woman should be called tomorrow and told to attend a mandatory meeting at Marafield next Saturday at 10:00a.m."

"What do we tell them when they ask what the meeting is about?"

"Tell them we are having a legal briefing regarding one of their former classmates from the novitiate and that's all you know about it, other than the fact that I expect 100% attendance. Advise them to share this information with no one: no one in their houses, no one in their families. Period." The Sister Diane who was calling the shots in this classroom bore little resemblance to the lightweight raconteur of Academy history that breezed from person to person, group to group in the reception down the hall.

Turning to Sister Dolorosa, the president informed her that she would be required to be at Marafield next weekend as well. In deference to her having been the Directress of Novices back then, Diane assured her that hers would be a separate meeting with the attorneys. She said, "Dolorosa, I'm glad you brought this to my attention. You did the right thing in telling me. The community has entrusted me to look after its welfare."

In a thin voice Dolorosa spoke. "Sister Diane, if I may . . ."

"Yes, Sister?"

"I think it would be wise to include Sister Gloria Penney in that meeting next Saturday. She was Assistant Directress of Junior Sisters then and, as I recall, Josephine's class was in her charge. I . . . she was never privy to any of the information I gave you . . . none of it. Quite by chance, she is the one who brought this to my attention today."

Diane asked in who's region Sister Gloria lived. The sister representing the northern region signaled that she lived in hers. "I think I saw her here; do you want me to tell her before we go?"

"No. Let's not engage in any unnecessary conversation about this till we speak with our lawyers. Add her to your list of calls tomorrow and tell her then."

Out of sheer habit Diane reached over to shake Dolorosa's hand and, as their hands were clasped, it was as though Diane looked into the very soul of Dolorosa whose eyes suddenly brimmed with tears that made the former directress wilt a little and look away. The others saw this and, not knowing the content of what she had just shared with Diane, went over to her and patted her on the back and kissed her gently on the cheek to console her.

Sister Diane, however, did not join them in their gestures of comfort but walked silently out of the room. She saw the sign for the faculty lavatory, went in, locked herself in a cubicle, wept copiously into a wad of toilet paper and then threw up.

Chapter 41

The last one to come downstairs for breakfast at Mimi Aroho's house was Annie Silo. When she got to the bottom of the staircase she was mildly surprised that she might be the first one down. No one was around. She followed the scent of coffee coming from the kitchen and found a tray of mugs on the counter between carafes of coffee and tea.

Breakfast plates, napkins, cranberry muffins and Galway Irish bacon, cooked and kept warm on a hot plate, were also arranged on the counter. As she stood quietly in the kitchen and took her first sip of coffee she heard the low murmur of voices from the pool area. Crossing over to the French doors that opened out to the pool, she saw the whole gang already out there. Kate was in the pool doing laps; Eily was lounging in the Jacuzzi; Mimi was sitting at the table reading the paper; Carrie and Siobhan were stretched out on chaise lounges and deep in conversation.

Mimi looked up from the paper and said, "Well, good afternoon!" The others looked up to see who Mimi was talking to and immediately began to give Annie the business.

"What are you a bat, you don't do daylight?" jeered Eily.

"Now, now! I have fifteen whole minutes of morning left. Good morning everybody!" Annie rolled with the teasing and walked over to join Mimi at the table. "Nice spa you run here. Do you give discounts to Marafield alumnae?"

"Marafield alumnae? Let's see . . . laity free; clergy double," Mimi quipped. "You want breakfast or lunch? These chickadees have been up for hours and ate breakfast around eight-thirty. I'm going to put some lunch out for them."

"Are you kidding me?" Annie yelled over to the others, "what's the matter, you geriatrics can't get a decent night's sleep?"

"No, lovey," Eily bantered right back, "you just spent a little more time with 'Mr. Gibson' than we did with 'Mr. Hennessey'!"

"Owww!" Annie feigned being wounded while the others all laughed.

Kate got out of the pool and announced she was going up to shower. Mimi negotiated with everyone that a lunch of salad and soup would be ready, poolside, at one o'clock. She suggested that they all 'put the good threads on' in the evening around eight and go out for a last hurrah dinner. That met enthusiastic consensus. Kate reminded everyone that whatever stories they had left to swap should be shared today since there were early departures lined up for Sunday.

"Right!" Siobhan concurred. "I want to know about this private investigator and how the hell he got my phone number! But don't start talking about anything good till we're all here for lunch. I have to get out of these jammies, take a shower and put on my sweats. Imagine . . . that is my entire schedule for the day! Is this a great Saturday or what?"

When one o'clock rolled around, Annie was the only one at the pool. She was the picture of relaxation, draped all over the Jaccuzzi like an over cooked noodle with her eyes closed. Mimi tiptoed back and forth from the kitchen to the poolside table setting up the lunch trying not to disturb the dreamily drifting friend. As the others started arriving they automatically joined Mimi in the preparations. Annie finally came to and saw that everyone had come down. She got off her little raft of reverie, towel dried, put on a plush waffle pattern terry cloth robe and pulled up a chair with the others at the table.

"Oh wow, this really is like a spa," Annie marveled. "What's this . . . spinach salad, French onion soup . . . yummy!" Mimi made the last trip from the Kitchen and said as she placed the last two items on the table, "and sour dough bread and ice cold Pinot Grigio, which completely blow your spa theory! Enjoy it anyway!"

About forty-five minutes into the meal, it was time for the private investigator story. Surprisingly, it was Annie who initiated it. She thought it would be better to bring it up herself rather than be tortured with waiting for it to be mentioned.

"I, uh . . . I was telling Carrie at the airport yesterday that a funny coincidence occurred that involved me and, uh, in an indirect way, uh, all of you . . ."

Kate knew instantly that Annie was the investigator mole. So did Mimi and Eily. All three sets of eyes connected for a nano-second signaling, "got it." With every other sentence of Annie's saga there were groans and gasps either at Annie's guilelessness, her plain stupidity, or her vulnerability. The most upset of all was Siobhan and she could not, would not conceal her annoyance with Annie for getting her involved again with this person from her past, no matter how remotely. Siobhan was in tears and let them roll down her cheeks unchecked. She wanted Annie to feel bad.

"How could you do this to me? To us?" Looking around at everyone as she spoke she said, "I would never give your names and addresses away to anyone! My God, who doesn't know the protocol for contacting people any more?" Looking directly at Annie she continued, "Annie, if someone called me and wanted to get in touch with you I'd take the person's name and number down and call you! I'd let you be the one to make the decision to speak to that person, not me! Now I have this guy leaving messages on my machine, sending me email. And for what? For what? To drag me –and all of us, I presume–back into the sick little world of Josephine Ahearn Quarters, who's still sticking it to anyone she can. Thanks a lot."

Annie's face had turned scarlet and she played with a thread on the end of her cuff not looking at anyone. Little muscles in her chin twitched much the way a child's does who is fighting tears. She whispered, "Siobhan, I'm so sorry. I'm so, so terribly sorry . . ."

Lifting her head, she looked around at the others as she repeated her apology to them. She was at a loss as to what else she could possibly say.

Chapter 42

It was Siobhan who managed to steer the conversation back onto some salvageable track. "Alright. The bloodletting's over. Let's at least try and figure this thing out. Kate, help us out here."

Kate put on her 'Sister Mary Perfect' voice and said with a straight face, "First of all, if we could just sing three verses of 'Kumbayah' I think we'd all feel ever so much better." Siobhan, on her right, and Eily, on her left, both swatted her with their napkins. Recovering, Kate changed her demeanor a few degrees to match her acknowledgment of what had just taken place.

"Annie, I've got to be honest and tell you that I agree with Siobhan; giving our names out to some guy you really don't know too well," Kate imitated George Bush Sr., "wasn't prudent, shunta dunnit, but it happened. Can you understand Siobhan's anger and all the other mini snits going on around the table?"

"Absolutely. I don't blame anybody for being upset with me. Honest to God, it was done so innocently. You know me; I can talk paint off a canvas. I say way more than I have to. Always did. I never dealt with a private investigator before in my life. He's a really nice guy with a very good memory. Then, when he said he knew some priest who was at 'Camp Horrendous' with us back in the novitiate days, I felt like we were kind of connected, you know what I mean? Oh Christ . . ."

Kate brought Siobhan into the conversation, "Siobhan, you okay now or do you need to say more to Annie?"

"No, I'm alright." She looked directly at Annie and said, "I'm okay now. I just get wild thinking about how much crap Josephine has gotten away with and she's still at it! Here we are, all these years later, talking about whom? Whom? Sister Flippin St. John!"

They all cracked up at Josephine's new name and were able let go of the tension that had enveloped them.

"Annie," Siobhan asked, "what does this guy want with us anyway?"

"From what I gathered, I think he's trying to establish a pattern of stalking allegations on her part. He knew about the diary. He knew about the private room she was given in the novitiate and in the motherhouse. I admit I told him I was one of those accused by her about the diary thing. He asked if I was the only one accused and that's where I screwed up and gave names. It didn't feel like an interrogation, it just felt like I was telling those ridiculous 'Boot Camp for Jesus' stories again."

Mimi spoke up. "Well, I think we should have a plan for when he finally does track us all down and gets us 'live' on our phones."

"So do I," Kate and Eily said together. "Got one?" asked Eily.

"I'm incubating one," Mimi stalled. "What would you suggest, Kate?"

"Hmmm . . ." Kate was thinking. "I won't lie to him and pretend I know nothing. On the other hand, I also don't want to offer him anything he doesn't already know and end up inadvertently doing what Annie got caught in." She was trying to work it through as she spoke. "I think, for me, I'll tell –what's his name 'Robert Young'?– I think I'll tell Mr. Young that I will not offer him any information, names, or addresses, but will only corroborate what he already knows. That seems reasonable. I mean, I really only know the parts that I actually participated in; all the rest is really just hearsay unless I was there."

"That's good," Eily assessed, "works for me. And you are right, Kate: each of us only has snatches of the whole cloth, not the whole cloth."

"Ah, but girls," Mimi said in a low voice, "we all know who sat at the loom and held every thread to that 'whole cloth' in her hands."

"Maybe. Isn't everybody who was "in charge" back then dead?" The doctor from the West Coast presumed. "Majella's dead. Her second-in-command is dead, I remember her dying. The whole Council was pretty old back then, they can't possibly still be alive."

Carrie said, "You're right, Eily; all those you've mentioned are long gone."

"No . . . not everybody," Siobhan was remembering with some satisfaction. "

"Right!" Mimi pointed at Siobhan for emphasis, then looked at each as she quizzed the group, "and who do we know who does know the whole saga, all the way from starving saint, to bleeding mystic, to burnt diary, to inquisition, and to things that go 'bye' in the night?"

"Dolorosa!" they all screamed.

"There's my plan. That's what I'm going to do when Mr. Young comes 'acallin'," Mimi said with conviction. "When he asks me, 'Ms. Aroho, to the best of your knowledge, who would you actually say can connect all the dots to these various pieces of information for me?' I'm going to tell him, Sister Dolorosa Feeney can, Mr. Young, Sister Dolorosa Feeney."

"We should all say that!" Siobhan opined. "After all, it's true. Let's lob the story right back to where it belongs . . . in Marafield's court. Deal?"

"Deal."

"Deal."

"Deal.

"Deal."

Everyone raised her wine glass to seal the agreement.

Carrie shyly said, "I really don't have a right to clink my glass with yours since I'm not in on any of that stuff and I'll never be called for anything, thank God! But for what it's worth, I do agree with you. Dolorosa knows where all the bodies are buried when it comes to that formation stuff." She thought for a moment, shook her head at the prospects of it all then added, "Boy, if anything ever does materialize and that private investigator ends up tracking down Dolorosa, you'll feel her knickers twisting all the way up the coast and across the country!"

Chapter 43

As Robert Young drove to his office, he was thoroughly enjoying his fantasy of walking in on the little reunion that had gone on during the weekend over in Glendarff that Annie Silo had let slip. "Imagine ringing the doorbell and announcing myself," he played. He was quite pleased with his efficiency that, by the time those women had gotten together at Mimi Aroho's house, they all would have heard from him. His introductory calling card dropped from cyberspace into each woman's home.

At all costs he didn't want to scare any of them off. Actually, they sounded like a good group from the stories he had heard. Solid citizens. Kind of an investigator or attorney's dream: a bunch of women who had actually been in the convent! He extrapolated his friend, James Carey's, still intact integrity and values onto them. He hoped he wouldn't be disappointed. He needed to see just how much of a pattern of any kind he could establish in Josephine's life and how far back it might go. Thirty years of an established pattern, if these gals could provide it, would take the wind out of the sails of any defense Miss Quarters could hire.

Whenever the weather forecast for the following day would indicate fair skies, Rob would plan to be in his office by 6:30 am. It was a ritual. He would stop at the Stop 'n' Shop one block from the office and buy The Globe and one fresh Kaiser roll that would still have a trace of warmth in it by the time he got to his office. He would make a fresh pot of coffee in the Braun he and Jim kept there and would go about the steps in this ritual without turning on the lights. He preferred operating in the early golden light broadcast from the horizon and its reflection off the still water of the harbor that softly bathed the office walls in warm pastels.

While the coffee brewed, Rob would stand at the window and take in the view. In this pristine hour of quiet he would not mull over problems, findings or leads. Instead, he presented himself to the wall of windows in a nearly blank state of perceptual expectation. Something in the sky or on the water would eventually catch his eye and he would follow its flight or course till it slipped from view. Or, something 'out there' would catch his imagination and his gaze would turn inward to his own spiritual landscape. He always waited for either with intrigue. A theologian might describe this little exercise of his as "awakening awareness and conscious attunement to the sacred." Rob Young just referred to it as "my time."

His time had nearly ebbed by the second cup of coffee. He would sip his third cup and take little pieces of the Kaiser roll while he sat at his desk and read the morning papers. By then he would hear the elevator click on and its doors open and close. Next, it would hum its passengers to their selected floors, pause four seconds till the door slid open and closed again then click off, a waiting silent sentinel. He heard the timpani of keys and banging doors begin the cadence of the workday. At any time, a whistling Jim Carey could be expected to tap on the office door politely signaling his entrance. Twenty minutes later, the morning choreography was completed with the arrival of his office partner.

"I'm just crazy about that cologne you wear . . . Eau de Starbucks! Can't wait to get some myself," the ever pleasant social worker said as he hung up his top coat. "How's 'Monsieur Pirot' today?" He poured some coffee into a mug and motioned to Rob with the pot, "ready for a refill?"

"No, I've induced a two-point-five tremor on the Richter scale already," Rob smiled back. "Thanks anyway. And I'm great. I just watched them hoist a brand new hull into the water. Enormous. Just the shell, no cabin or anything yet. I think it's for a new lobster boat. They look half their size in the water."

"How come I only get to see paint or welding barges when I come in early?" Jim said as he wandered over to the window to look out.

Rob had finished with the papers, folded them back up and offered them to Jim who gladly accepted them. "Thanks. These'll come in handy after I've corrected my sixty fifth paper on family systems therapy. Hey, what's this?"

Rob followed Jim's eyes to see what he had spotted on his desk and thought it was the tidy columns of information he had collected and collated. "This? It's that teacher case I told you about. I'm trying to line things up sequentially. Kind of 'get my ducks in a row' so I can figure this wacky thing out."

"Nice little system you have there. What I meant was what's that," Rob pointed to the last column that had a blue index card at the top with the word "Marafield" printed on it. Below "Marafield" was a black and white formal glossy of young novices lined up on the steps of a grand old building. Some of the faces were circled in red, some in green. Beneath that photo was a legend of names to go with the circled faces that Rob had typed out in their corresponding colors. Jim got closer to the desk and looked over Rob's shoulder. "Mind if I ask you what your growing interest in nuns and Marafield is all about? Can I take a look at that picture?"

Rob handed the picture to Jim, "Knock yourself out. Know any of them?"

"Who could tell? They all look alike except for 'Attilla the Nun' on the top step in the black veil. Yikes! Now there's a face that says 'no, nay, never!'" Rob looked to see if there were any more pictures in the Marafield column. "So what gives? What's with the nuns?"

"Nothing with the nuns, really," Rob leaned back in his chair as he answered. "I told you, I'm working for the woman who was accused of stalking that teacher who was on 'Crime Line.' Well," Rob stood up and pushed his chair back to give him and Jim room to view the roadmap he had made so far. "I've traced Josephine Quarters, the alleged stalking victim who's pinned all the incidents on my client, from her present job back to her first workplace." As he said that his hand touched the first column marked “CURRENT/ALPINE.” “Prior to where she is now, she was in this school district,” his hand touched the next card at the top of the second column labeled “Baratra.”

Jim followed and added, “and the third row means she worked in ‘QUEENSMONT’. Did you know that was a school for what they used to call ‘troubled’ girls?”

“You know,” Rob acknowledged, “the only reference point I have for that is way back when we were in high school. Remember how it used to rankle the girls if anyone said ‘Wahdayah, from Queensmont!’ It was a real slam, but that’s all I really knew about the place. I have leads for the other places, but nothing for Queensmont.”

Chapter 44

Jim tapped the blue card with "MARAFIELD" printed on it and said, "and what about this last column, Marafield? Did she work there too or was she a student there?"

"That's what the picture's for. Look, here," Rob pointed to a novice on the top row that he had circled in red. "That is the woman who was on 'Crime Line'. The one who's accused my client of stalking."

Jim took the picture and moved over to the window to get a better look. "Man, how would you ever know what she looks like today if this was all you had to go on? Skinny and wore glasses is about all you get. Well, how 'bout that." He handed the picture back to Rob.

"Yeah, how 'bout that?" Rob repeated with different inflection. "I gotta tell you, knowing she was a nun and all that has thrown me a little curve in terms of Judy Mazola, my client."

Jim leaned on the edge of his own desk facing Rob and looked puzzled. "What do you mean? How's that throw you a curve?"

"Well, I hate to admit it, but finding out she was a nun has me wondering who the hell is telling the truth here. The 'nun factor' tips credibility a little more to the stalking victim's side. On the other hand, my client's record is impeccable. I'm trying to pull back on my old fashioned conditioning that clergy trumps laity."

"What does that mean?"

"Well, you know, if she was in the convent once, surely she wouldn't falsely accuse an innocent person of the things she claims my client has done to her. That kind of curve."

"Hey, look, remember what good ol' Uncle Carl said: 'nothing is as it seems.' Jung knew all about that archetypal symbol stuff. No profession has a corner on the market of virtuous living. We just think some do. Human is human, pal and, subsequently, that means perfection ain't all it's been cracked up to be."

"Believe me, I know that all too well. Anyway, I've put that prejudice to rest. It only lasted for the weekend."

"Was she there when they had that fire?"

"What fire?" Rob asked.

"Come on! Don't you remember? They had a huge fire there back in the sixties. Their whole Motherhouse was destroyed, loads of nuns were injured; one even died."

"I was out of the country for a few years, complements of Uncle Sam if you'll recall. In fact, you weren't around either, complements of the Deity. You were in Seminary, then you got sent to some boondocks place for a while. How did you find out about the Marafield fire back then?"

"My mother. Don't forget, it was a big deal to be selected for altar boy duty at the Motherhouse. The Carey boys were the freckle faced favorites, so Marafield was always near and dear to my mother's heart. Anyway, Mom wrote to me every week of her life, God bless her. She sent me all the news clippings about it. It was a tremendous fire. All the dioceses around the country included prayers at all Masses for the nuns at Marafield during the week of the fire. I thought, how weird is this? Here I am all the way down in Appalachia, offering prayers for people who were practically in my own backyard."

"When was the fire, do you remember?" Rob was writing something on an index card as he asked.

"I'm pretty sure it was in 1966. It had to be sometime in winter. There was a ton of snow in all the pictures, that, I distinctly remember. I was missing a good old New England blizzard."

Jim went over to the coffee pot and poured another cup of coffee. He put the pot back and, while he stirred Creamora into the mug, he reminisced aloud. "Our old neighbor who lived down the road from us used to be the insurance broker for Marafield back then. He and my dad were great pals. I'm sure you met the guy at the house sometime, his name was Phil Tully."

"Was he the guy who always wore V-neck sweaters and saddle shoes? Had a crew cut?"

"Yeah! That's the guy. My mother used to call him 'Mr. Peeps.' Well every first Wednesday of the month he'd drag my father off to some 'Friends of Marafield' meeting and, after, they'd stop off for a beer." Rob could see Jim retrieving these scenes from his past and the smile it brought to his face in the telling. He continued, "In fact, I was home for a three week visit when the two of them went to one of those Wednesday night meetings. That night after Mr. Tully had gotten a little pie-eyed, I'm sure to my father's delight, he told my father something about the insurance money and the Motherhouse fire."

"Like what?" Rob was gaining interest. After all, every connection was to be examined. "Did the insurance company give Marafield a hard time?" Rob asked.

"Hell, no. Mr. Tully was their agent. He told Pop that the nuns definitely were all paid up. Somehow I think it had something to do with the Reverend Mother and the insurance money after the fire. Whatever it was, she and Tully got into a row and she practically had Mr. Tully blackballed from the diocese. Tully apparently told my father all about it over a few beers and all I know is that Pop came home and swore to my mother that he'd never go to another meeting of 'Friends of Marafield.'"

"But why?" Rob wanted to know, "what did Tully tell him?"

"Don't know. All I know was what Pop yelled before my mother shushed him to keep us from hearing him 'speak ill of those devoted Sisters.' She and Pop were in the kitchen and the more nervous she got about him saying something bad that we'd hear, the louder he'd bellow." Jim put on a brogue imitating his departed father and repeated what he had heard him say that night. "'If that eejit of a supeerie-yore won't listen to reason from as fine a man as Phil Tully, then I'll be damned if I'll crease me pants sittin' at another meetin' lookin' out fer

Marafield's welfare! Why should I, when that high and mighty Reverend Mother won't? That nune doesn't have the sense God gave a duck!"

Both Rob and Jim chuckled, shaking their heads at the vision both held of how "the old boy" sounded and looked when he went on one of his tears.

"And you never found out what the whole story was?"

"Nah. It never came up again as far as I knew and I left a few days later to go back to Appalacia."

Rob's mental computer was whirring now. "Jim, tell me: any chance that Phil Tully is still around?"

"He is, indeed! Can you believe it? He's about ninety-two now and is in residence at Hinesleigh Hall, the Carmelite's nursing home over by Marafield. I go over there on Sundays and take him some Scotch, The Globe, and a new book on tape. The guy's such good old stock. He's a little frail, but as sharp as ever. We chew the fat in the sunroom for a little while then he says, 'I've got something I want you to see in my room.' That's my cue: we go to his room, have a glass of Dewars and read The Globe. If you want to know anything about Marafield, he's your man."

"Think he'd see me?"

"What, are you kidding? Tell him you were the Carey's 'adopted child' and watch his reaction! He'll quiz you, though, just to see how well you know us. Ask him if he used to wear saddle shoes, that'll bring a twinkle to his eye; he'll like that you remember that." With that, Jim wrote down the name and address of the nursing home for Rob's new lead and handed it to him.

"Okay. I need to get cracking if I have any hopes of grading these papers by tonight's classes. I promise not to meddle with your investigation any more today," Jim assured his friend.

"No problem," Rob responded. "In fact, you've given me some good stuff to mull over. So anytime, bro, anytime."

Rob returned to his notes and noted that the fire had taken place while the nuns in the black and white glossy on his desk were at Marafield. According to the dates Sister Patricia Spillane had uncovered for him, the picture had been taken in 1963. This same class was then professed in 1965, and graduated in May of 1966. Except for Josephine

Ahearn Quarters, who graduated in 1968. The fire happened somewhere between the profession of these young faces before him and their graduation from Marafield. After his meeting with Mr. Tully, Rob knew it would be high time to start talking to "the girls."

Chapter 45

Hinesleigh Hall was high on a hill overlooking woods and a parkway on one side and, if you made your way to the very end of the property and to the other side of the buildings there, it had a sweeping view of Marafield's entire campus and, beyond that, mountains. It was so high up that Marafield looked like a miniature village that went with a train set. Just before the turn to go onto the property, there was a massive statue of "The Holy Family" bathed in floodlight. Next to it was a handsomely carved oval sign painted in blue and gold that hung from two posts and a crossbeam, "Welcome to Hinesleigh Hall."

Immediately across the driveway from that sign was an official looking warning: "Private Property. No Trespassing. No Hunting Permitted On these Premises. Violators Will Be Prosecuted." Bambi was safe with Jesus, Mary and Joseph. The entrance to Hinesleigh was a long windy, two lane private road dotted with bumper high little white hand painted signs that cautioned, "Limited view. Please proceed slowly. Thank you!" Two deer slowly meandered across the road just ahead of Rob's black Saab, apparently confident that the Carmelites and The Holy Family were watching out for them.

The sprawling complex that lay ahead through the blue spruce and fir trees was a beautiful brick American Colonial Georgian, unmistakably fashioned after Faneuil Hall in Boston, complete with cupola and weathervane. To the right of the building were formal gardens with a patio facing the grand view of the mountains. Far off to the left of the building were two out buildings, large red barns that housed machinery, tractors, snow plows and two golf carts in one and equipment, summer outdoor furniture, lumber and a tool shop in the other.

At the end of a lane of century old oak trees that deposited visitors at the front entrance of Hinesleigh Hall, was a circular driveway with a partially covered portico at the front door. Three quarters of the way around the circle was a turn that led to the parking lot. Rob parked there, walked over the to the front door and rang the doorbell. A buzzer sounded, signaling Rob to pull open the door and walk in.

His immediate impression was cleanliness and brightness. And civility. The large open foyer was busy with people getting off and on the elevators. Residents and staff addressed each other by name. Apparently it was the noon mealtime and the dining room, off to Rob's right, was the destination. Two nuns, in full habits and veils rarely seen any more, were part of the mix, giving and receiving greetings along with hugs here or kisses there from residents and staff alike. This was not at all what Rob's previous encounters with nursing homes had been like. He couldn't help but stand there and watch.

"Sir . . . excuse me, Sir?" a voice from his left was finally getting through. "Sir, you'll have to sign in over here, please."

Rob looked at the woman behind the reception booth and waived to acknowledge that he had heard her and went over. "Sorry about that! It's my first time here. It's quite a beautiful place, I was just taking it all in."

"Yes, we think it's nice too," the receptionist said warmly. "Are you here for an appointment or to visit one of our residents?"

"I'm here to see Mr. Phil Tully. A visit," Rob said, "I'm a friend. I just found out he was here."

"Oh, Mr. Tully, what a lovely man! He'll be happy for some company, I'm sure. Lucky for you it's not his card game day! Whoever's on duty gets strict orders from him right before their game: no calls, no company! Would you please sign the book right here and put his name in this column." She reached over and pointed to the column to be filled in.

Rob signed in while she watched. When he finished she reminded him, "If you can remember, please stop back here on your way out and sign out. Just write the time you're leaving and put your initials right after the time. Do you know where his room is?"

"No, I don't."

"He's up in 'the penthouse.' Top floor. The nuns are in 'the penthouse' too but on the other side of the building. Take the elevators on your right and go to the sixth floor. Don't take the ones on the left or you'll end up in the convent! When you get off the elevator turn right and go all the way down the hall, past the lounge. He's number 22 on your left. If he's not in his room, pick up any of the red phones and I'll page him for you. Have a nice visit."

Rob gave a wink and a nod as "thank you" and walked toward the elevators. On the right.

Chapter 46

As Rob approached Room 22, he heard the last phrases of a recording of Verdi's "Nabucco" being sung by a chorus. The door was opened half way and, sitting in a chair facing the mountains, was Mr. Phil Tully reading Tom Brokow's, *The Greatest Generation.* Rob knocked on the door and waited to be acknowledged.

"Come in! Come in!" the elderly gentleman yelled without turning around.

Rob walked across the room and stood just in front of Phil Tully who was surprised that a complete stranger was now with him. Before Rob could speak, Tully offered, "Are you lost, son? Who are you looking for, maybe I can help." As he spoke, he reached over and turned off the radio.

"No sir, I'm not lost." With that Rob put out his hand to shake the bony hand of the man in front of him. "My name is Robert Young. I'm a friend of Jim Carey's and I was one of the 'adopted sons' that was always over at the Carey house on South Morris Street."

"My God, Morris Street! Let me get a look at you, lad." With that, the tall skinny elder with thick pure white hair slowly stood up while taking Rob's hand and shaking it, studying his face the whole time. "Well, you're Jimmy's age that's for sure. Okay, let's see how well you knew them, then." Tully put his hands in his pockets and shifted his weight a little. He still had an athletic style about him. "Let's see . . . alright: what County were the Carey's originally from?"

"Too easy. Roscommon," Rob quickly answered, smiling.

"Or a bloody good guess!" Phil was enjoying this and behind his serious looking face and rheumy aqua eyes there was a glint of playfulness. "What nickname did we have for the big fella when he'd get a bit feisty?"

"Mrs. Carey's the only one I ever heard call him anything. She'd say, "alright now, 'Brian Boru,' calm down or we'll be after gettin' the doctor for ye!'"

Phil Tully put his head back and roared a good laugh, taking one hand out of his pocket to catch a drop at the corner of his right eye. "Ah, too good! A grand woman, that Maggie. And a grand 'Brian Boru' too. Like a brother. You'll do, lad! What's the name again?"

"Rob, Rob Young, sir. Now I have one for you."

"Fire away, Rob Young."

"Weren't you the trend setting 'saddle shoe man'? And you usually wore V neck sweaters? I think you also had a crew cut back then, right?"

"I'll be damned! So I did! Hell, I still do! The sweaters, I mean. I've gone the way of the tasseled loafer crowd now though, as you can see. They'd prefer me to wear sneakers, but the heels are too damn high on all of them and they're too God awful looking for my taste. I'm afraid I'd break my neck! I wear Docksiders most days. Depends on what I feel like when I get up. Pardon my manners, lad. Come over here and sit down," Tully motioned to the little sitting area by the window. His "suite" was like any at a Marriott Courtyard, nothing like the old dark musty rooms Rob had seen elsewhere.

"Now tell me about yourself, starting with what brings you here." A sudden worried look crossed the resident's face. "Nothing's happened to Jimmy has it?"

"No, Jimmy's great! He and I share an office down at the harbor in Boston."

"You're THAT Rob! Now I've got it all squared away! Of course! You and Jimmy were swim team buddies. Went to school together. I remember now. Your folks didn't belong to our parish then, did they?"

"No sir. We were not of the papal persuasion!"

"Oh Jaysus! And the old man let you eat there anyway!" Mr. Tully was as good a tease as the Carey's. "Talk about your 'lapsed Catholics'!" They both laughed and Tully continued. "So what brings you here, Rob Young?"

"Jimmy told me you were the insurance broker for a lot of institutions in the Boston area and some out this way."

"That's right. Handled most of the holdings for the Diocese: rectories, schools, convents, colleges. I'm not in the business any more, son. If you're looking for a good insurance broker for yourself I can probably put you in touch with someone at my old office. Don't tell me that you boys don't have insurance at your ages?"

"No, no, I'm all insured and buttoned down. You see, I was talking to Jimmy about a case I'm working on . . ."

Tully interrupted, "You a detective or a lawyer?"

"Retired state trooper. Now I do private investigation. Anyway, part of my research has lead me to Marafield right about the time of the big fire they had there."

"Spectacular, wasn't it?" the old man said as he sadly shook his head in the lingering disbelief that it actually had happened.

"I wouldn't know. I was in Viet Nam at the time. Jimmy was away too, so he's not a great resource. That's why he sent me to you. He said you'd know all about it."

"Well," Tully scratched his head as if to stir up some memories, "I'm not so sure I know all about it. Doubt anyone does any more. That was a long, long time ago, young Rob. I can tell you it was in February of '66. We had just had a blizzard and the goddamned fire trucks couldn't get close enough to the building to save it. Lot of nuns got hurt, badly hurt." His voice lowered and, again, he sadly shook his head, "One poor little thing died in it. They didn't find her body till the next morning. She was only about nineteen or twenty, just a kid, God rest her soul." He sat for a minute and stared out the window.

"Hey!" The elderly gentleman said, suddenly remembering something. He got up from his chair and went over to his walk-in closet. From inside the closet he yelled out to Rob, "Rob, would you come here and give me a hand?"

Rob was there in a flash. Tully had the lid of a trunk lifted up and pointed to one of three large metal boxes inside. One was labeled "Documents/Copies," another was labeled, "Pictures/Coins" The third was labeled, "Scrap Books." He pointed to the third box and asked Rob to lift it out for him and take it over to where they were sitting.

The meticulous old man went over to his desk, opened the drawer and took out a little black leather box. He examined the keys inside and extracted one that had the number "3" printed on it in permanent marker. As he sat down he handed the key to Rob and pointed to the box for him to open it. Rob obliged, lifted the lid and then turned the box around to face Mr. Tully.

Chapter 47

The box held exactly four scrapbooks and nothing more. He took out one, flipped through it, then handed it to Rob saying, "Take a look at that one while I search for what I'm looking for. You might see yourself or some people you know."

Rob was glad this was the only commitment he'd made for the afternoon and evening.

He got lost in the old photos while the organized gentleman across for him hummed his way through two more books. Tons of Carey pictures were in the scrapbook Rob had. Holidays, picnics, sports, hallmark events like graduations, proms, weddings, dances, awards dinners, ordination. He knew just about everyone in the pictures.

"Bingo!" Phil Tully said at full blast. "I wasn't sure if I held onto these or not, but here they are!" He turned the opened book around for Rob to see. Inside the protective cellophane were some aged and brittle news clippings and headlines about the Marafield fire. One headline blurted, "General Alarm Destroys Marafield!" Beneath it was, "Dozens of Nuns Injured, Critical." It was dated February 1, 1966. Another headline, dated February 2, 1966, cried "Fire Claims Life of Nun; Body Discovered In Rubble."

"Mind if I read these accounts, Mr. Tully?"

"You go right ahead. Say, young man, do you drink Scotch? I have my own bootlegger, you know.""

"So I've heard. I hope he doesn't unload his cheap swill on you!" Rob took off his sports coat and was tempted to sit in his underwear, it was so hot in the building. Mr. Tully, on the other hand, was wearing khakis, a Pendleton "Black Watch" plaid shirt and a navy blue pull over, looking quite comfortable.

"Now, now! It's not cheap swill. It's decent swill! Dewars. Neat or with a splash?"

From a shelf in the walk-in closet, Phil Tully took out a tan leather case the size of a shoebox and walked over to the table adjacent to where Rob sat. He unsnapped the flap on the case and removed two Irish crystal old fashioned glasses from one side, and the half full bottle of Dewars from its mooring on the other side.

"I'll take just a little with a splash; thanks," Rob said while he kept reading. He had finished all the clippings by the time both glasses were filled. He could see Mr. Tully straighten his shoulders as he held his drink aloft, ready to make a toast. Rob took the cue and stood, drink in hand.

The amiable resident of Hinesleigh Hall first offered, "Here's to the pleasure of meeting an old Morris Street friend. Or as the old boy would say, 'Here's to it and to it again. If you don't do it when you get to it," Rob knew Mr. Carey's toast by heart and recited the last line with the old Irishman, "*you'll never get to it to do it again*!' Slainte!" both said as they clinked their glasses and took a sip.

"Come over to the window. I want to show you something." Phil Tully said. "Take a look down there. See what looks like a park with buildings all around it? That's Marafield." Rob leaned his forehead on the window as he took in the view.

The man who had once drawn up insurance papers for a good number of buildings on the property below them pointed out the main entrance to the campus. "See those two fieldstone pillars?" Rob gave an uh-huh. "Go through them. See that big circle of lawn straight ahead of the pillars? There's a grotto in the middle of it, you following me?"

"Yes, sir. Got it."

"Well, that huge piece of unused land is where the Motherhouse stood. It was an enormous building. A landmark. Had a glass observatory on the top and a gold dome with a gold statue of our Blessed Mother on the top of that, 'Our Lady of Marafield.' The building was a tinderbox for sure. Burnt right down to the foundation. Damn shame."

The dapper Irishman continued. "My brother Liam, the Monsignor, God rest his soul, was the chaplain for the nuns over there. I'm sure he was my 'angel' who landed me so much business in the diocese. He'd never let on though. Always looked so surprised when I'd tell him about a new contract. I took very good care of him over the years, you know how it is: vacations, car, a little bungalow out on the Cape. Just about killed me when I got the call that he died. Heart attack." Phil snapped his fingers, "went like that."

There was that slow shake of the head again, then another sip of Dewars. "It's the best way to go if you're the one going, but a hell of a hit if you're the survivor. I pray I go that way. Quick and in my sleep. But hell, laddie," Rob could tell that the somber recollection was about to be diffused with a quip, "when someone's ninety-two you can hardly say 'he died suddenly' for God's sake!'" He enjoyed his own irreverence about age and death, as did Rob.

Wanting to reel the conversation back to the Marafield fire Rob tapped the window pointing to the campus below and said, "Why didn't they rebuild on that spot?"

"Well, I suppose they needed that spot to be a memorial of sorts. Unless you saw that building back then you'd never know it even existed. There's a plaque in that grotto about the history of the Motherhouse and that tragic night. I used to walk my dog all over that campus every night, but I stopped after the fire. The horrible smell of burnt wood seemed to hang in the air all the time. I found it just too sad."

The retired insurance broker sighed heavily and took another sip then continued.

"I have to give those women credit," he tilted his head toward Marafield, "though I do so begrudgingly." The two men, drinks in hand, stood looking out at the campus and talked to each other via the window. "They've managed to turn that campus into a pretty little spot all over again, even if they didn't collect the insurance on that building."

Chapter 48

Pay dirt. Rob definitely wanted to keep his ninety-two year old source on track now. He quickly reacted, "Wait a minute. A landmark building burns down and no insurance money is collected. Are you kidding me?"

"I know," the white haired man protested, "I know! It's absolutely crazy. Believe me, Rob, I went to the ropes on that one with the Reverend Mother who was in charge of the outfit back then. 'Reverend Mother Majella,'" the respectable gentleman pronounced the name slowly with an unmistakable derisive edge, "a name suspended in infamy, in my book."

Rob wanted to be sure he was getting this. "You mean 'never'? They never collected any insurance money whatsoever?"

"That's what I said and that's what I mean. Never. Period. Four floors of valuables from all over the world went up in smoke, not to mention all the expensive chalices and monstrances and the like. Why, just that magnificent pipe organ alone would have been worth a good claim fight, but no, they never pursued a goddamned claim on anything.

"A few other fellas –they were in this organization, 'Friends of Marafield,'– went and offered to help the Reverend Mother square things away regarding insurance matters.

"She thought I put them up to it. Thought I had broken confidentiality about her refusal to go after the claim money. I hadn't, of course. Next thing I knew, the head of my company removed Marafield from my portfolio and took it over himself. She was a real pip, that Reverend Mother."

"Do you think it was just a very bad case of naiveté on the Reverend Mother's part?" Rob played devil's advocate, "I mean, maybe the nuns were doing some kind of 'the Lord will provide' thing?"

"The Lord DID provide!" Tully raised his voice for the first time. "They were always provided with enough money to pay the premiums in full, on time, all the time! God's part was covered. Their job was to collect! Piece of cake!"

"Look, Mr. Tully, I'm a simple Protestant, not too versed in the ways of religious life. But I gotta tell you, a group of nuns that run a college just don't strike me as being that stupid."

Mr. Tully turned his head ever so slightly, arched his bushy white eyebrow and looked into the eyes of the private investigator. "That's exactly right, Robert Young. 'Stupid' they weren't."

"They had to have gotten money from somewhere," Rob mused to egg the man on. "A lot a displaced nuns, destroyed belongings, all that . . ."

Tully looked into his almost empty glass and muttered, "it's been my understanding that the Bishop helped them out and was very generous to them."

Rob put his finished glass down and turned to Tully, "so what do you think was really going on?"

Phil Tully's eyes twinkled and Rob knew before a word was uttered that he'd gone as far as he could. "You're the investigator, lad. I have every confidence that, if you put your mind to it, two and two will give you the same sum I came up with a mighty long time ago."

"I'm adding already, Mr. Tully," Rob said as he gave a wink of silent collusion to his host.

"Well, young man," Phil said, "the drink has made me mellow and I'm afraid a nap is on me now. Would you think me rude if I stretched out for a while?"

"No sir, not at all. You've been very generous with your time and your Scotch. I should be getting back anyway. You deserve a nap; I've grilled you all afternoon." Rob put on his jacket and straightened his tie. The two men shook hands and Tully patted Rob on the shoulder as they did. "I hope you'll come back, Robert Young. You're welcome any time."

"Almost forgot!" Rob said as he went to pick up the metal box and put it back in the closet. "I'll put this away for you before I go."

"Good man! Thoroughness is the necessary tool for an investigator . . . no loose ends. I had forgotten about putting the box back. Thanks, lad!"

"Okay, there you go. Everything's exactly the way you had it. Thanks again, Mr. Tully. It's been a pleasure, sir."

"Not at all. Drive safely on these grounds, son. You've got three land mines to clear to get out of here: deer, old folks behind the wheel, and nuns behind the wheel. Good luck!"

Mr. Tully closed the door after his visitor's exit and, as Rob walked down the long hall toward the elevator, he heard the distant click of the door's lock. "Good man," Rob thought to himself. He evaluated his time there as a very worthwhile visit. By the time he got to the lobby and signed out, he had decided to drive over to Marafield and check out the grotto Tully had pointed out to him. For Rob Young, the private investigator, it wouldn't be to light a candle. It would be to visit the scene of a thirty-year old crime.

Chapter 49

"Jane Early, Jane Early, Jane Early! Trying to make a fool out of me on national television! You pretty little prime time Barbie Doll with your perfect little ambush! DNA, DNA, DNA! How 'bout some DNA specimens of your own from an irate viewer in Sparrows Point, Massachusetts? And Lee Kelly, Lee Kelly, Lee Kelly . . . another one. Another 'Crime Line' sympathizer for that little bitch, the ever whining Judy Mazola. 'I have an attorney!' 'I have an investigator!' Oh, yeah? Oh, yeah?"

Ffrrrumph! went a telephone book as its pages wildly fanned just before slamming into the wall toward which it was hurled. Next went a notebook, then the entire contents of the pencil holder on the table, then a stack of magazines. The crashing of glass from a picture frame bumped to the floor by the flying objects startled the tantrum to a halt.

"Okay, okay, okay. Take it easy, take it easy. Don't let on. Don't let anybody know. Let's think. Just think. She's got an attorney. She's got an investigator. Big deal. Hey! She doesn't have enough money for that! That idiot can't afford attorneys and investigators! Anyway, she couldn't have enough money for them to be any good. Yeah. They're no good. Jerks. Idiots. Besides, what idiot would ever talk to them about me? They're all a bunch of babies. Little 'fraidie cats. Little weasels."

The phone rang and its shrill pitch whirled her around with fright. Involuntarily, she kept wetting her lips and swallowed repeatedly trying to gain control before answering. Finally, she picked up the receiver and, with an actor's skill, offered a cheery 'hello?'

"Oh, hi, Mr. Frezia!" Mr. Frezia, her attorney: another idiot. "Yes, I saw the show . . . Well, I didn't particularly like the last segment where Jane Early ambushed me with that DNA nonsense . . . How did she get those results? . . . Can you find out? . . . Why didn't you have them? . . . No, no, I'm not upset with you, Mr. Frezia. I'm just so tired of all this. Like I said in the show, I'm feeling victimized again . . ."

She looked catatonic as she spoke. She was ramrod straight and not a muscle moved except very few facial ones as she answered his questions. In containing her fury, her body correspondingly was contained. She was good at that. No, she was great at that. She had been raised, rewarded and esteemed for that . . . a mistress of emotional deceit.

"Mr. Frezia, you're so kind to call. You make me think I'll get through this nightmare . . . Yes, I know Miss Mazola 'means business.' . . . Well it's like you said from the beginning, it was just a matter of time before she tried to throw this all back on me . . . imagine? The nerve of her!" Easy, Jo, easy . . .

" . . . Yes, as a matter of fact, I was just thinking about it. . . . Well, no, I . . . I honestly can't think of anyone . . . Well, I'm not surprised . . . Let them go ahead and look at my other school districts . . . No, Mr. Frezia, I assure you, there are no 'little surprises' for them to find . . . Oh, I understand, Mr. Frezia; no offense taken. . . . I know, you have to ask these questions . . . No, sir, I haven't forgotten . . . . Next Wednesday at 10am, your office . . . I'll be there. . . . Yes? . . . Oh, thank you . . . yes, it was a big risk wasn't it? . . . I hope so, Mr. Frezia. . . . I'm counting on you. . . . Thank you for calling."

She replaced the receiver and began picking up the magazines with a chilly calm. Next she collected the pens, pencils and magic markers that had bounced off the newly pocked wall, landing helter skelter all over the kitchen. Mechanically, she went and got a dustpan and brush. She picked up the large shards first, stared at them a long time, then put them in the newspaper. She meticulously brushed up the splinters of glass and carefully deposited them onto the newspaper.

As she neatly folded the newspaper and placed it in the wastebasket, she began softly humming a few vaguely familiar bars of Gregorian Chant, improvising parts now forgotten. Chant was always so soothing whenever the dark bank of miasmal ether slowly began to curl around her.

Chapter 50

"So how'd it go? I thought I'd see you over at Dolan's last night. Figured you'd checked into the nursing home when you didn't show up," Jim Carey greeted Rob as he arrived at the office.

"Not a bad set up over there. Except for that crap Scotch he offered me!" Rob made sure he had eye contact on that delivery and wasn't disappointed in his friend's reaction. "He's quite a guy. I'd like to be like that when I'm that age: sharp, polite, clothes still pulled together, humor intact . . ."

"Jesus, you're not like that now, how the hell are you going to be like that at ninety-two?"

The answer to Jim's barb came in the form of a rolled up piece of paper aimed at Jim's head.

"You gave me a good lead, Jim; I owe you," Rob promised. "Listen, does that 'seal of confession' thing still hold any clout now that you've hung up the collar?"

"Sure it does. What's up?" Jim pushed back from his desk and put his feet up on the edge of the desk, settling in for a confab.

"I need to run something by you and then have you keep it under wraps," Rob said. "Can you do it?"

"Done," he waited for Rob to start.

Rob asked, "Did you know that Marafield never collected insurance on the fire?"

"No way!" Jim answered. "All that stuff? No way."

"Well, Tully told me 'no.'" Rob sat on the edge of his desk, hands in his pockets, facing Jim. "He said the 'Grand Pubah' for the Marafield sisters put a kibosh on retrieving any claims. He rode her a little –so to speak–about collecting the money, but the Reverend Mother wouldn't budge. In fact, she played hard ball and somehow managed to have him dismissed as the Marafield broker. He said he was practically blackballed from any more diocesan contracts, thanks to her."

"So that's what got my old man so bloody mad that night," Jim pieced together. "Doesn't make sense to this Carey either. I don't get it: why wouldn't they collect?"

"I'll bet you can answer that one yourself, Skippy. Think about it for a minute," Rob coached. "When is a claim not a claim?"

Jim thought a minute, then said slowly, "when an accident is not an accident." He put his feet back down on the floor and sat up straight. "Or maybe even when arson is arson."

"As your friend, Phil Tully would say, 'Bingo!'" Rob clapped his hands together as he belted out the last word. "If there's no claim, then there's no need for a thorough investigation. If there's no investigation, then there are no headlines, cops or courts. Somebody knew something, Jim. Something big, bad and shocking enough for those nuns to eat all the costs involved in recovering from such a major disaster."

"Or," Jim was working now too, "somebody also knew someone." He paused a bit then added, "but why would they want to protect someone if it was arson? Why not prosecute the fire bug and sue?"

Rob just arched his eye brows as if to say, "Come on, figure it out."

Jim rubbed his hands over both eyes and shook his head saying, "Can't be. No way."

"Okay, let's review your little didactic on Carl Jung yesterday . . . something about 'no profession having a market on virtuous living . . . '" Rob nudged Jim out of his denial.

"Oh, shut up!" Jim mumbled in good nature. Then he drifted a bit as he stared out the window musing, "wonder where they got all the money to have the ruins razed . . . and the grounds redesigned and landscaped, and have that memorial site built. That's not even considering restoration costs for about ninety some displaced inhabitants of the building. We're talking a lot of bake sales."

"Yeah, well, Phil Tully said his 'source' told him the Bishop picked up the tab for most of it."

"Birch? That miser?" Jim laughed. "He was the tightest Bishop on the East Coast! If those nuns could charm a dime out of him they'd be miracle workers!" Jim recollected. "Here's a true story for you: When that guy was a pastor, the other priests who were unfortunate enough to be assigned to his rectory actually wore their coats inside the house it was so freezing! Can you imagine? He was notorious for not parting with a penny. The Diocese needed bailing out of the red when he was appointed bishop. Needless to say, 'mission accomplished.' They called him 'Dollar Bill Birch.' Hard to fathom he'd be a sugar daddy for Marafield."

"Well Tully told it like it was gospel, that's all I know," Rob said.

"So where're you going to go with this?" Jim wanted to know. "How's this tie in with what you're working on?"

Rob admitted, "I'm not sure. There's this kind of convergence happening. I'm starting to wonder if the stalking victim, the fire, and the unclaimed insurance money don't somehow intersect. Look," Rob grabbed the picture from his desk and pointed to Josephine Quarters, "she was at Marafield at the same time that the fire took place. There's some story that these other gals know about her. Something about a diary of hers that was stolen and set on fire . . ."

"Oh come on!" Jim protested.

"No, wait!" Rob pleaded. "One of these gals," Rob looked up her name on his sheet, "Annie Silo, told me that this woman right here, the very same Josephine Quarters, accused other women in this picture of stalking her and setting her diary on fire!"

Jim stared noncommittally at Rob. "And?"

"And it just makes me wonder. Aren't you wondering, Jim? Tell me, as a counselor to the world's walking wounded, that you're not wondering . . . just a little?"

"Okay, I'm wondering, but mostly about you!" Jim conceded.

"Oh for God's sake, Jim, just play with this a little, will you? If the pieces all fit, there's a much bigger issue here than the little hissy fit I was hired for," Rob assessed.

“Like what?” Jim ventured.

“Like murder. Arson changes the mode of death for that young sister who died in the fire from ‘accidental’ to ‘manslaughter.’ Oh, and try this on for size: it also means ninety-five counts of attempted murder.”

“And you think that’s why the Reverend Mother never collected on the fire, because she knew ‘the real deal’?” Jim wasn’t resisting Rob’s theory so much any more.

“You got it! Hey, James, back in those days of ‘The Sound of Music,’ when nuns and priests were high up on pedestals, I ask you: what price scandal?”

“Good God, exactly . . .” Jim shook his head sadly, just like Tully did, as he repeated Rob’s words, “what price scandal . . .”

Chapter 51

In Washington, D.C., Sister Dolorosa Feeney sat in the back of the large darkened convent chapel in her nightgown, robe and bedroom slippers. She had been there for nearly an hour and was oblivious to the passing of time. She had felt a clenching anxiety growing within her ever since her chance meeting with Sr. Gloria Penney at the Academy's Centennial celebration. Her meeting with the President of her order, necessary as it was, was when it all went sour. She had not had a decent night's sleep since. Now here she sat, wide awake, while the others in the convent serenely slept.

The dream that agitated her into wakefulness tonight was yet another vivid playback of scenes from thirty years ago. This time she was accompanying Mother Majella down the spotless marble corridor of the Chancery. They were led by the Bishop's secretary, a ghostly, silent monsignor in long black cassock with purple piping and purple satin buttons down the front and around and on the cuffs. His perfect fitting cassock was finished off with a wide purple cincture that dropped off the left hip and hung down the length of the cassock, flapping with his stride.

They were shown into a room filled with antique furniture. "Please be seated, Sisters. His Eminence has not yet finished his meeting. May I get you a glass of water or some tea?"

“No thank you, Monsignor,” Reverend Mother Majella answered for both.

The Monsignor made no attempt at small talk but said simply, “When His Eminence is ready to see you, I will knock on these doors. At that time, I will escort you to Bishop Birch’s office.” He bowed slightly while taking both doors in his hands pulling them shut as he backed out saying, “Until then . . .”

The two nuns sat in ornate chairs covered in rich tapestry and did not speak. Any conversation would be at Mother Majella’s initiation. After she was certain no one was nearby, she turned to Sister Dolorosa and said in a barely audible matter-of-fact voice, “Sister Dolorosa, you are here with me because I feel you can be trusted.” Dolorosa was about to form the words “thank you” but was abruptly stopped by Majella’s hand raised to indicate “don’t.”

The Reverend Mother continued, “You have the makings of more than just ‘Directress of Novices,’ Sister Dolorosa. One day, you may bear this very burden of office. In so believing, it has been my intention to ‘groom’ you for that occasion which is why you are the one who is accompanying me on this meeting with His Eminence. You are to say nothing in this meeting whatsoever. You are to listen. And you must listen dispassionately, Sister. What you hear in this meeting is to go to the grave with you. Do you understand?”

Wide eyed, Sister Dolorosa nodded and said, “Yes, Mother.”

“Do you give me your solemn word?”

“I do, Mother. You have my solemn word.”

“Now, until we are summoned by the Monsignor, you are to pray as if the very life of the congregation depends on it.”

The memory of that exchange made Dolorosa close her eyes and cringe with disgust at her own guilelessness back then. In both her pride and her youth, she was more taken with verbally having been crowned Majella’s ‘fair haired’ apprentice than with trying to comprehend the complicity to which she blindly had just pledged her fealty. And now what? Now, three decades later, she found herself trapped anew.

“Honoring your word,” “strength of character,” “‘going to the grave’ with what people had asked you never to betray,” all codes of conduct that had their places back then. She had fashioned a modus operandi out of such standards. Now the trend was justice, equality, diversity. What a muddled mess morality is, she sighed in silent frustration.

Right on cue the tears came. They always did whenever she judged herself as having had a part in saving the congregation while losing her soul.

Chapter 52

"Dollar Bill Birch" looked as though every story about him could be true. When Mother Majella and Sister Dolorosa were introduced to the Bishop he was seated in the center of his large office on an ornate high backed chair. He made no motion to stand as the two women entered. To Sister Dolorosa, he looked like a very cross leprechaun who did not want his time wasted. To the left of his chair and two steps behind it stood the Monsignor who had delivered them to this chamber.

"Your Excellency, I am grateful to you for honoring my request to see you. I assure you that my personal presence here is indicative of the urgent and sensitive nature of the matter for which I seek your counsel." With her eyes riveted onto the Bishop's as she spoke, the Reverend Mother glanced at the Monsignor with such deftness that the message "lose him" could not possibly have been missed.

"Reverend Mother Majella, does this 'sensitive' matter require that I dismiss my Secretary during your visit?" the Bishop asked with a tinge of incredulity.

"It does, your Excellency," the direct Reverend Mother said unflinchingly.

"Then should not your sister companion also leave?"

"No, your Excellency."

The Bishop shifted in his chair with unchecked annoyance and flicked his left hand at the Monsignor signaling that he should leave. As the Monsignor came around to face the Bishop he gave a slight bow and turned to leave.

Reverend Mother Majella spoke to him, "Thank you, Monsignor." He offered an insipid smile, nodded, and left.

"Mother Majella," the Bishop began, "it grieves us that, so soon after the tragic fire that took the life of one of your young Junior Sisters and injured so many other sisters, you come now with additional concerns. First, we must ask, how are the hospitalized sisters doing now that a month has passed?"

"They are improving, your Excellency, thank God. However, I'm afraid that between the burns and the seriousness of their injuries many will remain in hospital for some time. Some face additional surgeries."

"Their recovery is prayed for every day. Are you satisfied with the care they are receiving; is it adequate?" the Bishop seemed interested.

"Quite. We will be happy for the day when all of our sisters are returned to Marafield," Mother Majella responded.

"I should say you will be," Bishop Birch agreed. "We presume the expense for their care is being covered by the insurance your community has on each of your sisters."

"Yes, your Excellency, the hospitalized sisters are covered," Reverend Mother Majella emphasized the words 'hospitalized sisters' as she answered. The Bishop did not miss the nuance in her response and picked up on it.

"And all other insurance matters are in good order?"

Mother Majella, whose hands had been hidden in her sleeves, sat a little straighter in her chair and folded her hands on her lap as she answered. "Your Excellency, that is precisely the purpose of this call."

"Yes?" Bishop Birch intoned clearly indicating "go on."

As Reverend Mother Majella recounted to his Eminence the moral plight in which she now found her congregation, he rose from his chair and slowly paced back and forth in front of her and Sister Dolorosa with his hands behind his back, head bowed, jaw clenched. He understood all too well the damaging ripple effect that the least impropriety could have throughout a diocese, an arsonist in veil and habit not withstanding.

Chapter 53

Bishop Birch had not been prepared for what he had just heard and was totally stunned by it. He stopped no more than a foot from Mother Majella and asked, "When did you come into possession of this Sister's Book of Prayer that had the page in it from her diary?"

"Last Friday, your Excellency. I met with my other Councilors that evening about it. I did not read the contents of the page to them, the fewer who know its contents, the safer."

Majella paused to see if she should continue. The Bishop waved his index finger motioning for her to go on. "I entered the chapel by the side door at about nine o'clock. Rather than take my usual place in my own pew at the back of the chapel, I simply slipped into one closest to the door. I wanted to read the psalms before retiring for the evening, so I reached for the book of prayer that was in the book holder on the back of the bench.

The Sisters are instructed to keep their prayer books neat and free of anything other than a holy card or two to mark their places. As I opened the book to the psalms, a folded paper filled with writing tumbled out. I opened it to see whose book I was using and there, in wild scribble, was the entire plan for the fire, intending to trap the Junior Sisters while they slept, methodically outlining the precise times for each step that lead up to the final act of setting it. The discovery of such a demonic plan was horrific enough; the prurient venom that filled the rest of the page was evil and chilling."

"Did you bring that page with you?"

"Yes, your Excellency." From somewhere up her cavernous wool serge sleeve she produced a sealed envelope and handed it to the Bishop. He opened it, went to the window and read it. He quickly finished, threw the paper down in disgust and exclaimed,

"What hateful, shameful bile!"

Approaching the place where she sat, the Bishop leveled an accusation at the head of the order that now teetered on the brink of disgracing the whole diocese. "Reverend Mother Majella, tell me: how does an extremely troubled person such as this manage to go all through your novitiate? And further, can you tell me how she is allowed to profess vows which I believe, Reverend Mother Majella, this Bishop before you received himself at the Profession ceremony in your chapel?" His face was crimson and, having sputtered so furiously, little spits of white froth had formed at the corners of his thin lips.

Mother Majella coolly rebuffed his slur with a question of her own, bishop or no bishop. "Your Excellency, does not your own seminary occasionally ordain a few cunning men who've successfully managed to become psychological and spiritual chameleons, that no rector lacking a degree in psychiatry could detect?"

The bishop glared while his nostrils worked overtime. "Indeed. Indeed!" he yelled, wondering if she was privy to the scandal that had just erupted about one of his priests or was her analogy sheer coincidence.

"This is grave, Reverend Mother, very grave!" The Bishop returned to the window where he placed his hands on the windowsill and leaned over deep in thought. Time seemed suspended in such charged grim silence. Finally, he straightened up and returned to the chair in which he sat when this session had begun.

"Have you any more to tell us?" his Eminence said flatly.

"I have, your Excellency. Mr. Tully, the congregation's insurance broker, is daily pressuring me to move forward with the claims for the building and its contents. If I do as he urges, I am told that an independent and rigorous investigation into the cause of the fire certainly will be conducted. Should anything more be determined than what our local Fire Chief mercifully has labeled as 'spontaneous combustion' or 'cause unknown,' I fear for what those findings may bring upon the congregation and upon the diocese that has so many devoted Catholics. Your Excellency, if the cause of fire ever was determined to be of a criminal nature, it would be at once scandalous and disastrous."

The Bishop sat in silence resting his forehead on his upraised hand. At long last he wearily said, "Mother Majella, I must speak with you in private." He pointed his arm toward the door and said to Sister Dolorosa, "Sister, I must ask you to leave us and wait in one of the chairs in the corridor."

"Of course, your Excellency," Sister Dolorosa said as she rose to remove herself from the discussion about to take place. Curious as she was, she was relieved by her dismissal.

Chapter 54

After Sister Dolorosa left the room, Bishop Birch walked over to where she had been sitting along side Mother Majella and sat in that chair. "Mother Majella, I bind you to complete confidentiality on what I am about to say. It is to be regarded as a matter to be kept in 'Grand Silence,' is that understood?"

"Of course, your Excellency."

"Last week the Holy Father officially accepted my invitation to him to grace our diocese with his presence during his tour of the United States in the fall. This week, today in fact, I have been meeting all morning with our diocesan attorneys to try and figure out how to keep out of the newspapers an embarrassing indiscretion committed by one of my priests. I am advised that his actions are tantamount to a serious criminal offense. I need not tell you how our Holy Father's visit here would have a profound impact on reviving the spiritual stagnation of our people, on filling our churches back up again and, of course, on filling the coffers. However, His Holiness will never set foot in this diocese if this scandal is ever found out and made public. And now you come to me with this!"

He paused to think for a minute then continued, "Mother Majella, did I not understand that 'The Friends of Marafield' have been actively raising funds for your congregation since the fire?"

"Yes, your Excellency, they have and still are."

"And tell me, Mother, the Sister who died in the fire . . . how many brothers and sisters did she have?"

For the first time, Majella's face had a hint of expression that flashed a genuine pinch of pain. "Sister Hildegarde was the oldest of six, your Excellency. The Noonans are now left with three girls and two boys."

"Reverend Mother, I want you to take whatever money 'The Friends of Marafield' collect for your order and put it in escrow for the Noonan children. No one is to know that you are doing that. Your college is to provide full scholarships for the three girls when that time comes. Full scholarships will be arranged for the boys at our university."

Mother Majella looked worried. "But, your Excellency, if we refuse the claim money and then reroute donations as you have just ordered, it will be impossible for us to bear any recovery costs. At minimum, we have the removal of the remains of the building, the restoration of the grounds, and replacement of all that was lost in the fire."

"I will assume all expenses for those concerns. You are to assume all expenses for the education of the Noonan children. I will meet with our financier tomorrow and direct him to contact you about forwarding all bills for the purposes you've mentioned. I also will have him draw up a substantial check for Mr. and Mrs. Noonan when the time is right . . . a token of the diocese's deep regret at the loss of their daughter who so selflessly dedicated her life to the Church."

The Bishop thought some more. "We should include in the restoration project a memorial of some kind on the site of the fire that includes a commemorative plaque in honor of Sister Hildegarde. I want this completed by the fall. When the Holy Father comes, I will invite the Noonan's as my guests and have them see the memorial. While they're here, I'll arrange for them to meet His Holiness. Then, in private, you and I will present the Noonans with the check and a promissory note guaranteeing a college education for all their children."

"Your Excellency, may I ask why you are doing all of this?"

"There must be some form of restitution exacted from us both, Reverend Mother, if we are to enter into such an unholy alliance as putting out an even greater 'fire' than the one that destroyed Marafield."

"Then how do you suggest we handle the situation at hand," Mother Majella asked.

"Dismiss that sister immediately!" the Bishop roared. "Send for her when no one is around and act swiftly!" He moved in closer and instructed Mother Majella, "Do exactly as I say, Mother: Immediately before she leaves, have her understand that you know all that you told me today. Make her sign an agreement to never discuss her days at Marafield with anyone. She'll do it. Even in her state she would have to know the alternative. Then get rid of her! Put her in a taxi and get rid of her!"

Regaining composure he said, "Now bring Sister Dolorosa back in. I want to give her an opportunity to speak."

Dutifully, Mother Majella summoned her companion apprentice and the two of them stood before Bishop Birch ready to bring their meeting to a close.

"Sisters," he asked, "have we discussed everything that needed discussion?"

"Yes, your Excellency. You have been most generous with your time and your guidance. I . . . I . . ." Mother Majella's voice trailed off. She wanted to ask a question that she sensed would be Dolorosa's too.

"What is it, Mother?" the Bishop asked, intuiting what was on her mind.

"Your Excellency, I can't help but wonder . . . where 'sin' is in all of this?"

"The sin is on the one who committed the crime! Regrettably, Sisters, the residual effect of her sin has splattered on us who are left to clean up this mess." The Bishop went to his desk and sat down heaving a great sigh and continued, "Sometimes there are vying principles placed before us. In this case, the choice is between 'the greater good of the faithful' or 'truth telling.' You know what our choice must be." He removed the cap from his pen, ready to write, then said, "now leave me, Sisters, and may God have mercy on us all."

It was always back to that day that Sister Dolorosa traced the uneasy feeling that her moral compass never quite knew 'true north.'

Chapter 55

The private investigator had one goal for the week, to conclude his five month long marathon of interviews. Unmistakably, a pattern was emerging. Six teachers from Josephine Quarters' previous school in the Barata School District had the same "take" on their former colleague. She had a "thing" about a teacher, in this case a male, who was very popular and who barely acknowledged that Josephine existed. Not out of maliciousness. He just was too involved with too many other people and students and projects. Probably the most well liked teacher in the school they said.

The six faculty members all knew that Josephine brought charges of sexual harassment against him to the school principal. The rest of the faculty knew there was some brouhaha going on between them, but only the six knew what the nature of the brouhaha actually was. It seemed this group happened to have been in the teachers' lounge after school one day when the accused teacher, Jeff Baderi, came in and fell apart right in front of them. He had just come from the principal's office where he had been confronted with the charges against him. He was devastated. He had been set up. He didn't understand why.

The principal wanted the matter settled "in house." He didn't want it blown out of proportion. He called in a mediation team. What was worked out was that neither teacher could be in the same room at the same time as the other, barring faculty meetings. If either was going to be in the building after school, she and he first had to get authorization and then had to sign in and out of the principal's office for the time either was there, stating where they would be.

Josephine was content with the arrangement, letting her "relief" be known that some one would be watching out for her safety. Jeff Baderi, on the other hand, was crestfallen, demoralized and furious that his character had been tainted by this woman's baseless allegations. He kept it all pretty quiet back then. He was young and too shocked to do anything beyond what the principal and mediators had recommended.

Rob asked Jeff Baderi and his six colleagues if they would ever consider being witnesses for the plaintiff, Judy Mazola, in the upcoming hearing should they be needed.

Baderi didn't hesitate when he heard about Josephine's allegations against Judy Mazola.

"You bet I'll help," he told Rob. "I think Miss Quarters just gets her jollies trashing innocent people. I'm a little older, a lot wiser and definitely more 'in your face' when it comes to being pushed around. It took a long time for me to get over what her lies did to me." Rob just listened. "I guess I'm glad her little 'thing' for me was all handled 'in house.' God knows I'd hate being the center of all the media attention your client's been getting."

"People have to start standing up for one another when stuff like this happens. And I'll tell you what, Mr. Young, I'm going to work on the others to agree to go to the hearing, too, if we're needed." Rob made the notation next to their names: "subpoena." Judy Mazola's attorney would use this less friendly language later.

In the Alpine School District, where Josephine Quarters and Judy Mazola were employed at the time of the most recent and publicized alleged stalking, no one had a bad word to say about the very warm and likeable Judy Mazola. There was a significantly large pro Judy Mazola group. There were, as always, the predictable "middle grounders" who had no comment about anyone or anything and who wanted to be left out of it all. There were two women, young teachers, who rallied to Josephine's defense. One of the older teachers had likened these two and Josephine to The Witches of Eastwick, very clique-ish and odd.

Rob easily had elicited over a dozen solid agreements from among that faculty to be called upon as witnesses, should the need arise. He made the same notations next to their names as he'd done the other subpoena candidates from Barata.

By the time winter began melting into spring and spring began flowering into summer, Rob was well into his longest and most tedious round of interviews. It took all of April, May, June and now July to contact the nearly fifty novitiate classmates of Josephine Quarters. Rob Young always honored the rule that private investigation should never be reduced to something that smacked of a telemarketing campaign. Phone interviews were out. Whenever possible, his canvassing was conducted nose to nose and toes to toes. He needed to see people's eyes and mannerisms when they spoke.

Canvassing the ex-nun crowd actually proved more interesting than he could have imagined. This was a distinct group. All of the women with whom he spoke gave him the feeling that they had worked for the CIA rather than having been in the convent. They were tight-lipped, extremely cautious about talking to him, and they would only corroborate what he already seemed to know. Which was a heck of a lot more than he got when he tried talking to any of the nuns who were still part of the Marafield order. "Sister is not available," was the patent response he got. Enough of those lines made for an easy guess that the nuns had been put on alert.

What Robert Young had "squeaked" out of Marafield's alumnae was a nearly unanimous acknowledgement about Josephine's diary, its having been set on fire, remnants of it having been discovered by Josephine, and her incredible accusation of five possible stalker-novices. All also remembered the subsequent arrangement made by Josephine and the "higher ups" that she no longer live "in common" with her sister classmates for her "protection," and that she be given her own private room.

Had it not been for Annie Silo's regaling him with so many stories at their first meeting out in Colorado, he would have had a much harder time getting anyone to "give anything up" about those swell "good ol' days." Once one of the "formers" heard he already knew something then she'd chime in with "that's right," or, "Yes that happened," or,

"Correct." What he couldn't understand was how no one knew whether or not the matter had ever been cleared up or if the actual culprit had been discovered. It seemed only fair to him that, for all the havoc they went through for months on end back then, someone would have told them it was over, solved, or a terrible mistake.

Usually Rob asked three final questions of the Marafield crowd: "Do you know any of the people who were accused by Miss Quarters of stealing and burning her diary?" Most never knew who all five of the accused were since it was such a cloak and dagger operation and since "The Silence" they had been placed under prohibited discussion. Another question he put to the former nuns just for kicks was, "Would you say that the Josephine you knew then was psychologically sound?" That question always got two responses. On the one hand, "Well, all I can say is that she had a very different approach to spirituality than I did . . ." On the other hand, "Mr. Young, I'm not qualified to make such an assessment."

The final question was always, "Is there anyone you can think of who would know all of the missing pieces that you are unable to provide about those days as novices and newly professed sisters?" At first, it would be recalled that everyone who had been a member of the Council, along with the Reverend Mother, was dead. Then, to a person, the name of the one surviving person who would know "A" to "Z" about Josephine's days at Marafield was given without hesitation: Sister Dolorosa Feeney.

Chapter 56

Rob called Sister Dolorosa regularly to set up a meeting with her and, as he grew to suspect would be the case, she was ever "unavailable." Finally, he was forced to go to D.C. unannounced and went first to the Cathedral, her place of work, to see if he could spot her there. He asked for her at the main office and was told she was conducting a tour of the Cathedral with a group of visiting art students and that the tour should be winding up in about twenty minutes. He sat on a garden bench across from the main entrance to the Cathedral in the steamy hot July weather, waiting to catch a glimpse of her when she and the tour group would emerge from the coolness of the stone building into the blast of Washington humidity.

As the bells began to chime that it was five o'clock, a small group filed out of the front doors and stood for a few minutes on the apron in front of the steps chatting. Rob studied Sister Dolorosa as she answered a few final questions. As she spoke she glanced up and caught Rob square in the eye. Something in that instant gave Rob the feeling that she had just registered who he possibly could be. Finally, the leader of the visiting art students and their tour guide shook hands and parted ways. Dolorosa hurried into the front door of the main office and closed the door.

Rob followed. When he got to the office the door was locked.

"Office closes at 5:oopm" was on a professionally printed sign hung from the inside on the window of the door. Rob went to his rented car and waited in it down the street from the property's exit for about thirty minutes. While he waited, he took off his tie and jacket and put on his Red Sox baseball cap. It was such a simple change, yet she wouldn't be watching for a guy in shirt sleeves, cap and sunglasses.

Finally, a plain gray Oldsmobile pulled out with a woman driving. He followed it. At the first light he pulled up next to it. Sister Dolorosa was so busy looking in her rear view mirror that she didn't see him immediately to her left. When the light turned green, he allowed several cars to cut in front of him, putting a good screen between his car and hers. He followed her to her convent where she pulled into a garage and parked the car.

He watched from down the block as she hurried to the convent, put her key in the front door and let herself in.

Rob stepped out of the car and put his tie and jacket back on and fixed his hair. Then he walked to the convent door and rang the bell. An elderly sister answered.

The investigator put on his best charm. "Good evening, Sister. My name is Robert Young. I'm here on business from Boston and I'm wondering if I might be able to see Sister Dolorosa.?"

"Would you be kind enough to wait right there, young man?" the nun pleasantly asked through the locked storm door. "I'll see if Sister is in." She closed the door.

In a few minutes the door opened and the same sister said through the door, "I'm very sorry, sir, but Sister Dolorosa is not available. I'm terribly sorry." She began to close the big door.

Rob stopped her by speaking loudly through the door, "But, Sister, I just saw her park her car and let herself in this door not five minutes ago. Please, Sister; if you would . . . it's very important and I've traveled a long distance on a beastly hot day."

"I'm sorry, sir. Sister has retired for the evening."

"At six o'clock?" he said incredulously. "Aw c'mon, Sister, really . . ."

"Sister is not available." And that was that. The old nun closed the door and turned the dead bolt. Rob, ready for this eventuality, reached in his jacket pocket for an envelope. He dropped the envelope with

Sister Dolorosa's name on it into the mailbox with a brief note asking her to please contact him. Of course, it was a request never to be acknowledged.

Rob decided to not waste any unnecessary time wilting in Washington in July when he could be in cool, cool New England by night. He knew when to fish or cut bait. As he walked to his car, he said a few unseemly words that would have twirled the old nun's beads. Then he took solace in the Grey Goose vodka tonic he envisioned himself sipping at Reagan International Airport while he waited to catch the shuttle back to Logan. Tomorrow he would call Annie Silo's pals and arrange meetings with them. He doubted they would "retire for the evening" before the sun went down.

Chapter 57

Of the four friends, Eily McVetty was the least resistant to meet with Robert Young. He called her at The Crofford Institute in California and got her on the first try. Her secretary had just stepped out and the unpretentious Director worked the phones from her office herself until her assistant came back. Doctor McVetty was completely caught off guard to hear the caller identify himself as Robert Young, a private investigator. She knew she had heard the name before but, for a beat or two, couldn't retrieve from where. His mention of his client, Judy Mazola, as the woman who had appeared on a 'Crime Line' show about stalking last winter, triggered instant recall.

"You e-mailed me after that show . . . me and a few others," Eily verified for him that she knew exactly who he was.

"I did. Very good!" He liked her sharp memory. "That e-mail was my electronic foot in the door, Doctor McVetty," Rob offered politely. "I thought I'd have been in touch with you much sooner than this, but the list of people I had to contact got a little longer than I anticipated."

"I'll bet it did, Mr. Young," the Doctor laughed knowingly.

Rob started, "I was hoping that I could arrange a meeting with you, Doctor."

"You mean fly out here?"

"Sure, why not? Do you have any time in the near future that would be convenient for you?" The vibes Rob got made him feel she'd cooperate.

"Well, let me see . . . hold on, Mr. Young, I'm flipping through my day planner. Let's see, next week is totally booked so that's out. Well 'lookee here,'" Eily said affably as she discovered an opening. "The week after that I'm actually heading east. I have a two day conference in New York on July 16 and 17, that's a Monday and a Tuesday. Why don't we try to nail something down for then, how would that be?"

"That would be perfect. I can be in New York any time; so let's make it your call," Rob proposed.

"Tuesday at 4:00. I finish at 2:00, have a short meeting after that, and then I'm expected to attend the gala dinner that night at 7:00. So it'll have to be 4:00."

That certainly put parameters around their meeting. There'd be no long dinner or idle chat, so he knew he had to make their meeting as business-like as possible. "Where shall I meet you? I'd offer to take you to lunch or dinner but it sounds like that's already spoken for . . ."

"That's very nice of you, Mr. Young, and you're right, it is. Let's see . . . it would probably be better if I left the hotel that the conference is in so we're not interrupted. How 'bout we meet at the Irish Pavilion on 57th Street? You'll be able to slake both your thirst and your curiosity there!"

"That's great. Thanks so much for being willing to see me." Rob was appreciative of this uncomplicated connection. "Doctor, before I hang up, may I ask you one quick question?"

"Just one, Mr. Young, I've got a meeting in five minutes."

"Let me preface the question by saying that I've heard from other Marafield classmates about the burnt diary incident back in the novitiate. Any chance you'd know any of the women accused by Josephine Quarters about that?"

"I do. Intimately," Eily McVetty said with just a little clip in her voice. "You're speaking to one." Suddenly she sounded like a busy Director, "Look, Mr. Young, let's make a little deal for our meeting on the 17th. No cat and mouse routines, okay? You already knew I was one of the people Josephine accused, didn't you? What were you doing, testing me?"

"Guilty, and I do apologize. Doctor McVetty, believe me, it's been more than a little challenging trying to get the Marafield alumnae to say anything to me."

"Well you won't have that problem with me. I'll . . . what's the expression people in your line of work use . . . 'give up' whatever you want to know." Doctor McVetty was sounding relaxed again.

"That'll be sweet relief after what I ran up against this week! Why are you being so cooperative?" Rob thought he'd ask.

"My line of work I suppose; I try to save lives, Mr. Young. Now that was your second and last question. I've got to run. See you in New York."

Rob quickly added, "thank you Doctor. See you then."

Chapter 58

Like Boston, New York virtually emptied out in the summer. Most people preferred the beaches in July and August to the gritty and hot mushy tarred streets of Manhattan.

Rob walked in to the Irish Pavilion at quarter to four and sat at the bar having a "black and tan" while he waited for the California doctor to arrive. The place was practically empty.

Rob asked the bartender if it was always this quiet. "Nah, it'll pick up," the large silver haired man said. "July and August are a little slow though. The Hamptons, you know. How come you're not out there?"

"I go to the Cape. Next month." Rob said it almost as a reminder to himself that better days were just around the corner.

A tall attractive woman in an expensive sage colored linen suit stood in the doorway scanning the pub. Rob was certain this must be Eily McVetty so he went over and asked,

"Doctor McVetty?"

"Call me Eily." She offered her hand as she said, "you must be Mr. Young."

"I am! Please call me Rob. Where would you like to sit?"

"The bar's fine." There was only one other person sitting there reading the paper and having a pint.

Rob steered her to the short end of the bar where there were only two high swivel chairs, limiting the likelihood that they'd soon be surrounded by the after work crowd.

"What would you like to have?" Rob asked.

"Does your two week old offer of a meal still hold? I missed lunch and I could stand a bite to eat. First, I'd like a glass of cold water." Rob caught the bartender's eye and asked for a glass of water that was immediately delivered. "Wonder what I could get that wouldn't be huge. I just need something to tide me over. Is there a menu?" Rob reached for a menu from behind the bar. She looked it over and saw the smoked salmon, brown bread and capers appetizer and decided to have that along with a glass of Chardonnay.

"That's not exactly what I'd call a meal," Rob commented, "are you sure that's all you want?" She nodded her head as she took a long drink of water. Rob, on the other hand, opted for the mixed grill. The bartender saw they were ready to order and came over. He placed their orders through a doorway behind the bar and came back with another black and tan for Rob and a wine for Eily.

The visitor from Boston raised his glass in the direction of the visitor from California and said, "Here's to you, Doctor, thanks for showing up!"

"Not at all, Mr. Young. Slainte! And please, it's Eily, remember?" She took a sip of her wine, put the glass down on the cocktail napkin and asked the first question. "Tell me, Mr. Young . . ."

"Rob," he reminded her.

"Rob," she repeated with a smile, "what, essentially, are you looking for when you conduct an investigation?"

"It depends on the case really," was Rob's lame answer. The way the woman next to him looked into her wine glass with an ever so slight smirk made him remember his promise to her not to play "cat and mouse." He started over. "Okay, I remember the agreement: 'no cat and mouse,' so here we go. This particular case seems to have an interesting pattern that's emerged and I'm trying to follow the thread as far back as I can."

McVetty continued that thought, "and that thread has wended its way back thirty one years to the wool serge 'warp and woof' of me and my classmates. So what's the pattern you've discovered, Rob . . .

Josephine's penchant for allegedly being stalked by more people at every turn of her life than anyone you've met so far?"

"That pretty much sums it up," Rob said, "but, hey, don't hold back!" They both laughed softly. He took a sip from his pint, returned the glass to its coaster, then turned to look at Eily as he said, "Eily, I'm hoping I can get you and your friends to agree to testify should the need arise. What do you think my chances are?"

"Which friends?" Eily now tested him.

"Now, now, now, Doctor McVetty," Rob played, "I thought the no 'cat and mouse' agreement was mutually assured! Alright, I'll take your quiz: I mean your friends Kate Fitzmaurice, Mimi Aroho, Siobhan Greene and Annie Silo. How'd I do?"

"Very well," she said with exaggerated encouragement.

"Why thank you. Now back to the original question. Do you think your friends would agree to testify?"

Eily thought a while before saying, "Tough call. We had a little pow-wow about all this."

"I know. At Mimi Aroho's house in the winter."

"So I see you've been speaking again to our beloved mole, Annie," Eily said lightly.

"You know how it goes . . . it's important for me to keep the lines of communication open and working. She's been a big help up till now."

Eily caught the inference. "Why 'up till now'? Did you scare her off?"

"Yeah, I think I did," he admitted. "I asked her if she'd be willing to testify –like I just asked you–and she completely panicked. She said she's worked too hard to get where she is now and doesn't want to jeopardize her career. She's afraid 'Crime Line' will be all over the trial as a follow up to the show and she doesn't want to be part of the story."

"I know how she feels." Eily sympathized. "I'm pretty sure that's fairly representative of how we all feel. That's a normal initial gut reaction, don't you think?"

"Oh sure. People don't usually like to get involved in hearings and trials. You never know how long and drawn out they're going to be."

Eily countered his considerations about time with other reasons. "I think there's a little more to it than what a court case can do to an appointment calendar. We've got legitimate professional considerations about not wanting to be dragged through something unsavory that could in any way negatively impact our images or standings in our various fields." Eily paused a minute and looked blankly out over the pub. "Maybe even bigger than that, is the personal safety issue."

Rob was very attentive. "Meaning what?"

"Meaning simply that people are afraid," she said, implying by tone that she thought he should have gotten that one.

"Afraid . . . hmmm . . ." Rob mused a bit then asked, "None of you are fugitives from the law are you? You don't have criminal records or tax shenanigans you're trying to keep under wraps, do you? Please 'say it ain't so'!" He looked at her pleadingly.

"Oh bloody hell! Of course 'it ain't so'!" She looked at the investigator with incredulity then said clearly, "People are afraid of Josephine, Rob! They're afraid of her."

Chapter 59

The bartender brought the appetizer for Eily and the mixed grill for Rob. Eily devoted her attention to constructing little brown bread squares with horseradish sauce, smoked salmon and capers that kept rolling off the top. Rob started in on the Irish sausage, cut a piece of Galway bacon, separated the lamb chop from the mashed potatoes and sliced a quarter of the broiled tomato then began with the sausage.

"Perfect!" Eily pronounced after taking her first bite.

Rob was doing a few mental laps about the case while he simultaneously studied the black pudding uncertain whether to try it. Finally he spoke. "I'm not 'zoning out' on you, Eily, I was still back at your last remark. Do you really think your friends are afraid of Josephine Quarters?"

"Well, I know Annie is. Siobhan definitely is. Mimi lives the closest to her and expresses the least anxiety of those three. Kate lives far away enough not to give it too much thought and I'm on the other side of the country, lulled by distance into not caring."

She took another bite of her food and while she dabbed the corners of her mouth with her napkin she qualified her previous remarks. "I'm talking about their being afraid of Josephine causing them bodily harm some how."

"Based on what?" he quizzed.

"Based on reality. We all have past experiences involving her. Not pretty either. Then we found a few news clippings about some other 'misfortunes' that befell her and the people near her. Frankly, I think she has the makings of a dangerous woman. And no, I will not be an 'expert witness' for your client's case! You'll need a shrink for that. I'm just telling you 'off the record' how I feel about her."

"Not to worry. You know, I've seen those newspaper reports too," Rob said wryly adding, "She's had quite a run of fires and stalkings in her life, wouldn't you say?"

That was the first time anyone outside of the "circle of friends" attributed both to her and it jarred Eily a little. "You could say that."

"Tell me honestly, do you think your friends ultimately will choose to protect their own careers rather than help my client who's been so injured personally, professionally, and financially by Miss Quarters?"

"Well, first let me ask you how much you've found out about Josephine."

"Okay: Feigned illnesses. Stigmata. Diary: stolen, burnt, and planted. Accusations of being threatened and stalked by nuns. Domestic fires. More accusations of harassment, threats, and stalkings by decent colleagues in various places of employment. How'm I doing?"

"Dick Tracy lives," Eily said, impressed with his chronicle.

He smiled appreciatively at her couched compliment. "Now that you know I really do have some grasp of Josephine's anecdotal history, will you answer my question? Do you think your friends will protect their careers or help my client?"

"I only can represent myself here, Rob. My sentiments have long been that the people in charge in the novitiate back then never took seriously the signs of psychopathology that were flapping in their faces every time they considered Josephine to be a 'sound' member of the community. This may sound hard nosed but, in my book, I think they were derelict in their duty then and, because of that, look at how many more people have been hurt by her over the years. I'm sure you've seen over and over again how these things go. Events just keep on escalating and, often, till someone finally dies. God help us, I don't want that to happen."

"Aren't you worried about your career?" Rob tested.

"Hey, you bet!" she quickly admitted, "but the real issue here, the overarching virtue, is really justice, isn't it?"

Rob nodded appreciatively for the insight and, respectfully, for the woman.

The bartender came over and cleared away their plates. Rob asked for a coffee and Eily asked for tea. She asked Rob, "If your client's case goes to trial, do we actually have any choice about being called as witnesses?"

"I've tried taking the friendly approach with everyone about that, but the bottom line is you can be subpoenaed," Rob informed his luncheon guest.

"Now there's a word sure to spike some blood pressures!" Eily joked. "What would you say is the likelihood of that happening?"

Rob poured cream into his coffee and said, "Highly probable. That's why I was trying to estimate how strongly any of you would try to fudge out of cooperating. I think some of the fright about testifying can be reduced if I could just speak with all of them, kind of like this, up front and low keyed."

"Maybe."

"Tell me if this is this too wild an idea: Do you think you and your pals would be willing to sit down together with me for an afternoon and have a kind of group 'deposition'?" Rob was trying to think of what would elevate the comfort level of Eily's 'circle of friends' so that they'd be more confident in laying out their parts of information about Josephine's established pattern.

Eily thought about that a minute then said, "Actually, that might not be a bad way to go. There's comfort in numbers. Why not ask them? I'd come in for it if it would help."

"Can I ask you for a favor?" Rob looked sheepish.

Eily knew exactly what it was. "Oh, here we go . . . you want me to be your 'advance person,' don't you?"

"I'm just being practical. They'd listen to you and stiff arm me. What do you think? Think they see this situation through the same lens of virtue that you do and can be moved to help my client?"

"Rob, if you know nothing else about these women, just trust that their hearts are used to being in the right place. Call me next week. I'll let you know when they can meet with you," Eily said with a wink of unwavering confidence in her friends.

"You're that sure?" Rob double checked.

"Look, it isn't often that a pub inspires the recollection of Aristotle's definition of the moral life," Eily said reflectively, "but, believe me, these gals are no strangers to 'the habitual disposition of acting well.'"

Chapter 60

Eily was grateful to have the next morning to her self at the Marriott Marquis. She decided to relax in her room till check out time, when a car would be waiting to take her to La Guardia for her flight back. She called room service and ordered some breakfast and decided to fill the time by contacting her friends Kate and Mimi about getting together as a group with Robert Young.

She called Kate at her office first.

Kate's secretary, Rosemary, picked up the phone and replied to Eily's request to speak with Kate by saying "I'm not sure if she's in her office. Let me check. Who's calling, please?"

When Eily identified herself, Rosemary's voice took on a whole different tone, "Oh hi! I know you! You're Kate's friend from California! Hold on, I'll put you through . . . What? No, she's in her office; that's just my 'line' if I don't recognize the voice. You ought to come east to God's country sometime. Take care. I'll put you through."

Informed that Eily was on the line, Kate picked up the phone and started right in, "If it's nine o'clock here you must be sleep walking there, Eily McVetty! What's going on at this hour in California? You okay?"

"I'm just ducky, Kate, and I'm in New York," Eily said in a voice that still had traces of a late night in it. "Your secretary's a riot! I hope you know she takes very good care of you."

"Oh, I know that alright. She's a good egg." Kate knew Eily had been duly screened. "I hope you're calling to say you're coming up. What are you doing there . . . meetings?" Kate wanted to know and added, "Who goes to Manhattan in July? Yuck."

"I had a two day conference here in the city and you're right, it's steamy and the streets suck the shoes right off your feet, it's so bloody hot!"

Kate offered an invitation, "So are you coming up to get in a little 'R&R' before you go back?"

"I wish I could," Eily sighed, "but I have a board meeting tomorrow 'back at the ranch' and I have to be there. But I'll take a rain check for the weekend after next, the 27th, if you'll be around."

"Hey, I'll be around, even if you are full of beans . . . like you'd fly all the way back here in another week!"

"I would! I have to start putting a dent in my 'frequent flyer miles,' so I thought maybe we could have another one of those 'spa weekends' at Mimi's. What do you think? Can you drive down that weekend?"

"I think you have an ulterior motive, that's what I think," Kate toyed back. "What might there be about a Californian coming east for a spa weekend that sounds just a tad 'off'? Come on, spill it, McVetty, what's up?"

"Okay. I met with Robert Young yesterday, Kate. He came here to have a little pow-wow. Looks very much like we're going to be subpoenaed for this Josephine deal."

Silence. Then in a low, serious voice Kate made sure she heard correctly, "Are you kidding me?"

"Wish I was, hermana. This investigator, Rob, has done his homework. I think he's uncovered a very convincing pattern of Josephine's sordid little ways in every place she's been. He feels his client's attorney will definitely want us on deck."

"Well, Eily, this is the call I've been dreading. In fact, I've had a little talk with myself about this possibility. I'll do it, though. I'll go. How 'bout you?"

"I'm in. As the saying goes, 'ya gotta do whatcha gotta do,' Eily said in her best New York accent, resigned.

Kate continued, "Boy, are the others going to love this! Poor Siobhan . . . she'll be in buckets. As for Mimi, she's already made it known that she'd do what she could to help that poor teacher and her family. Wonder how Annie will take it?"

"Word has it: 'not well,'" Eily answered. "Rob said she flipped at the suggestion that she might be called as a witness. She's very worried about her career, her reputation, the publicity . . . all that. Which is very legitimate, Kate. I'm not exactly thrilled to find myself lined up to perform in this circus either. However, I feel even stronger that Josephine has to be stopped."

"I agree. She does," Kate concurred. "So what's with coming east on the 27th?"

"Well, my new best friend, Rob, thinks it might be beneficial to him as well as to us if we met with him as a group. I agree. One big yahoo on Saturday afternoon and we can all fill in the blanks together and be done with it till or, pray God, if we're subpoenaed."

"Robert Young seems to be a decent guy. It shouldn't be too bad." Eily sounded encouraging.

"If you say so. The 27th is a good weekend for me. I go on vacation in August and I'll be in Dingle for the month." Then Kate teased, "Maybe I should just apply for citizenship while I'm over there and stay!"

"Gee, you don't sound well at all, Kate; I think you'll need to have a physician with you!" Eily quipped. Realizing she had other calls to make, Eily quickly said, "Look, let me call Mimi and get this set up before I leave town. I'll have Mimi do a relay to the others."

"Yeah, I'd appreciate that. I'm pretty socked in all day and into the evening. Eily, when do you think you'll arrive for the 'spa weekend from hell'?" Kate asked.

"I'm going to book my flight today when I get to the airport. I'll come in Friday, the 27th. Robert Young will be at Mimi's on Saturday, the 28th, around 1 o'clock." Suddenly Eily realized she was making a plan that involved someone else's house. "Guess it would be nice if I called Mimi and asked her to host another reunion weekend!"

Kate chuckled, "Are you kidding . . . she'll love it! That girl loves a crowd! I'm sure I'll talk to her tonight. She'll be all gung-ho for this, you know."

"I know. I think we're all for it in theory. It's the damn praxis that's killing us!" Eily joked. "Okay, Kate, I'll see you on the 27th."

"Want me to pick you up at Logan?" Kate offered.

"Hey, that would be great; thanks Kate! I'll come in earlier than last time. I'll call and let you know when my flight is. Thanks again!" Eily added, "Have a wonderful rest of the day. Ta-ta, lovey!"

"Oh yeah . . . 'wonderful' is happening already, thanks to you!" Kate teased. "Have a safe trip, Eily. See you soon!"

Chapter 61

"Good afternoon . . . Kelly, Baker, Dowling and Greene. How may I help you?" the pleasantly modulated voice greeted the caller. Whenever Rob called Judy Mazola's attorney's office and got this particular receptionist he was always tempted to suggest that she have her own radio show. A "lite music" gig like that syndicated "Delilah" show, minus the saccharin. Better yet, a nice classical station.

"This is Robert Young, may I speak with Ellen Kelly, please?" The receptionist with the mellifluous voice directed his call to Ellen Kelly's office and her secretary answered.

"Ellen Kelly's office, may I help you?" asked a voice fit for C-Span.

Rob repeated, "this is Robert Young, may I speak with Ellen Kelly, please?"

Ellen Kelly was principal partner of the law firm and was handling the Judy Mazola case herself as a favor, of sorts, to various acquaintances that had prevailed upon her to come to the aid of the extraordinary teacher who had been wrongfully accused and publicly humiliated. This was a 'small potatoes' case for the firm and everyone was surprised that it was being handled by this high powered group and shocked that Ellen Kelly had opted for it.

Ellen Kelly possessed the kind of presence that spoke eloquently, even though her words usually were few. Her head of premature pure white hair, perfectly styled in a modified wedge, softly framed her high cheek bones, fair complexion, and deeply set blue eyes. There could be little doubt about her Celtic lineage. Nor could there be any doubt about how much of "Brigid's fire" crackled within her. She was precise in dress and demeanor and when she was engaged in conversation her eyes locked onto the one speaking. She had a happy capacity of charm and challenge in equal measure and, in legal circles, an enviable record of wins. Judy Mazola was far luckier than she might realize.

"Hello, Robert, how's my favorite P.I.?" a friendly sounding Ellen asked.

"I'm tying the bow on my work product for you, Ellen," was Rob's chipper response. "I should have the investigation all wrapped up by July 30th, Monday. Just wanted to check in and let you know."

"Great, and not a day too soon, Rob," Ellen replied. "We received a notice from the court clerk yesterday."

Rob guessed, "Got a trial date lined up?"

"We do. Monday, September 11th. I have to send over a witness list and that means I've got to get out some subpoenas, tout de suite. Any more names I need to add to the list you already gave me?" Ellen wondered.

"Yes, indeed," Rob hastily responded. "I have six more names to fax over to you. Any chance you can hold off on the subpoenas till after the 27th?"

"Not on your life," Ellen was firm.

"That's not exactly what I wanted to hear. Anyway, Ellen, one of them's a nun. She wouldn't have any special 'dispensations' or anything like that from court appearances, would she?"

Ellen gave a quiet laugh, "No, Rob, no 'clergy specials' or 'dispensations.' Do I hear special interest on your part about her appearing?"

"You sure do. She's been 'the artful dodger' of this whole hunt. It would give me a certain amount of satisfaction to see her finally get cornered."

"Cornering is what we love to do. Listen, Rob, can you come in before the 30th to give our team your preliminary findings?"

"Absolutely. Tell me when."

"This Thursday at eight works for me," Ellen offered, "or is that too early for you?"

Rob shrugged the hour off and said, "Thursday at eight it is."

"Say, Ellen, the people I'm meeting with on the weekend of the 27th have some concerns that the defense's client, Josephine Quarters, will find out if –or that– they're subpoenaed. What are the chances of that?"

"Nothing 'chance' about it. There's a hundred percent certainty she will find out," Ellen said in an off hand way. "You remember how this goes . . . witnesses are public record. All her attorney has to do is look up the court file to see if there's any activity on our part. The court clerk can tell them whether or not things are heating up. It's all part of 'discovery,' so they'll definitely know. Rob, tell me, are these people you're meeting just 'concerned' or are they actually afraid?"

"They're afraid, Ellen," Rob's voice sounded sympathetic. "You'll hear the legitimacy of that when we meet this week. You might want to leave your naiveté at home that day."

Ellen's voice dipped, "Well, I'm sorry to report that my naiveté has stayed home ever since I tried my first case twenty five years ago. This will probably be a pretty straightforward case, I should think."

"Think again, Counselor," Rob hinted ominously. "See you Thursday."

Chapter 62

"Mimi, dear, if you're at the drawing board, please pick up. It's Eily . . ."

"Hey, I'm here, hold on, hold on!" Mimi picked up the receiver from the answering machine, "Eily! What's up?"

"Hi, Mim. Thought I should let you know that I met with Robert Young yesterday. I've been at a two day conference here in New York and he met me here for a little chat before I fly out this afternoon."

"You have your clinical voice on, Eily, and that doesn't bode well in my book. What did he say?"

"You won't like it, but here goes: he's pretty sure we're going to be subpoenaed."

"All of us?" Mimi's voice rose as she said each word, then she exhaled a softly audible, "Crrrap!"

"All of us but Carrie," Eily clarified. "Now before you start hyperventilating, this guy seems to think it would help all around if we met with him as a group . . ."

"So we'll do it," Mimi offered right away, "I agree. A group meeting is a lot better than one to one. Jeez, I can't believe this is really happening. God! Well anyway, want to meet here?"

"Good ol' Mim, always right on the dime, aren't you? That would be great. This is what you get for having the best tent! How does the weekend of July 27th sound to you?"

"Wow! That's soon. Let me check . . ." Mimi tapped her Palm Pilot to see what was on the calendar. "Looks good here; I'm clear. Are you going to come all the way back here just for that?" Mimi sounded like flying across the country twice in one month was prohibited.

Eily explained, "Well, I think it's pretty important for my own comfort level. I'm hoping this guy's going to give a little tutorial on what to expect at trial time. I've never done this before. I've gone for jury duty a couple of times, but I never get picked. I do think talking to him might help."

Mimi asked, "Have you delivered this good news to anyone else yet?"

"Just you and Kate. I thought if you two went for the idea the others might be a little more at ease with it. Do you mind calling Siobhan and Annie?"

"Not at all. I'll call them tonight, though. I'm in the middle of a project right now and I know neither one will be a quick call." Mimi predicted, "Siobhan will be a wreck, but you know how strongly she feels about this. Annie will practically faint with worry that she'll be out of a job this time next year, God help her."

"I told Robert Young about those kinds of reservations. But I also told him that we all feel pretty convinced that Josephine should be stopped," Eily explained. "Hey, Mim, let me ask you something: Do you have any concerns about safety? I mean, you live the closest. What if Josephine finds out that our names are going to be put down as witnesses?"

Mimi rarely let on if she was concerned or anxious, but Eily did detect a rather thoughtful pause at the other end of the line. "Hmmm . . . it's worth thinking about, I suppose." Another pause. "Look, Eily, I'm the architect, you're the doctor. You tell me what you think. Knowing what you might about Josephine's type of personality, should I be scared? Never mind, the hair on my arms is standing at attention . . . guess that answers that!"

"I certainly don't want to alarm you or any of the others, but I did surprise myself yesterday when I told Robert that I feared for our safety if Josephine ever found out we were helping out Judy Mazola's case. Think I'm being melodramatic?" Now Eily was second guessing herself.

"Nah, I don't think you are, Eily. The name 'Josephine Ahearn' always evoked the word 'caution' in me anyway," Mimi confessed. "Maybe we should talk about this with the others, not to scare them, but just to encourage a little extra vigilance on everyone's part. What do you think?"

"I think that's wise. I'm sure that on the 27th Kate will give a clinical profile of this kind of personality and some behavioral predictors we should know about and file. That'll really scare the bejeezus out of us!" Eily tried for lightness.

"Oh great!" Mimi said with mock sincerity. "I'll just have the liquor store delivery guy back the truck up to the garage that Friday!" Changing her tone Mimi shared with Eily, "You know, I sit here at my board for hours at a time doing numbers and angles and degrees and renderings. Then, all of the sudden, I think of this bizarre situation we're in and I find myself shaking my head to try and come out of this weird dream I'm having in the middle of designing a building."

"I hear you. We're all probably doing that." Eily glanced at the clock on the night table and was startled, "Oh my God! Mimi, I have forty-five minutes to shower and meet my ride for La Guardia! I'll call you this weekend to find out how the others took the 'glad tidings.' Thanks for offering 'Claddagh House' again. See you on Friday!"

"Try coming earlier this time, will ya? Take care, Eily. Be safe!"

Chapter 63

Michael Frezia, Josephine's attorney, was planning to go away with his family the first two weeks in August and decided to call the clerk's office to see if there was any movement going on with the case. Lynn Goldberger was a clerk of the court and had signed the subpoenas for the people Ellen Kelly wanted to have on deck for the trial.

"As a matter of fact, it looks like things are starting to perk, Mr. Frezia. Ellen Kelly's office had a hefty stack of subpoenas that I signed and put in the court file. They should be in everyone's hands this week."

"Really?" Michael Frezia was stunned and annoyed. The 'discovery' period was going to require more work than he had imagined. Another damn working holiday. "Look, Lynn, I'm going to have to come down and take a look at that file today. Think you'll still be there for another hour or two?"

"Sure. Stop by my desk and I'll save you some scouting time," she kindly offered. "I hope you don't have plans for a big August holiday. With the court date I've seen you're going to have to do some fancy dancing."

"Yeah, who'd of 'thunk' it?" Frezia said to himself as much as to the clerk. "Thanks, Lynn. See ya later."

When Michael Frezia got back to his office at around six o'clock, he studied the list of witness names. He wasn't too surprised to see the names of former school colleagues of his client's. He was totally puzzled about the last six. He was sure that Ellen Kelly had folded in a one-two punch somewhere in those last names and it worried him. Even though he already had asked Josephine if there were any 'surprises' he should know about, he decided to call and ask her again.

"Hello, Josephine? This is Michael Frezia . . . is this a bad time to ask you a few questions? Great . . . I really appreciate it and I won't keep you long."

"Now I did tell you that the trial date is set for the 9th of September, didn't I? Good . . . Yes I do, as a matter of fact; it's Judge Catherine Thomas. What's that? Well let's just say she's formidable. Well . . . meaning she runs a very 'no nonsense' courtroom.

"Anyway, remember when I mentioned to you that there is always a possibility that opposing counsel may drum up a list of witnesses? Right, they have . . . Josephine? You there? C'mon now, take it easy, it's all part of the process . . ." He waited uncomfortably before continuing.

"You okay? Maybe we should have the rest of this conversation in my office, would that be better for you? . . . You sure? Well, let me just ask you if you recognize these six names . . ."

For the first time since he took on this case, Michael Frezia had misgivings about his client. By the time he had hung up the phone he felt as though he had been talking to a very different Josephine. Maybe he was just tired and grouchy about this dorky little case interfering with his fun in the sun.

On the other hand, it wasn't all that unusual for people to freak out when they found out who's going to be on hand as rebuttal witnesses. He usually had to listen as the client trashed each witness and for what reasons. It was all part of it. But man, she was spitting, she was frothing, she was foaming at the mouth over five of those names. At least he got her to calm down a little before he hung up. Good thing she can come in to see him tomorrow. As he turned out the lights and closed the door of his office, he made up an eleventh commandment: never call a client at home in the evening.

As the defense attorney crossed the street heading for the parking garage he saw just ahead of him, Robert Young who also kept his car there. He walked a little faster to catch up to him. It was no secret that Ellen Kelly had 'Mr. Clean' do her footwork.

"Hey Rob-O!" Michael Frezia gustily hawked. "You've been one busy hound dog, haven't you?"

"I'm gainfully employed, if that's what you mean," Rob coolly countered. "Boy, Frezia, don't you just hate it when you have to actually earn your outrageous fees?" He razzed back.

"Smart ass!" Frezia laughed. "So tell me . . . who the hell are these legions of people Ellen Kelly's nabbed as witnesses? Talk about overkill! Christ, that woman probably has pictures of Ken Starr all over her bedroom! I mean, this is just a stupid little 'tit for tat' case and now you've both gone and screwed up my vacation by forcing me to depose so many people."

"Hey, I'll think of you while I'm sailing off the Cape," Rob teased.

"What a minute, before you go," Frezia moved in closer and got serious. "I get the school chums, past and present, but who are those others? And what's with the nun? Come on, Rob, throw me something, anything."

"This is all you're getting: They were in the convent with your client," Rob said, looking to see how well the attorney knew his client. The wide eyed "huh?" told him. "That's it from me," Rob cautioned, "anything else you want to know you'll actually have to 'discover' . . . get it, Mikey? Either that or try and talk to Kelly."

"Yeah, I will . . . when I ask her to handle the divorce my wife will file over the vacation I'm going to miss. You can be the P.I. for my side! Thanks for the word, Rob-O. Enjoy that sailboat, you dirty rat!"

They shook hands and got into their cars, one lighter for a job well done; the other now burdened with doubt and weeks of tedium ahead.

Chapter 64

"Start with what you know.' 'Start with what you know.' That's what I always tell my students just before a test. Now I'm being tested. Dear God! Siobhan Greene, Eily McVetty, Kate Fitzmaurice, Annie Silo, Mimi Aroho . . . How did they end up in this trial? How did anybody find them? Didn't they learn their lesson? What do I have to do? What the hell does a person have to do?

"They're probably all rich little bitches with fancy cars and perfect homes and perfect lives and perfect careers and perfect clothes and perfect hair and perfect teeth and . . . oh yeah, perfect memories. Well, we'll just have to see about that, won't we? Yeah, we'll just have to see.

"Okay, Jo: 'Start with what you know' . . . come on, Jo, 'start with what you know' . . . Let me think, let me think. Ooooh . . . I know . . . I know! . . . I think Mimi Aroho still lives here! She's been in the paper. Yeah! She's some big shot architect. Yeah . . . she lives right here in Massachusetts! Now I can start with what I know! Phone book, phone book . . .

"Let's see . . . 'Armus' . . . 'Arnovi' . . . 'Arocchia' . . . 'Aroho!' . . . I win! I win! Aroho! Right here in black and white: 'M. Aroho, 14 Locknell Way, Glndrf.' . . . Glendarff . . . where's Glendarff? Here mappie, mapiee, mappie, show Josie where Glendarff is . . . Glendarff: '3C' on the map . . . let's see . . . hmmm . . . Glendarff! There you are! Only about forty-five minutes away. Now that's really what I call 'perfect' . . . Gotcha, you little bitch!"

Josephine was so excited, so nervous, so frightened that she could barely tap a cigarette out of the pack that she took from her pocket. When she finally extracted it, it had little creases from the package buckling under the force with which she tried banging out a smoke. Her Bic lighter, out of butane, added to her frustration so she slammed it onto the floor for failing her in her moment of need. She went to the kitchen and opened the top drawer next to the refrigerator and rummaged frenetically through it for a light. Finally, she found a box of matches, pulled out a kitchen chair and sat down to think and have a smoke.

The need for an immediate plan began distracting her from lighting up. "Oh, my God; wait a minute! It's almost August. Dammit! People go on vacation. Dammit again!" She reached over and flipped the calendar from the wall next to the phone, grabbed a pen and notepad from the counter and began calculating.

"Okay, Okay . . . easy Josie, easy; just get organized. Today's Wednesday, the 25th. August 1st is Tuesday. Let's see . . . if she goes away in August, summer rentals run from Saturday to Saturday. Damn, this is going to be close. I've got to get to Glendarff by the 27th," Josephine completed the sentence by singing, "'in the wee small hours of the morning . . . '" as she finally struck the match to light her cigarette.

Josephine took a long, deep drag from the cigarette and held the lit match in front of her face to blow it out when she finally exhaled. She began studying the flame, watching it stretch higher then drop down to a low blue sputter. She turned the wooden matchstick to a sideways position, helping rekindle the dwindling fire back to flame. The burnt top portion curved over like the handle of a cane. She gingerly took that spent end and turned the match completely upside down, guiding the flame to its total consummation of the tiny stick. There was something so mesmerizing about watching a flame, something so soothing about fire.

She struck another match and now she saw herself, in dark habit and white veil, lighting the taper in the sanctuary of the chapel, readying to go out to the altar and light the candles for Mass. When that match went out she lit another and now she was at the back of the darkened chapel at the beginning of Easter Vigil and the starting of the fire that would light the new Paschal candle. Striking another she intoned, "Light of Christ . . ." she stared at the flame, transported. She struck another and chanted, "Light of the world . . ." She struck the last match in the box and sweetly sang, "light of my salvation . . ."

When Josephine finally came out of her reverie, she picked up her wallet and car keys and walked out to her gray 1998 Taurus parked in the driveway. She got in, turned on the engine and sat a few minutes, waiting for both the air conditioning and a direction in which to go to kick in. At last, she remembered there was a Home Depot in the mall in Kittonden, two towns away. She pulled out and headed there.

This was only her second time in this shrine to the gods of home improvement, so rather than waste time by wandering around the cavernous warehouse, she asked a red vested employee if they carried gas cans. He said they did, and then directed her to the lawn mower and yard work section. She found the aisle of lawn mowers and at the end of the aisle she also found a variety of gas carriers. She selected a red five-gallon container made of some plastic or rubberized composition. It had a top mounted carrying handle, a "no spill" pouring spout at one end, and a smaller cap at the top of the other end. Attached to the handle was a funnel that had a card stapled to it exclaiming, "Bonus Gift: Free Funnel!"

At the check out counter were sundry last minute tempters: tape measures, utility knives, work gloves, putty knives and a ten pack of Bic lighters. Josephine, lifted a package of the Bic lighters off the display hook and added it to her purchase.

As she pulled out of the parking lot, she decided to take the local roads back rather than the highway. In the town between Kittonden and her own home in Sparrows Point, she pulled into a gas station at a busy intersection and asked an attendant if he would please fill up the container with gas.

"Somebody outta gas or ya cuttin' the lawn?" the friendly young attendant asked.

"Cutting the lawn," Josephine answered pleasantly.

"This is the week for that alright," he remarked as he watched the gas near the can's capacity mark. "It's supposed to be dry all the way through to next weekend."

"Is it really?" Josephine gushed, pleased with the forecast.

"Guy just said it again on the radio." He took a twenty dollar bill from Josephine and said, "let me bring you some change back and I'll put that in the car for you."

When the attendant came back with her change, he advised her to keep the can on the floor of the backseat. "I don't like to put these in the trunk," he explained, "they can tip over without you knowing it and they get better ventilation here. You goin' far?"

"No, just around the corner," she said casually.

"Well, there you go! You might want to keep your windows down a speck; the fumes are pretty strong."

"Thank you so much," Josephine said sincerely, "you've been very helpful. I hope you get to enjoy some of the nice weather we're having."

"I will! I start vacation on the 28th. Gonna spend the whole week on my boat." He double thumped the top of the car as he walked away saying, "Have a good one!"

"You bet," Josephine said back. The attendant had moved too far out of earshot to hear her finish, "that's just what I'm planning, gasoline boy: a really good one . . ."

Chapter 65

As promised, Kate and Eily arrived at Claddagh House early in the afternoon on Friday, the 27th. They had only been there about half an hour when Siobhan called from her cell phone to say she was only two exits away. Mimi told her she'd leave the garage door up so she could pull in next to Kate's car. Annie Silo was not expected till about seven that night and would be arriving by car service from Logan.

Since it was such a perfect cloudless day, they decided to lounge around on the deck and patio in the back yard. Eily had changed into shorts and tank top and headed, barefoot, straight for the hammock. Kate opted for the canvas director's chair and turned it to prop her feet on the deck railing. This way she could take in Mimi's 'Monet gardens,' the Japanese fountain of slate and copper that bubbled in the center of the putting green perfect lawn, and the cobblestone labyrinth at the far end of the property that was curtained with a backdrop of wispy miscanthus.

Mimi brought out a tray with lemonade, cheese and crackers, and a bowl of fresh sliced peaches and blueberries. She poured three glasses of the cool drink and passed them around to her thirsty friends.

"Oh, thank God you're not making me get out of this thing," Eily said appreciatively as she took the glass from Mimi. "I have visions of doing a complete flip when I finally try to get up!"

"Why get up? You can stay there all afternoon and night," Mimi said. "I thought, since it's such a gorgeous day, maybe we could just grill tonight and eat out here. Is that okay or would you rather go out?"

"Oh, I'd rather go out," Kate deadpanned, "preferably to a place without air conditioning, really crowded . . . greasy food and bad acoustics. I mean, listen to that . . . do we really want to be annoyed by song birds and breezes faintly purring through the evergreens?"

As though part of a well rehearsed routine, Eily chimed right in, "I'm with you, Kate! I mean, Mim, really, who could eat out here with all these fragrances wafting through the air from the flowers? Kate, do me a favor will ya? See if you could turn off that aggravating water fountain."

Mimi quietly chuckled as she pulled her bay recliner around to face the others. Then, in answer to her guest's obstreperous comments, she silently took the ice scoop and tossed a quick volley of crushed ice on each of the two fake whiners. "Yeow!" "Brat!" were the satisfying responses.

"Well, girls, here's to life, liberty and justice for all," Mimi offered as she tipped her glass toward her friends. "Here, here!" "Cheers!" were the replies.

"Yoo-hoo! Wait for me!" Siobhan yelled as she walked from the garage breezeway to the deck stairs.

Siobhan was greeted with cheers for her early arrival. She began her round of hugs with Eily who held her two arms straight up in the air, signaling for her hug to be delivered to the hammock. "Hi, sweetie pie," she said to Siobhan, "I'd get up but I know I'm going to twirl in this thing if I do!"

Kate and Mimi went up to Siobhan and welcomed her. Eily reached for Siobhan's hand and said, "Now Siobhan, please talk some sense into Mimi. She's insisting we all go out to dinner tonight but we just want to stay here and have a cook out."

Siobhan fell for it and, gesturing to the yard, quizzed Mimi, "why on earth would you want to leave all this? It's a perfect day to cook out. Then we don't have to worry about getting dressed up. I'm staying!"

"Okay, you win," Mimi went along, "I know when I'm out numbered!"

Mimi handed Siobhan a glass of lemonade and Siobhan said, "Now what was that toast I caught the tail end of . . . 'life, liberty and justice for all'? You girls just get right to it, don't you! Well, phooey on that! Here's my toast: To October! Which comes after September. Which is after the trial that I hope to survive!"

"Well said!" Mimi laughed as she gave Siobhan a pat of encouragement on the back.

"I thought the next time we'd all be together here it would be for our annual 'just for fun' gathering," Siobhan wistfully owned. "After this episode of 'Law & Order' we're all being dragged into, we'll have to make arrangements with the 'Witness Protection Program' just to get together again!"

"You could all move to California, my lovely little 'Subpoena Sisters'!" Eily shouted back.

"Everything's going to be alright," Mimi reassured Siobhan, the others, and herself. "Tomorrow, when we're meeting with Robert Young, let's just remember to get equal time and ask him all the questions we want answers to before he leaves."

"Right-o! I've got my list," Eily responded and then asked, "Are we going to get into this stuff right now or are we going to wait till Annie gets here? I need to know if I should go with this nap I feel coming on me."

Kate answered, "Go with the nap, Eily, you've had a long trip. We'll just sit here and talk about you while you doze, so make it a good long one!"

"All I need is twenty minutes. This hammock is working on me like an anaesthetic," Eily's voice faded as she spoke. The other three looked out on the halcyon scene of gardens and birds and greens before them and drifted off in comfortable silence, subtly carried away on the raft of cognition that beauty noticed, heals.

Chapter 66

Josephine was starting to get annoyed with how long this summer day held brightness. She wanted it to be dark and late. Her nerves were not helped by how long she had to rummage through her basement looking for that box of fatwood kindling sticks she uses in winter to light logs in the fireplace. She thought she had put it over with the Christmas decorations, but it wasn't there. For a couple of heart stopping minutes she thought she had used all the fatwood. Then what would she do?

She hoisted down box after box from the deep shelving that lined one whole wall of the dark, unfinished basement. When she got to the third section and pulled out the boxes on the floor from underneath the bottom shelf, she gave a victorious "Hah! There you are! Hah!"

She picked through the box for sticks of a certain length and heft. Not too short and not so light that they could blow around like bark if a breeze picked up. She selected five pieces. She really only needed one, two at most. She opened the back door of the basement and stepped outside to test the dryness of one of the pieces. The sticks would be useless if they were damp from the humidity of the basement.

She reached in her pocket and pulled out a new Bic lighter, flicked it once and adjusted the tall flame to low. Then she held the end of a stick of fatwood over the flame and, to her great relief, it caught immediately. Josephine laid the piece of burning wood on the rusty barbecue grill and studied it. It burnt steadily, then slowly curled into a blackened strip that finally glowed a bead of orange between the tiny crags of ash.

"Nicely done," Josephine whispered.

She went back into the basement, scooped up the other sticks of fatwood she had chosen, and picked up the filled can of gasoline that was sitting in the corner and carried them around the side of the house to the driveway. By now the setting sun left the gray Taurus in the driveway in the cooling shade of the house. Josephine placed the can of gasoline on the driveway between the front of the car and the house, out of view from passersby. Next to it she laid the sticks of fatwood out in single file; the more air they got, the better.

Josephine went back into the house through the basement, locked up, and went upstairs to shower. She had to be on the road by 8:00p.m. Her plan to leave at that time was to avoid being noticed leaving her house at an unusual hour. Then she would drive to Glendarff and find Locknell Way, Mimi Aroho's street. She would orient herself to the house, "Number Fourteen," but not slow down or look too interested. She'd look like she knew exactly where she was going. Then she'd do all the side streets and scout the best place to later park her car.

From there, she estimated that she would arrive at the nearby movie theatre by around 9:45p.m., just in time for the 10 o'clock showing of "The Sixth Sense." She had called the theatre the day before and asked if there were any places nearby that served food after the movie got out at midnight. The young woman who answered told her about "The Silver Streak," a new all night diner that was three miles from the theatre. She would go there after the movie and kill as much time as possible. If the place was too empty and staying there would be too dicey, she'd go sit in her car in the parking lot till about 2:30 a.m. Glendarff would be her next stop and, with any luck, Mimi Aroho's last.

Reviewing this plan while she got dressed in dark blue jeans and a long sleeved black cotton pullover, Josephine felt a rush of excitement mixed with exoneration. As she walked toward the bathroom to put on some make-up, she stopped at her dresser one more time and picked up the old 1996 copy of Affinity, the Marafield Alumnae Newsletter with the special Directory supplement for that year's reunion classes. A rubber band stretched around and held the first several pages to the front cover so that the directory flipped open to the "Thirty Years" section. Her eyes followed the little arrows she had drawn in the margins pointing to the five graduates' names and the states from which each hailed.

She just couldn't help herself. Even though she was on her way to Glendarff this very night, she was already in mental transition to the next venue, Thistle, Connecticut, where Siobhan Greene lives. After that, a little trip to Kate Fitzmaurice's Cape Porpoise, Maine, would be equally worthwhile. Colorado and California she hadn't figured out yet since they were antithetical to her rule of "start with what you know." Besides, this order was panning out to be almost too good to be true. It serendipitously matched the hierarchy of her loathing for those five "fair haired" bitches.

Josephine glanced at the clock and saw that it was 7:45. She quickly put the journal down and half skipped to the bathroom to put on some makeup. When she finished, she ran down stairs and into the kitchen. She opened a bottom drawer and took out a brown paper lunch bag; the sticks of fatwood would go in there. Next, another drawer was opened and, from a neatly folded pile of cloths, two old worn dishtowels were taken.

She picked up her wallet and keys and headed for the back door, opened it and then stopped short. She hurried back and opened the door to the cabinet underneath the sink. Josephine yanked a few disposable rubber gloves from a dispenser box, stuffed them in her jeans pockets and left.

In the driveway, Josephine gathered up the fatwood sticks and put them in the lunch bag. She opened the front passenger door and put the bag in the glove compartment. Then she lifted the red gasoline can and placed it on the floor behind the driver's seat. She took the gas station guy's word for it; she didn't want to chance gasoline spilling in the trunk of her car. Next, the two old dishtowels were loosely laid over the gas can.

She got in the aging car, turned on the engine and then the lights, adjusted her mirrors, and opened the two back windows just a crack. The clock on the dashboard glowed "8:00." Right on schedule. Pulling out of the driveway, Josephine had a flash of the movie, "The Sixth Sense," that she would be seeing tonight. She cracked herself up as she took on the character of the eight year old actor, Haley Joel Oment, and whispered chillingly in the dark as she pulled out of the driveway and onto the street, "I see dead people . . ."

Chapter 67

"I hear car doors and a trunk closing; that must be Annie," Siobhan said as she carried a tray of wine glasses, paper plates and cocktail napkins out to the deck. Eily and Kate followed with two bottles of chilled Vouvray, pretzels, chips, a veggie platter and dips. "C'mom, let's go see," Siobhan said.

The three reached the front door of Mimi's house just as Annie was about to ring the doorbell. "Welcome, welcome, welcome!" Eily effused as she held the door open and the others helped Annie in with her suitcase and shopping bag.

"Well, don't you look relaxed!" Annie observed, "You must have gotten here way ahead of me. Where's Mimi? Did you bump her off and change the locks?"

"She's here; she just ran around the corner with a pie she baked for one of her neighbors," Eily explained, "some little old lady who's husband died last week. The son went back to Texas today so 'Mother Teresa' thought a homemade peach pie and a little visit would help cheer her up. Isn't she a love? People don't seem to do that kind of thing anymore."

"That's our Mim," agreed Annie, "guardian angel to the world."

Kate came down from taking Annie's bag upstairs to her room and said, "Why don't you get comfy and meet us out on the deck. We timed cocktails around your arrival, so don't dawdle! The three of us are in a summery white wine mood . . ." Kate caught Annie's nose wrinkling in disapproval and continued, "and I guess that look means you're in the four seasons vodka Gibson mood" Kate lightly interpreted.

Annie playfully reached into her shopping bag and pulled out a jar of cocktail onions, a split of dry vermouth and a litre of Absolut as she chirped "Absolute-ly!" Kate took the ingredients for the Gibson from her and retreated to the kitchen to concoct Annie's elixir.

"I also brought these," Annie handed Siobhan a gift bag of cheeses and crackers and ended the presentations by handing Eily two beautiful earthenware terrenes of pate that had become her trademark hostess gift for this crowd.

"Wow! Thanks, Annie! This is the best pate this side of France!" exuded Siobhan. "I'll put these over on the counter for Mimi to see when she gets back," Siobhan suggested. "How 'bout if we have these tomorrow night? That okay with you, Annie?"

"Of course!" Annie shrugged, "on the condition that I don't have to wait till then for that extra crisp clear beverage with the onions in it that Kate's mixing!"

Kate yelled in, "Coming right up! You want it now or when you come down?"

"I'll wait till I come down. I just hope I don't trip over my tongue on the stairs!" Annie joked as she headed up to the second floor.

By the time Annie had changed into khaki shorts and denim shirt and came out on the deck to join the others, Mimi had returned from her good deed for the day.

"Hey, Annie, welcome!" Mimi said as she left the grill that she was cleaning to give Annie a hug. "I saw all the goodies you brought; thanks! I know it's like talking to the wind when I say this to you girls," Mimi turned to get everyone in her crosshairs, "but you do not have to come laden with gifts every time you come here!"

They blew her off, muttering in unison, "yeah, yeah, yeah . . ."

"So was the lady home that you took the pie to?" Annie asked Mimi.

"Yup. Poor little thing. Mrs. Eihler and her husband were married fifty-two years," Mimi said. "She's such a cutie. She walks every day around the neighborhood, about eight in the morning and again around six in the evening. Her husband was diagnosed in March with cancer. Hospice just started coming in only three weeks ago, so it all feels pretty fast to her."

"Hey, Mim, did you want to invite her to have dinner with us?" Kate asked.

"Oh, I already did that," Mimi said as she lit the grill, "she said it's a little too soon for her, which I had presumed, but she was very touched by the offer."

Eily chimed in, "How'd she like the pie . . . and by the way," she continued impishly, "I'm sorry for her troubles, but I hope that was an extra home made pie you gave her!"

"You are so terrible! I made two, but none for you now!" Mimi sparred back. "As it happens, peach is her favorite, so she was delighted. Poor little thing, she said she's having trouble sleeping these nights and that now at least she'll have something to snack on when she starts walking the floors."

"Which house is hers?" Eily wanted to know.

Mimi went over to the middle of the deck facing the gardens and said as she pointed east with the bristled grill brush, "See the property that backs mine down there? Well, if you cut through that yard, pass the house on that property and stand on the sidewalk in front of it, the Eihler house would be the one right across the street. That's Clapham Lane or, as the bird flies, it's two houses that-a-way."

Mimi got to the business at hand, "Okay, here's the menu: grilled halibut, grilled marinated shrimp, grilled zucchini and grilled spuds . . . okay with everyone?"

"Oh my God," moaned Annie, "what's not to like? That sounds fantastic!"

"Well, let's relax a little, catch up, and have some hors d'oeuvres. Let's see . . . it's seven thirty now. How 'bout if I start grilling around eight-thirty?" Mimi asked. "Okay if dinner's at nine?"

"Suits my Pacific clock just fine," Eily registered. Everyone else nodded approval.

Kate playfully admonished, "And no peach pie for anybody till we talk about our meeting with that investigator tomorrow!"

"Bartender!" Annie yelled as she held her martini glass aloft, indicating her sentiments about the conversation to come.

Chapter 68

"Well I'll be damned! Look at the size of these homes in Glendarff! Jesus Christ, what do these people do for a living, rob banks? I should have been a goddamned architect! Holy cow, this is her block coming up . . . number eight . . . ten . . . twelve . . . number fourteen, corner house . . . Jeee-zus! This is an all the way around the corner, 'corner' house. Holy crow! Will you look at that thing! Well . . . hot diggity dog, Mimi Aroho, get a load of all those nice old wooden shingles on your all wooden house. Mmmmm . . . somebody in the neighborhood must be having a cook out . . . smells good.

"Well doesn't this just get better and better? It looks like she's home tonight: and boy, every light in the house is on too. Oh, what the hell . . . no cars are coming . . . I might as well turn right here and go down the side of good ol' 'Number Fourteen.' Let me see . . . what side street is this? Salcombe Road. Remember that: Salcombe Road. Now don't go too slowly, Josie girl, you don't want to be noticed. Mama Mia! Will ya look at her house? This thing just keeps going and going! Oh, I see: an ivy covered brick wall enclosing a yard back here. Wish I could see in . . . looks like she has lights on in the yard. Just wish I could see in . . .

"Okay. Let's check this place out again from a different approach. Hey! Wait a minute! Where the hell are all the cars? Don't tell me you can't park on these streets! Easy, Jo, easy . . . What's this sign at the corner say? 'Parking on Street Prohibited' Dammit! Dammit! Okay . . . alright . . . don't

panic yet . . . Drive around, Jo, drive around. Go one more block and turn left. Hey! Parking! Good. Okay, turn left . . . cross Locknell Way . . . go two more blocks and turn left . . . okay: parking! Go two blocks . . . good, here's Salcombe Road again. Now turn left: hmmm . . . no parking again. Oh, I get it! Locknell and Salcombe must be the through roads; that's why there's no parking.

"And there's her house again, straight ahead. Wow! This is definitely the best view . . . look at that huge wrap around porch . . . and the big driveway . . . and that manicured wall of boxwood trees before you turn into the driveway . . . and the carriage lights all over the place. Wow! I didn't even see that turret from that other direction. My God, that place even has a third floor. That house is mammoth! Well, all the better, little Miss architect. All the better, with those great big open spaces and high ceilings and three stories of dark wood . . . all the better.

"C'mon now, Josie, let's step it up a little. Let's see what the street behind Lochnell looks like. Guess I'll turn right here and pass by the front of the house again on this side. Coast is clear. Man, her property is practically the size of my whole damn block! Oh yeah, Aroho . . . you really wanted to be a nun back then, didn't you! You really would have kept those vows, wouldn't you! Yeah . . . everybody thought you were so great . . . big champion of the poor . . . big 'why can't we do something to help the migrant workers?' . . . big 'we've got to do more than just say prayers about the war in Viet Nam' . . . big 'if you feel so compelled to fast all the time, Sister St. John, why not fast from false accusations?' God I hated her for that one . . .

"Where's the damn cross street? Oh there it is . . . okay, make a left. Now try this street . . . left on Clapham Lane. Great! Look at all the cars parked here. Slow down, slow down . . . Her house should be right behind this left one on the corner. Perfect: Salcombe Road straight ahead. Yeah, this is perfect. I can see the lights on in her yard from here. If I park right about here later on, I can walk around the corner without crossing any streets and make it to the back of her house without being seen. Okay, let's see . . . I need a landmark . . . there! I'll try and park in front of this house with the mailbox painted 'Eihler.' Oh yeah . . . this is going to work out just fine."

"Okay . . . Nine-thirty. Am I good or am I good? Alright, Josephine, rehearsal's over. Time to go to the movies . . . then time to go to the diner . . . and then: 'Show Time!'"

Chapter 69

"Mimi, that dinner was fabu!" Kate offered. The others joined in with their own raves about its lightness, the unbeatable char flavor, and how they couldn't have done better at a restaurant.

"Know what my favorite part is?" Mimi asked. "No pots and pans. All the rest just goes in the dishwasher," with that, she automatically began collecting everyone's dishes.

"Oh no you don't! Sit," Siobhan ordered Mimi, "the cook doesn't do dishes: house rule!"

As everyone got up to clear the table, Mimi took a poll, "Are you warm enough out here or should we go in to have our dessert and tea?"

"Please! Don't say the 'D' word! Let's wait a while for dessert. I'd love to stay out here . . . look at that sky! There must be a million stars out tonight. But I'll need to borrow a sweatshirt if you have one," Eily said. The consensus was to stay on the deck with some extra layers.

No sooner said than done, Mimi appeared with an armload of sweatshirts and cotton throws and dumped them onto a chaise. "There you go, girls, take your pick." While Annie, Eily and Shiobhan loaded the dishwasher and tidied up the dining table, Mimi and Kate moved the bay recliners over to the other end of the deck where the chiminea was. Mimi sent Kate under the deck to the weatherproof storage box to retrieve some pinon wood while she got rid of the old ashes. Then she showed Kate how to load the portable clay fireplace with the pinon and handed her the lighter.

In no time, a cozy fire started to take the chill out of the night air and the distinct aromatic fragrance of the wood was wonderful. The others soon filed out of the house, mugs of tea in hand, and scooped up the throws Mimi brought out, settling in the chairs that had been moved into a horseshoe around the chiminea.

Siobhan marveled at the difference that the chiminea made, "You know, I've always wondered about these things. They really do throw off heat. This feels great!"

"I've been wondering . . ." Eily began ad random, "has anyone else noticed that when we've been together specifically to talk about the Josephine case –which automatically reverts to impassioned discussion about the Marafield fire– Mimi builds this conflagration of leaping flames and makes us all sit and stare at it?" Eily was setting the hostess up again. With a little wink she tossed the remark to Kate. "What would you call that, Kate, Mimi's not so subtle attempt at 'reality therapy'?"

Kate went right along, "Hmmm, let's see . . . could be some latent 'PTSD' . . ."

"I know that one!" Siobhan joined in, "Post Traumatic Stress Disorder!"

Kate continued, "Or it could be 'OCD' . . ."

"Obsessive Compulsive Disorder!" Annie decoded, "God help me, I know that one intimately!"

Kate offered one more, "or she could simply be 'JPN.'"

Even Eily was stumped, "You got me there, Kate; I don't know 'JPN.'"

This time Mimi jumped in laughing and said, "Oh, Eily, sure you do! You have all the classic symptoms of it. 'JPN,' Eily: 'Just Plain Nuts'!" Everyone applauded Mimi for finally getting Eily at her own game, including the good natured Eily.

"Now listen, girls, you've got to earn your dessert before you go to bed tonight," Mimi established. "We've got to get organized about tomorrow and it's already quarter to eleven."

"You're right," Kate agreed, "where should we start?"

Surprisingly, Siobhan began. "Well I'd like to know if Josephine already knows we've been subpoenaed, or will she just be knocked off her pins when she sees any of us walk into the court room. I mean, I'm not embarrassed to tell you that I'm really scared about all this. I'm sorry, but I just don't trust her."

"Siobhan, lovey, I think we all feel that way," Eily said calmly. "I let Robert Young know that when I spoke with him in New York. I think this is something worth bringing up again as a group in our meeting with him tomorrow."

"Definitely!" Mimi seconded. "I also want to be sure that the attorney for Judy Mazola, Ellen Kelly, knows we feel this way too. So be sure you all tell her this when you meet her, as I'm sure we will." Heads bobbed in agreement.

Eily wanted Kate's opinion, "Kate, do you think we're just blowing this fear thing out of proportion because our resistance to testifying is so high, or is there merit to our concerns for our safety?"

"Oh, I think there's merit alright," Kate warned, and then explained by starting with a disclaimer. "Based solely on anecdotal information alone and not really knowing Josephine well enough to make a valid diagnosis, if you will, I would venture that she fits a certain profile warranting caution on our parts."

Annie was visibly shaking as she asked, "Like what?"

Mimi noticed her shivers and interrupted Kate's answer, "Annie, are you cold?"

"Hell no, I'm a freakin' nervous wreck talking about this stuff! Go on, Kate, what do you mean?"

"Jesus, Annie, we're going to have to get a seatbelt for that recliner, you're shaking so much!" Kate quipped, attempting to ease a little of the tension. "You sure you want me to go into all this?"

"Yeah, sure, I love creepy stories in the pitch black . . ."

Chapter 70

"Come on, Kate, I want to hear this," Siobhan coaxed.

"Well, first, let's look at what we know. Josephine has had this stalking thing as far back as 1963 when we were all novices with her. Mimi, you said that some of your 'sources' told you she was involved in stalking events in her early teaching days in her school district. Eily, you said that Robert Young had witnesses from other teaching sites who had likewise been accused by her of stalking."

"Yeah," Siobhan interjected, "and let's not forget that the stakes get a little higher each time she does one of these routines."

"Which is exactly why we're here, sweetie, we don't want any more people to end up getting injured or . . . even worse," Eily added. "Sorry, Kate; go on . . ."

Kate continued, "I ran some of this by a friend of mine who's on the board for one of the societies dealing in psychiatry and the law, and he had some interesting statistics about stalking. He said that twenty three percent of all stalkers are in professional relationships with their victims. Eleven percent had other work related contacts with their targets, and seventy-seven percent of the stalking victims who had been threatened ended up being assaulted."

"So far my brain is saying yes, yes and yes to what you're saying, Kate," Annie registered, "but my gizzards are saying no, no and no. I want to hear this stuff, I honestly do, but these statistics aren't helping my bad vibes about being involved with this and it's very unsettling."

"Annie, why don't you just to go inside and do a few laps in the pool while we talk about this?" Mimi asked with respect for Annie's obvious anxious state. "We'll come and get you when it's time for the peach pie . . ."

"No!" Siobhan countered, glaring at Annie. "You have to stay right here and listen to this. There shouldn't be any of this 'protecting each other' crap! We have to talk about this stuff tonight and we all have to be on deck ready to talk at our meeting with that guy tomorrow. I'm sorry, Annie, but I don't like this any more than you do, so you'll just have to deal with it . . ."

"Take it easy, will you, Siobhan!" Annie snapped. "You're still mad at me for giving your name to Robert Young, aren't you? That's what this is really about! Just get off your goddamned high horse! I'm not going anywhere and I'm not swimming any laps. I just made one lousy comment about how I feel. God Almighty!"

"Alright, alright . . . everybody take a deep breath," advised Kate. "If you two think we need to get into this now we can, but I think the whole group needs to decide how we want to spend this time."

Siobhan and Annie were silent. Siobhan's foot was wildly gyrating back and forth. Annie stared into her tea mug so closely that only the top of her head could be seen.

"Well, girls, I love you both, but I didn't make this trip to join an 'encounter group,' Eily bluntly said. "Look, short fuses are predictable for all of us. Let's just move on."

Mimi agreed, "Yeah, let's not give our anxieties any more power than they already have. I want to keep on point . . . even though it was my big mouth that started this."

Siobhan thawed first. "Annie, I apologize. I did snap at you and I shouldn't have. I want to get back to what you were saying, Kate. This is the last time we're going to be together before the trial, so I want to focus on that."

"Annie?" Kate checked to see if she wanted to say anything.

"Let's keep going," was her only reply.

"Okay . . . moving right along," Kate picked up, "delusional disorders are a big part of the picture in stalker profiles. And even though Josephine is the one who cries 'victim,' she herself is the actual stalker, transferring and projecting onto others the predacious behavior which she, in turn, perpetrates upon herself for verisimilitude in her attention getting drama."

Chapter 71

"That is one nasty boomerang," Eily thought aloud.

"You're not kidding," Siobhan responded. "and we've all been grazed by that boomerang too! Kate, before you go on, say a little more about delusional disorders for me."

"I was just about to!" Kate gladly complied. "In one study, the categories of the delusional disorders associated with stalking are erotomania, morbid jealousy, morbid infatuation, and persecutory delusions."

"Wow! Didn't we talk about this the last time we were here?" Siobhan was trying to remember. "Didn't somebody say that she thought Josephine was jealous of Eily and Annie . . . ?"

"Yeah," Mimi recalled, "and I said that I thought Josephine was infatuated with you, Siobhan. She was always doing little things for you, always trying to get your attention in some way and you never seemed to notice."

"And you two," Eily pointed to Mimi and Kate, "she wasn't even on your radar screens! I think a lot of that delusional stuff really kicked in with her 'I'm an emaciated-mystic-burdened-with-a-tiresome-ol'-stigmata' routine. When that didn't get your attention and win your devotion, as was the case with most of our classmates, she upped the ante to 'persecutory delusion.' And thus commenced her whole 'they're out to get me' cabal."

Mimi augmented the discussion. "You know, I saw 'Larry King Live' a couple of weeks ago. He interviewed a psychiatrist who wrote this book about stalking. She said something on the show about some stalkers being socially immature loner types and I thought, 'that fits.' She also characterized stalkers as becoming angry with their victims over some slight, real or imagined, and that they're the disgruntled employee we see in the news who targets the boss, the co-workers, or the whole company."

Siobhan checked with Mimi, "Did you tell everybody what you told me about that?"

"I'm not sure I said anything to Annie," Mimi hesitated.

"Well say it!" urged Siobhan, giving her a look.

"Go ahead, tell me" seconded Annie.

"I think you're going to need that seatbelt Kate teased you about," Mimi warned. "My sister, Kathy, found out somehow that Marafield never collected insurance on the fire and . . ."

"What? What did you just say?" Annie bolted upright.

"Kathy found out that Marafield never collected insurance money on the fire and she swears that her little tidbit of information is rock solid," Mimi repeated. "It got me thinking some pretty unpleasant thoughts. Then I saw that Larry King show on stalking. Now with what Kate's just said, I mean . . . "

"Yeah?" Annie murmured waiting for the rest, yet not wanting to know it.

"Well, Annie, here's how I see it. Maybe, for Josephine, the Motherhouse was 'the company.' Maybe all of us, including our classmates, were 'the co-workers.' Maybe she was the 'disgruntled employee.' And maybe her mysterious dismissal in the stealth of night just one month after the fire . . ." Mimi posited and waited with the others to see if Annie was computing. She was.

"Oh my God . . . you think she started the Motherhouse fire, don't you?" Annie's eyes blankly skimmed over the wooden boards of the deck while she worked at reframing the most terrifying event in her life. "I'm the last person who saw her completely dressed in her full habit when everyone else was asleep in bed . . . I remember registering how unlike her it was to be up so late, and how flustered she got when

I stopped to see how she was. I always thought she was embarrassed that I caught her still in her habit after 'lights out' . . . you know, being 'caught' kind of breaking one of the rules."

Annie looked from face to face and whispered in horror, "oh my God . . . oh my God!" Then, a sudden pained look widened Annie's eyes simultaneously with her realization, "Hildie!" she exclaimed, "Oh my God, poor Hildie died in the fire! Oh my God! Oh my God!" Annie flopped back in her recliner and stared up at the sky in such a way that it almost seemed she was scanning the heavens for some meteoric flash from Hildie's very own effulgent spirit.

Chapter 72

Mimi spoke, "Annie, when I heard Kathy's reports of all the fires in Josephine's life since she left the convent, coupled with the repeated stalking incidents, I thought that was a convincing and telling pattern. Then Kathy unloaded her insurance story on me and I was physically sick at the implications."

Mimi continued, "Siobhan called me, just by coincidence, the very same night that Kathy told me about the insurance. I told poor Siobhan what I just told you and she was terribly upset. We all were. Are."

Siobhan jumped in, "Tell her about your conversation with Robert Young this week."

"Right," Mimi was glad for the reminder. "Robert Young called to thank me for hosting this meeting tomorrow and to get directions to the house. He also brought up the Marafield fire. He certainly knows a lot about it. He was a bit cryptic with his information but said that he had bumped into some interesting facts that had piqued his curiosity about it."

Mimi continued, "So, I said that if he ever 'bumped into' any info about whether or not Marafield collected insurance on the fire, I'd be interested in knowing about it. He sounded a little surprised that I would be wondering about the insurance. He tried to wheedle out of me why I wanted to know about it. I told him I had a 'source' who had some information about it that I found disturbing. Then, get this, he said, 'that's funny, I have a source who also knows about the insurance and what he told me I also found disturbing . . . '

"Well let's nail him on this tomorrow," Eily advocated. "What's so distressing to me, if it's true that the administration didn't collect insurance on the fire, is that it looks more like cover-up than fiscal ignorance. I mean, you don't collect a claim if it's arson. If arson is suspected, there's a thorough investigation. You can't tell me the people in charge just dropped the ball on filing a claim for something so monumental."

Annie was figuring things out aloud, "and if there had been an investigation that determined it to be arson, it would have been all over the papers. Then there'd be a hunt on for the arsonist." Annie fell quiet for a minute then resumed, "Just picture the headlines: 'Nun Torches Nuns!'" She thought again then blurted, "My God, what if they hid it! What if those cowards hid it? I feel sick! They really couldn't sit on something as grave as that, could they? I mean, this is murder we're talking about now!"

"Yes, it is! Not to mention how many other deaths there could have been that night . . . *ours* included! Now do you understand why we're hell bent on stopping her? She's just going to keep going till someone else ends up dead," Siobhan said.

"Oh my God . . . oh my God . . ." Annie muttered. Then with tight-lipped fury she said, "Forget my damn job! What the hell have I been worrying about? I should be ashamed of myself. I'll talk to the attorney! I'll sit on the witness stand! This is terrible, just terrible! We've got to stop her. We've got to do something about this!"

Annie put her head in her hand and was motionless. Between her fingers could be seen a sparkling trail of tears rolling down her cheeks. Eily reached over and put her hand on Annie's shoulder. "I'm okay," Annie whispered, " . . . just give me a minute."

Finally, speaking through teeth clenched in anger, Annie picked up her head and growled, "Dolorosa better have received a subpoena the same as we did! She's the one who knows a hell of a lot more than all of us combined! I hope Robert Young and that attorney know where she lives and that she got subpoenaed too."

"If it's any consolation to you, I think he said she was on the list to receive one," Eily offered, then expanded. "Now there's a picture for you, girls . . . Dolorosa and all of us waiting in the same holding room at the courthouse to be called to testify!"

"That wouldn't happen, would it?" Siobhan looked alarmed.

"Listen, sweetie, we can wait any ol' place we want. You can be sure Dolorosa wouldn't want to be stuck with us either! She'd have a 'tic' that you could measure on the Richter scale by the time they called her!" Eily laughed.

"I have this fantasy that I'd have the nerve to say something to her," Siobhan yearned. "Something like, 'so Dolorosa, did you and Mother Majella and the others send Josephine home because you knew she torched the Motherhouse?' How's that?"

Eily answered, "Well, it wouldn't be very fair to me . . . I'd have to work up a sweat in my good clothes right before I testify, from doing CPR on her after she keeled over in cardiac arrest!"

"Hey, if you think we're nervous about this trial, just imagine the state she's been in ever since she got her subpoena!" Mimi gloated a little then tempered it by, "I've wondered if Dolorosa's somehow managed to block all that stuff out and never look back, or has she actually had nights when she laid awake because of a troubled conscience over it all?"

"Not that I wish for her to have nights wracked with sleeplessness," Kate said, "but I would hope for the latter. If she did have a troubled conscience, she would have to know that it would be the soul's invitation for healing . . . I hope she accepted the invitation."

"I think this is a good time for some comfort food . . . some peach pie and a fresh pot of tea!" Mimi declared.

"Screw the tea!" Annie yelled, "Kate, get in there and wake up Mr. Gibson! Tell him I need to see him and his three little onion friends in a stem glass immediately!"

Chapter 73

By around midnight, the peach pie, the hot mugs of tea, the dying fire in the chiminea and hours of being out on the deck in the fresh air, all conspired with the quiet pockets of conversation now taking place to finally take their soporific toll on these friends.

"Want me to throw some more wood in the chiminea?" Mimi asked, "or are you campers fading with the embers like I am?"

"Fading? I'm gone! I've got to go to bed, girls. What time is it anyway?" Kate asked.

Eily squinted at her watch and said, "This can't be right. I have quarter after twelve! No wonder I feel like my bed is calling me! Mimi, everything was out of this world; thank you so much. Okay, girls, I'm outta here. Goodnight! See you manana!"

Everyone else, equally unable to fight sleep any longer, followed suit and began folding throws, putting lounge chairs back and restoring the deck to its original order.

Mimi and Kate went down beneath the deck and pulled out two large filled trashcans and rolled them over to the side gate that opened out to Salcombe Street. The wooden gate opened easily with a simple handle latch. Once outside the high ivy covered brick wall that enclosed Mimi's yard, the trash cans were placed at the curb for pick up in the morning.

"Is that it?" Kate asked Mimi.

"That's it. Thanks. Now I don't have to get up early to do this. I hate when I forget to do this the night before."

"Mimi, thanks for such a nice day and evening; everything was great. You're going to go to bed too, aren't you?" Kate checked.

"You bet; I'm beat," Mimi said wearily as they climbed the deck stairs. "This emotional stuff is exhausting, isn't it?" When they got to the door to go in, Mimi hesitated a minute and confided to her sidekick, "Listen, Kate, you know how calm and cool I look when we talk about Josephine and when people say they're worried about her finding out we've been subpoenaed? Don't fall for it. I'm really worried. So is my sister, Kathy." Mimi gave Kate a searching look. "Come on . . . isn't this the part where you're supposed to say I'm just being neurotic and everything will be fine?"

"No, Mimi," Kate was serious, "this is the part where I say watch your back, be aware of your surroundings, and maybe consider having a sensor system put in around this rambling place. You've got to be smart, Mimi. If Josephine ever did want to get back at any of us, you're the one who's available first by proximity. Just don't take any chances. You mean too much to too many people not to follow your gut on this one."

"I have followed my gut," Mimi admitted. "I'm having a sensor system put in next Wednesday. I booked a home security company the day after I got my subpoena. Kathy really leaned on me to do it. I hate living like that though, with alarms and locked doors. I feel like I'm severing my last thread of belief that the world can be a beneficent place."

"Mimi, the world is a beneficent place, but it's sadly scarred with violence committed by the unchecked hand of vengeance."

Mimi nodded reflectively at what she had just heard and flipped off the lights on the deck and opened the door for them both to go in. They went around and turned off lights and locked doors as they made their way to the second and third floors. When they got to the landing just outside of Mimi's suite, Kate patted Mimi on the back and said, "Goodnight, Mother Teresa."

Mimi called back over her shoulder, "Goodnight, Oprah!"

Chapter 74

The sleep disorder that Sister Dolorosa had started experiencing back in March had escalated enough in July to warrant clinical intervention. None of the sisters with whom she lived at The Academy in Washington knew about her involvement in an upcoming trial, about her occasional meetings at headquarters with the congregation's attorneys, or that she had just been subpoenaed to appear in court on September ninth. When she failed to take her place at table for the special birthday dinner, celebrating those who had birthdays that month, it was noticed.

One of her tablemates asked, "Has anyone seen Dolorosa? Is she home from work yet?"

Someone at the next table volunteered, "I saw her come in about twenty minutes ago. She picked up her mail and went straight up to her room."

The one who had inquired said, "I'll go page her; maybe she forgot we're celebrating birthdays tonight."

When the sister who went to page her returned to the dining room she told the others, "Go ahead and start without me. I'm going to go up and check to see if she's okay."

The two sisters at the side table who were opening the wine bottles had just started to go around to the tables offering red or white wine, when yells for help from the second floor pierced the low tones of conversation that had begun.

Three tables of four emptied instantly and headed upstairs at varying gaits. The cook heard the commotion from the kitchen and followed the others, as worried as the rest. When they got to the hallway, Sister Dolorosa was on the floor being propped up from behind by the sister who had gone looking for her. Dolorosa's feet were pointing toward her room and her body was slanted across the hall. It looked like she was leaving her room when she collapsed or fell.

"Dolorosa? Sister?" asked the house 'Coordinator,' Marianne, as she knelt on the floor next to her. Dolorosa was a ghastly white and began making little smacking noises as she tried moistening her dry mouth. She had her eyes closed but was coming to and was very slowly rolling her head from side to side.

"I'll call 911," the cook said as she turned to pick up the nearest phone.

"Don't you dare!" came the weakened but stern voice of Dolorosa. "I'm not going to any hospital!"

"Dolorosa," the Coordinator appealed, "what if you're having a heart attack? Please don't be foolish . . . or stubborn. You need medical attention."

"I'm not going!" she reiterated adamantly. "Just let me catch my breath. I'm not having a heart attack, that much I know. I fainted."

"Does anything feel broken?" the woman holding her gently asked.

"No," came the terse reply.

The group in the hall all exchanged glances about what to do . . . call 911 against her wishes or take Dolorosa's word for it that she didn't need to go to the E.R.

"Dolorosa, I'm going to ask you again to please reconsider and let us call 911. Something has to be wrong for you to have fainted like this . . ." the Coordinator tried one more time.

Dolorosa freed herself from the assistance of the sister on the floor behind her and sat up straight, regaining more strength. "I know exactly what happened. I fainted, that's all. I will not go to the hospital for something so ridiculous as that. Now if you would be kind enough to help me up, I'd like to go to the ladies room . . ."

Two sisters escorted a shaky Dolorosa down the hall to the dorm styled lavatory and returned to the others who waited outside her room. Some urged the Coordinator to override Dolorosa's stubbornness and to call 911 anyway, but she explained that she couldn't do that as long as Dolorosa had her wits about her. They had to respect her decision and take her word for it.

When she returned to her room, she said "I think I'll go in and get under the covers for a while. Would one of you please bring me a cup of tea? My mouth is so dry."

Half the group, seeing that she seemed alright, returned to the first floor. The others scurried about turning her bed down, helping her into her robe, and adjusting the shades on the window. The Coordinator sat on a chair across from the bed and asked after Dolorosa settled into the bed and was propped up with pillows, "Why do you think you fainted? Have you eaten anything all day?"

"Yes, I had some lunch," Dolorosa said. "I've been having a terrible time sleeping for weeks on end. I'm awake practically all night. It just seems to get worse and worse. I think I'm just exhausted from it. I may have just collapsed from sleep deprivation, if that's possible."

"Well, whatever the cause, you can't go on this way. I agreed with your decision not to call 911, Dolorosa," the Coordinator leveled, "but you're going to the Doctor tomorrow and I'm taking you."

"Alright," she conceded, "I'll go. Maybe she can prescribe something to help me get some sleep at night."

There was a light tap on the door and a sister came in carrying a tray loaded with a pot of tea, a cup and saucer, milk and sugar. There also was a plate with a sandwich cut in four quarters, a small bowl of fresh fruit, a small dish of shortbread cookies, and a linen napkin. "Now, there you are!" she said as she put the tray down on the desk in the corner.

She poured Dolorosa a cup of tea, handed it to her and quietly edged toward the door.

"Thank you," she said as she took the tea in her still trembling hands. "I'll be fine as soon as I get some of this tea in me. You girls run along now. Your dinner's ruined enough, no use missing it completely. I'm sorry this happened . . . and on birthday night too. Please apologize to the others for me. Tell them to have a glass of wine on me!"

"Are you sure you're okay?" The Coordinator wanted to know. "I'd be happy to stay till you eat a little something and, hopefully, drift off."

"Drift off . . . wouldn't that be grand?" Dolorosa said wryly. "You go on, Sister. I'll be alright. You can check on me later if you want. Will you call the Doctor or shall I?"

"Why don't I call her for you and get her answering service tonight. Maybe she can fit you in first thing in the morning."

Dolorosa said, "I'd appreciate that. Thank you. Now, please, go join the others."

Dolorosa knew she could never tell the others what she had sensed to be the cause of her fainting spell. When she was leaving work at the Cathedral in time to be home for tonight's festive dinner, a well-dressed gentleman approached her while she unlocked her car. He waived so amiably to her that she was sure she knew him. He seemed so pleasantly familiar as he drew near saying, "How are you this fine day, Sister Dolorosa?" Then, that quickly, the private "process server" put into her hand a subpoena.

"What's this?" she asked the courteous man who began backing away to turn and leave.

"You've just been served a subpoena, Sister. Good evening."

How she made it to the convent she'll never know. Now, finally alone in her room, she took the stack of mail off the night table and withdrew from underneath it the subpoena she had been tricked into receiving not even an hour ago. She looked at it again, then folded it, tucked it back under the stack of mail, and returned the stack to the night table. Pressing the linen napkin against her mouth, she first gasped, then took short spasmodic breaths and finally gave in, crying tears of sheer terror.

Chapter 75

The next night at about nine o'clock, the Coordinator tapped on Dolorosa's door.

"Enter . . ." called the voice from inside.

"I brought you some goodies," the Coordinator said as she pushed open the door while balancing a tray. "I picked up your prescription this afternoon, Sister. The pharmacist said you should drink some milk and have a little something in your stomach when you take this stuff, so here you are." She put the tray down and handed the bottle of pills and all the directions that went with it to Dolorosa, who put on her glasses and began reading all the warnings.

"Thank you, Marianne, you've been so kind. What are these called," Dolorosa said squinting at the name on the bottle, 'Ambien?' They try to give these drugs friendly names anymore, don't they?"

Marianne began tenuously, "Dolorosa . . . Doctor Courtenay told you that you have symptoms of anxiety and depression, probably contributing to that elevated blood pressure. What do you think that's about? Are you worrying about something? Are things okay at work? Is anything here in the house bothering you?"

"Sister, I'm probably just a woman resisting turning the big '8-0' next month, that's all. Don't people my age have occasional bouts with these things?"

"Not necessarily, Dolorosa. Usually the theory of cause and effect applies. Your "spell" and your sleeplessness have to be responding to something. If there's something troubling you I hope you know you can always talk to me, or to a priest, or to a therapist."

"Oh good Lord! Sister, I'm depressed because I can't sleep!" Dolorosa countered, "and I'm anxious because I'm afraid I'll faint one day from fatigue! That's all there is to it; case closed. Maybe these magic pills will restore some sleep to my life and I'll be back to my old self again."

"I hope so, for your sake. Are you going to start the pills tonight?" the Coordinator, Marianne, asked.

"Yes I will. I'll take one around ten. Now stop checking in on me. I'm fine. Maybe this little bottle will cure all my ills."

Marianne kidded, "If those pills prove to be that good, save a few for the rest of us!"

Signaling to the younger sister that she was being dismissed, Dolorosa said, "Goodnight, Marianne, and thanks again for everything."

"Goodnight, Dolorosa. I hope tonight you sleep the sleep of the angels," she said as she closed the door and left.

To no one at all, Dolorosa quietly uttered, "My thought, exactly . . ."

Dolorosa got out of bed, went to her closet and took out her very best suit and hung it on the front of the closet door. Then she slid hangar after hangar to one side of the closet till she found the new blouse that went with the suit. She took that out and hung that with the suit. Next, she looked at the four shoeboxes and read the magic marker descriptions printed on the end of each box. She reached for the box labeled "Dress/ Patent Leather" and pulled the box from the stack, closed the closet door, and set it down on the floor right beneath the suit and blouse.

Moving to the desk and turning on the table lamp, she pulled out the chair and sat, opening all the drawers one by one. They were, of course, in perfect order. The few things she no longer wanted she shredded and threw into the trash can. She took out of the center drawer a clump of opened notes and letters that had a rubber band around them. Briefly, she glanced at each one, tore it up and threw it away. She repeated the process till there were none. Finally, she took out her address book and ceremoniously placed it on the center of the cleared off desk.

She went over to the night table, picked up her Bible and thumbed through it till she found the card she was looking for, removed it, replaced the Bible, and returned to the desk and sat down. She read over the vow card that she and every sister in the community had received. Used for renewal ceremonies on her Community's "Feast Day," the vow card would be placed, finally, in the hands of each sister at the time of death, throughout the wake, and would be buried with her. Dolorosa carefully placed the vow card on top of the address book and turned off the desk light.

Dolorosa took the pillar candle that had been given to her at Christmas and placed it on the night table next to the bottle of pills, lit it, turned off the overhead light, and knelt in its golden glow at her bedside. She made the sign of the cross and, leaning her elbows on the bed, bowed her head into her raised hands.

"Into you hands, O God, I commend my spirit . . . let my cry come unto you. Mary, holy Mother of God, come to my assistance. Angels and saints of God, surround me and give me strength . . ." Dolorosa could barely continue she was so choked with emotion. For a time, she simply knelt in hushed silence till she regained her composure and then continued. "Eternal and Loving God, I beg you, turn not your ear from me. What should I do? How can I go on? Is it better that I give my life for the sake of the community that I have loved all these years, or is it better that I tell the truth and risk ruining the community?"

"I am an old woman. I have sinned by omission as boldly as I have sinned by commission and I have lived in these sins for thirty years . . . too weak to right a dreadful wrong . . . too confused to discern the right path . . . too proud to seek counsel. And now, Eternal and Loving God, I come before you stripped bare, unable to flee, unable to hide . . . unable, I' afraid, to go on . . . Finished. Look upon me, your errant and sinful daughter, and have mercy."

Dolorosa lifted her head and her eyes settled easily on the framed 11x14 "Psalm 139" calligraphy print that hung on the wall above the bed, just opposite her. She had seen it hundreds of times, noting more its colors and design than its content. Perhaps it was her heightened state of anxiety and search that so keenly focused her mind on its message. She read it now as though the words were brand new to her:

"Where can I go from your spirit?
From your presence, where can I flee?
If I go up to the heavens, there you are.
If I sink into the greatest depths, there you are.
If I take the wings of the dawn,
If I settle at the farthest limits of the sea,
There you are, your own hand guiding me,
Your right hand holding me fast.
If I say 'Surely this darkness will hide me,"
For you, night shines as the day,
For you, darkness and light are the same.
Probe me, O God, and know my heart.
Try me and know my thoughts.
And if my way is crooked,
Lead me, again, in the ways of your Love."

From within the deepest, most neglected regions of her soul came a cry that could not, would not be deferred another day, another moment. She convulsed and heaved and finally doubled over onto the bed sobbing as she had never before sobbed. She wept thirty years of ignored and compartmentalized truths. Within her, there finally rent the secret that had so tightly bound her heart, constricting it from feeling anything but fear.

Such potent catharsis was, at once, invitation, cleansing, freedom and commissioning. Tonight, sleep would finally enfold the troubled body of Sister Dolorosa, and in the morning she would rise again in the light.

Chapter 76

"Is it always this busy here at this hour of the morning?" Josephine asked her waitress at The Silver Streak diner.

"Nah, not usually. A lot of these people were at that 'Antique Road Show' you see on public television sometimes. It was held at that big hotel down the road. See that fella over there? He and his wife just got some silly antique snuff box appraised for fifteen hundred bucks! Can ya believe it? Geez, I wish I had some good antiques hanging around my house. My stuff's more like what ya'd call 'early Bohemian' if ya know what I mean!"

"Sounds like my house," Josephine said kindly to the waitress.

"You know what ya want for dessert or should I come back to take your order?"

Wanting to spend as much time in the diner as possible, Josephine politely asked her waitress to take her time and come back later. "Take a hike, Laverne," Josephine jeered under her breath as she resumed pretending to read USA Today.

She checked her watch; it was one forty-five. The after movie crowd was practically gone and two whole sections of the diner were darkened and roped off now. There were still enough people for her to not be noticed as some loner with no place to go. However, by two o'clock she'd be pushing her luck. Then she'd have to go sit in the car in the parking lot for a while.

The waitress returned to Josephine's table, wet her thumb with her bottom lip, peeled back pages of other orders in her little receipt book till she found "table 12's," then asked, "Now which of those desserts do you think you'd like?"

Josephine replied, "Actually, I think I've changed my mind about getting dessert. Could I just have another cup of coffee?" She was going to ask for the check too, but held back knowing that flagging the waitress down and having her make another trip would use up more time.

When at last she finished the coffee that had been brought, she asked for the check and paid it at the register by the door. The Ladies Room was next, an important detail not to be overlooked. Finally, she exited the diner at 2:15a.m. She went to her car and drove it to another part of the lot, parking it among the other remaining cars. She didn't want it to be noticed sitting all alone. Turning off the engine, she slumped down in the seat a little and sat quietly listening to the pings and tics of the cooling engine in the early morning stillness.

Josephine surprised herself with the little "cat-nap" that befell her. She thought that, with the excitement of what lay ahead in the game plan, she'd have been too wired to doze. Maybe too much adrenaline had flooded her system and made her drowsy. At any rate, she felt the benefit of the forty winks and was ready to go. It was three o'clock.

Before she left the parking lot, Josephine got out of the car, opened the back door, took out the gas container and put it on the floor on the driver's side. She managed to get back in and reach the pedals with the container pressed between her legs and the seat. One thing she didn't want was a lot of car doors opening and closing on a neighborhood street at three in the morning. Next, she opened the glove compartment and took out the bag of fatwood. She removed the pieces from the bag and laid them on the passenger seat. "Okay, here we go," she said with a trace of excitement

She passed by Mimi's house, this time via the side street, Salcombe Road. From this approach she could see the front of the house and drive down along the side of the house, checking to see if there were any lights on in any part. She drove at precisely the twenty-five mile an hour speed limit intending not to draw attention to a car going too slowly.

"Looks like you're all tucked in for a good night's sleep, Mimi Aroho. I'll bet you don't have a care in your pretty little world to worry about, huh? My, my, my . . . how quickly things can change . . ."

Josephine drove several blocks away then made her way back to find the street that she had discovered on her earlier expedition, Clapham Lane. When she turned onto Clapham Lane she was several blocks higher than during her evening run. She watched frenetically for her designated spot marked by the mailbox painted "Eihler," which would place her directly behind Mimi's property.

"Where are you? Where the hell are you? There are so many trees on this street I can hardly see anything! Where the hell's the house with the 'Eihler' mailbox? Oh for God's sake, I'm in the wrong damn block! It's the next block! Here we go . . . here we go . . . Got it: 'Eihler!' Oh good, a spot right on the corner. Perfect!"

As soon as Josephine pulled into the parking place at the curb she turned off the motor. She sat motionless for several minutes to see if any nut job was out walking a dog or if any teenager was slinking home. She studied the street behind her through her rearview and side mirrors. Checking out the houses on either side of the street, she was relieved to see all homes in darkness. Remaining in the car, she shimmied the disposable latex gloves out of her jeans pockets and put them on. She reached up and flipped the overhead car light to the "off" position so it wouldn't go on when she opened the door.

She checked for her lighter and felt it in her pocket, picked up the fatwood sticks and opened the car door. She lifted the gas can up and set it down on the ground. Swinging her feet over the gas can as she got out, Josephine held the car door and pressed it shut, making as little noise as possible. She looked carefully in each direction, then bent over, picked up the can, walked between two parked cars to the sidewalk across from her and hurried around the corner to the side wall that marked the beginning of Mimi's yard.

Chapter 77

Josephine was so glad for all that training in the convent about how to walk, rolling from heel to toe, heel to toe, without making a sound, preserving The Silence. She moved like a cat, walking as close to the wall as possible, hiding in its shadow, unpleasantly catching a few dew-laden spider webs from the ivy that clung to the brick. Finally she reached the gate.

She put the can down and used both hands to lift the latch and muffle the click of the lock. Then she held the gate tightly to preempt any squeaking and carefully eased it open only wide enough for her to slip through. She tentatively let go of the gate to see if it would stay in place and, when it did, she picked up the can and entered.

She walked under the deck and went to the far side of the house. She immediately began pouring some gasoline on the shingles of the house the entire length of the deck and inched her way backwards toward the gate as she did it. The "stalking victim" then went back and doused a little for good measure on the back posts of the deck. Next she poured a line of the excellorant along the side wall of the house, also shingled with wood, heading toward the front of the house on Locknell Way. The star of "Crime Line" capped the gasoline container when she got to the front corner of the house and turned to go back to the yard to start the fireworks. Suddenly, she froze.

"Hey, wait a minute! Have you completely forgotten everything? Don't

you remember how well you trapped everybody by setting the stairs on fire last time? God, girl! Get with the program! Uncap this can and do the job right."

Josephine, corrected by memory, turned and skulked her way back to the front porch. Lightly, she tread on each step and made it noiselessly to the front door. In front of the entrance and along the edge of the house that lipped onto the wrap around porch, she poured a small stream of gasoline. She'd come back to light this section of the house last, then go to her car and drive away.

Tiptoeing back down the front stairs of the porch, Josephine hurried along the side of the house and went back to the deck area where she had begun. Standing just outside the overhang of the deck, Josephine took three fatwood sticks from her back pocket and lit all three at the same time. Their combined ignition gave her such a start that she nearly dropped them. Collecting herself, she tossed one to the left corner, one to the center that was right in front of her, and one to the right.

"Whoompf!" "Whoompf!" "Whoompf!" complied all three sections, as the lethal combination of gasoline, wood, and flame coalesced. She ran to the front of the house and, crouching low at the side of the front porch, the ex-mystic lit the last piece of fatwood, made sure it had a good strong flame, then tossed it up over the railing toward the front door. To her trepidation, it was a lob that proved to be beyond her athletic prowess. The burning stick fell well short of its incendiary mark, panicking her.

"Shit!" was the only word she hissed during the entire exercise. Now smelling the back of the house cooking along nicely and hearing the blister, sizzle and pop of the fire consuming the treated deck wood, Josephine knew that she was dangerously close to running out of time. "Do it, you idiot!" she commanded herself. Leaving the gas can on the ground, the former Sister St. John ducked through the bushes at the corner of the porch, gave a quick furtive look around, then once more gingerly began ascending the stairs to more effectively reposition the burning fatwood. She was only on the second step when an explosion from the rear of the house rocked the neighborhood.

Her heart was pounding so loudly within her as she dove back into the hedges, she was nearly oblivious to the car alarms that had been set off. This much she knew: she had one chance only to make a run for her car before the people who were jarred from their beds by the blast would be peering out of windows or coursing onto the street. She picked up the gas can and raced back to the gate. As she turned to scramble through it she felt the warmth of the deck ablaze behind her. Using the shadows of the yard wall for cover, Josephine lunged ahead to the end of the block, her shoulder glancing now and then off the brick wall that hid her.

When she reached the end of the block, she braked abruptly before emerging from the shadows to pull off the white latex gloves, shove them in her pockets, and then lift the gasoline container to a cradling position against her chest. No one would be able to distinguish what it was she was carrying in the short distance between her and her car.

She stepped to the curb and in three quick strides opened the car door and jammed herself into the driver's seat. She heard voices of people approaching from behind her who were hurrying down the street to see what had happened. She slid as far down on the seat as she could and held her breath till they passed. Their eyes were too busy alternately watching the uneven pavement underfoot and the orange glow of embers above the rooftops to ever notice the arsonist in the car parked at the corner.

When they scurried left and were well up the street, Josephine turned on the motor and drove straight ahead for eight blocks to the very end of Clapham Lane. Then she turned right and headed as far in the opposite direction of the fire in Glendarff as she possibly could while making her way back to the diner parking lot. Minutes later, she pulled into the parking lot of The Silver Streak. She grabbed the gas container from the seat next to her, got out, opened the trunk and put it in, nestling it between two plastic crates filled with magazines and books intended for the town recycling bin.

The parking lot light shone on her at such an angle that she caught a glimpse of gasoline stains blotched all across the front of her black cotton pullover. Her jeans also were marked on one leg from her dive into the hedges. When she got into the car, she pinched the fabric of her pullover between her thumb and forefinger and pulled it away from her body so she could reach the stains with her nose to sniff for gasoline. It was there alright, along with a mixture of barely detectable Jean Nate body splash and the acrid musk of her own sweat.

She started shaking so badly now that she leaned her arms and head on the steering wheel to rest a few minutes. This little venture had been more of a workout than she bargained for. Originally, she had envisioned herself coolly strolling away from the done deed, certainly not doing body slams into bushes and sprinting hundred yard dashes. She was grateful that she didn't have a heart attack or break any bones.

Above the still labored puffs of her own rapid breathing, the sound of sirens heading into the village of Glendarff cocked Josephine's head. She sat up straight and held her breath, the better to hear not one, but definitely two and possibly three trucks racing to Locknell Way. She turned on the motor and pointed the car in the direction of Sparrows Point. She could hear the sirens fading in the distance as she drove away. As always, their wail, which heralded someone's woe, was music to her ears.

Chapter 78

"Oh my God, no! Fire! Get out! Get out! Go!" Siobian screamed immediately after the blast went off that launched her to an upright position on her bed. All she saw was smoke and debris. She, Kate and Eily were all sharing the third floor apartment. The living room section of it overlooked the deck and the dorm-style bedroom overlooked Locknell Way. A staircase divided the two areas. Windows, casements, shades and curtains were blown all over this third floor living room in pieces.

Eily was thrown out of bed by the blast and began wildly foraging in her suitcase for the leather emergency medical kit she always carried with her. Kate, stunned for a second as she found herself standing by her bed trying to decipher what was happening, finally snapped out of it, pulled open the closet door and yanked all the blankets from the top shelf. All three knew there was glass everywhere and tried jamming their feet into sandals, loafers or tennis shoes . . . whatever was closest and went on fastest.

"Siobhan! Here!" Kate threw a blanket around Siobhan's shoulders and together they yelled, "Eily!" who couldn't be seen since she was on the floor at her bag.

"Here I am!" Eily yelled from out of the cloud of smoke that was gathering. She took the blanket that Kate threw to her and put it around her shoulders too. "Cover your mouths, stay low, and let's get out of here! Hold onto each other!" Eily ordered. "Siobhan, you find the stairs for us!"

"Here they are! Come on, hurry!" Siobhan said as her hand felt the tip of the banister.

Mimi was yelling on her way up the same stairs toward the others, "Siobhan! Kate! Eily! Can you hear me? Where are you?"

"We're right here Mim, we're coming . . . you okay? Where's Annie?" Kate asked as they felt their way down the staircase and met Mimi's hand reaching to guide them.

"I'm right here behind Mimi" was Annie's choked response.

Mimi reported, "I called 911. Fire Department's on the way. Must have been the grill on the deck . . . I can't believe it . . . I'm so sorry. Come on, this way. We can get out."

Only when they grouped momentarily on the landing of the second floor did everyone realize that they were being soaked by overhead sprinklers. Kate draped blankets around Mimi and Annie and then Mimi led the way to the first floor. Emergency lights dotted the staircase and hallway with enough light to take the guess work out of which way to go.

When they reached the first floor it was swathed in bright yellow orange cast from the back of the house. A thin slice of smoke had begun to glide across the living room. The back of the house menacingly spewed flames licking in through the blown out glass doors that separated the deck from the indoor pool, which mercifully, was serving as a fire wall slowing the fire's spread to the front of the house.

Mimi unlocked the front door to usher the others out and onto the street. Because she had assumed that the grill was the cause and general location of the fire, she was stunned into wide-eyed disbelief that the front porch floor was burning in the area over by the railing. The heavy coats of paint and thick topping of polyurethane fueled the section on fire, helping it to spread steadily.

"Get going! Get out! Go into the street!" Mimi shouted and pushed the others toward the steps. Then she ran inside and pushed open one of the hidden doors on the nearest pillar, grabbed a fire extinguisher from inside of it and ran out onto the porch blasting the porch floor with it in sweeping motions. Kate and Eily heard the whooshing bursts from the extinguisher and saw what Mimi was trying to do. Eily grabbed the extinguisher from Mimi and shouted "I'll do this. You and Kate go find more extinguishers! Hurry!"

Mimi and Kate ran in and tapped two more pillars, pulling two more extinguishers from their moorings. They joined Eily in containing the fire on the porch and, together, triumphantly succeeded in extinguishing it. Then, suddenly remembering something, Kate walked back to the front door went through it, turned around, and walked right back out. She did it again, this time standing in the doorway, clearly trying to figure something out.

"What are you doing?" Mimi wanted to know.

"Come here," Kate said to the two others. "I smelled something before. Walk around here . . . what do you smell?"

"Something . . ." Eily sniffed, "I definitely smell something . . . and it's different than burnt wood."

Mimi picked up the doormat from outside the front door and smelled it. "Jesus, Mary and Joseph!" she blurted, "what in the name of God is this?" She held the mat for Eily and Kate to whiff and they both blanched at the familiar scent soaked into the mat: "Gasoline!" they confirmed with alarm.

Annie and Siobhan were in the street waiving to the arriving engines and trucks to go around the corner to the back of the house where the worst damage was being done. Another engine and a rescue company stopped right in front of the house and firemen ran up to the porch.

"Everyone's out and accounted for," Mimi told the men. Some went right by Mimi, Kate and Eily to quickly assess things from the inside. The Battalion Chief and another fireman stopped and asked who the owner was.

"I am," Mimi answered, "Mimi Aroho. Thanks for getting here so fast. Do me a favor, smell this." She held the doormat up to the firemen's faces. For a second they weren't sure whether she was crazy or not. Eily saw them both searching Mimi's face, and hers, for clues.

"She's not nuts, gentlemen," Eily defended, "we think we smell gasoline on that thing."

They firemen obliged, did the nose test, and nodded affirmatively. “Where’d you find this?” the Chief with the name “McKavanagh” printed in day glow on his bunker gear wanted to know.

“Right there,” Mimi said, pointing to the area just outside the front door.

The other fireman knelt at the spot on one knee while the Chief slowly examined the rest of the porch. “Hey, Chief, over here,” the fireman called. He pointed to a shiny smear that had established itself under the mat. Then he pointed to how the shine moved from that point outward in a line along the porch, flush with the house. “What do you think?”

Before the Chief answered, he walked along the narrow liquid line, bent over, rubbed the pads of his fingers in whatever it was, smelled what was now on his fingers and said, “No thinking about it, Danny. It’s gasoline. We’ll need to get the Marshall over here.”

Chief McKavanagh turned to Mimi and said, “You ladies have any ideas how this might have gotten here?”

Chapter 79

"Mimi . . . Mimi!" Mrs. Eihler, wrapped in a raincoat over her nightgown and wearing sneakers, called from the sidewalk up to the porch to get Mimi's attention. When one fireman went into the house and the other went to the truck to make a call, Mimi walked down to the sweet elderly woman with the worried look on her face.

"Oh Mimi, you poor, poor dear!" Mrs. Eihler said as she put her arms around Mimi. "What on earth happened? Thank God you're alright!"

"I'm not sure what happened, Mrs. Eihler. It sounded like the deck grill might have blown up. I haven't even seen the back of the house yet . . . that's certainly where all the action is. I need to go around there now," Mimi said as she stepped out of the yard to walk around to Salcombe Road.

"You can't see this alone, dear, I'm going with you," Mrs. Eihler asserted and hooked her arm into Mimi's. Kate and Eily saw Mimi heading toward the back and caught up with her and her concerned escort. As they made their way down the side of the house on Salcombe Road, neighbors came up to Mimi and kissed her, or hugged her or just started drifting in the same direction with her.

"Jesus, Mary and Joseph!" she gasped as she saw the entire back of the house smoking away while it was being flooded by several fire hoses. There were firemen on the roof doing God-knows-what with axes. Of all the things to notice, Mimi saw that the water fountain in the middle of the yard was in smithereens, which puzzled her until she figured out that a projectile piece of the grill had smashed into it and embedded itself in the lawn behind it. She turned her attention back to the house. The floodlights allowed her to see that the deck was gone. The doors and windows were all gone. The back of the house would have to be ripped out and rebuilt, along with the roofline over it.

"It's just a house, Mimi. I know it's your house and all the work you've put into it, but no lives were lost, thank God," Mrs. Eihler said.

Mimi's face was unreadable. "You're absolutely right, Mrs. Eihler. It can all be replaced. I have four friends visiting me this weekend and I can only thank God we're all safe."

Mrs. Eihler saw the others with blankets and wet hair and realized that's who they were. She reached to shake each one's hand, saying, "Forgive me, girls, I was so worried about Mimi I didn't even register why you had those blankets around you. Please, won't you all come down to my house and get away from this and dry off?"

"That's very kind of you Mrs. Eihler," Kate said, "but I think I'll stay here with Mimi for a while." The others nodded that they'd do the same.

"Very well, I certainly understand." Then the recent widow turned to Mimi and said, "You can't stay in that house today. When the firemen leave, come down to my house, all of you. You know I have plenty of room, Mimi. You can make phone calls and shower and have some tea or coffee and settle your nerves a bit. God knows I won't be going back to bed after all this. I've been awake most of the night anyway. Come down when you're ready. I'll leave the lights on and watch for you."

"Miss Aroho?" a tall fireman dripping sweat and looking exhausted came over.

"I'm she," Mimi stepped forward.

"Can you tell me if you had any combustibles under the deck? Chemicals, firewood, gasoline, stuff like that?" the fireman inquired.

"The only thing under there was a container of pinon wood, but there were only about three pounds of it left," she recalled. "No gasoline or chemicals . . . I have a lawn service and gardener, they bring everything with them. I did have a gas grill on the corner of the deck over on the far side. That's probably what blew up, though I can't imagine why. I've never had any problems with it."

"Yes, M'am, we can see that there was a grill explosion. But it looks like the deck and back wall of the house had been burning before the 'Bleve.' Do you know approximately where you had the pinon wood stored under the deck?" the fireman pursued.

Mimi said, "Right here. Right on this end of the deck nearest to these steps closest to us. What do you mean 'Bleve?' What's a 'Bleve'?"

"It's an acronym for 'Boiling Liquid Expanded Vapor Explosion.' Essentially, your grill blew up. Now M'am, you're sure that's the only spot that had any combustibles, just that one location right there?"

"Yes sir. What are you thinking?" Mimi already knew.

"Well, we're trying to figure a few things out. The Chief and the Fire Marshall will be right over to speak with you. Thank you, M'am." The fireman left in a hurry.

"What's that all about? What do you think he was looking for?" Mrs. Eihler was curious.

"Well, to tell you the truth, Mrs. Eihler, I have a funny feeling that this thing didn't just start by itself," Mimi postulated. Tired, shaken and distraught, she had let her guard down now and said out loud what she had been thinking since she picked up the doormat.

Chapter 80

"Dear God! You mean to say that you think there's a pyromaniac loose in our neighborhood?" Mrs. Eihler looked frightened at the mere thought of it.

Kate interjected, "Mrs. Eihler, you mentioned a few minutes ago that you've been awake all night. Do you mind if I ask you a question about that?"

"Yes, of course you may. My husband died last week and I'm all discombobulated with my sleep," the widow spoke not taking her anxious eyes off of Mimi or the activity of the firemen.

"Mimi told us about your husband," Kate sympathized, "these must be such difficult days for you." The elderly woman nodded sad agreement. Kate continued, "Mrs. Eihler, about your sleep, or lack of it tonight and this morning: Were you asleep and got wakened by the explosion, or were you already up?"

"Actually I was already up. I was in the kitchen having a little slice of the peach pie Mimi brought over last night. I needed to take some medication and I had to have a little something in my stomach. I made the dumb mistake of taking my last pill at seven and had to get up to take the next one at three so I wouldn't mess up the cycle. That's why I was awake."

Kate asked, "Is there any chance at all that you heard or saw anything, anyone at that hour?"

"No . . . no dear, I didn't. The only thing I saw that was unusual to me was a car just like mine parked in front of my house on the corner. We're the only ones on this block that have a Taurus." Then Mimi's neighbor gave a mild nervous chuckle and said, "That, I remember, because it really made me think that I was loosing it! I saw it when I first came downstairs.

"You see, I have this routine when I prowl around at night. When I go downstairs at night I don't turn on any lights. I don't want anyone outside to see me padding around in my nightgown. Anyway, my routine is that I always stop in the living room and look out the window . . . mostly to see if there are any shooting stars. My husband and I always watched for shooting stars. Anyway, I looked out the window and got all flustered."

"Why did you get flustered?" Kate encouraged Mrs. Eihler to continue.

"Well, like I said, I thought I was loosing my marbles! I thought I had put my car in the garage this afternoon when I came back from the grocery store, but when I looked out the window, my God, it was sitting out front! Or so I thought." Mrs. Eihler nervously played with the lapel of her raincoat as she relayed her saga. "I never leave my car on the street so I thought, 'Good Lord, Harry's not gone a month and I'm losing my mind already!' I was so upset! I went right to the kitchen and turned on the garage lights praying I'd see the car and, thank God, I could see the roof of the car through the window. So I don't know where that other car came from."

"What kind of car did you say you have?" Kate followed up.

"A gray Taurus. It's really too big for me. Harry drove most of the time. I'm going to have to get a smaller car for me now that I'm the only driver, maybe a Honda."

"Siobhan, Annie . . . stay with Mimi till we come back, okay?" Kate called over to them. "Eily, walk down to the corner with Mrs. Eihler and me, will you?"

"You girls don't have to walk me to the corner, stay here with Mimi," Mrs. Eihler offered.

"No, no . . . we insist, Mrs. Eihler," Eily spoke up. "If we're going to come down later and take you up on your offer of tea, we'd better find out where you live!" she said amiably. Eily gave Kate a look over Mrs. Eihler's head that said, "What the hell are we doing?" Kate just motioned with her eyebrows to keep moving.

When they reached the corner of Clapham Lane and Salcombe Road, Kate paused at the curb. "Mrs. Eihler, before we cross the street, show me the car you were talking about." Kate clued Eily in on what they were doing when she said to her, "Eily, Mrs. Eihler noticed a car like hers parked here before the fire."

Mrs. Eihler put her hand to her collarbone and looked perplexed. "Dear me, I feel like such a fool! The car was right there not even an hour ago. It was there when I came downstairs. Now you girls will start to think I don't have all my marbles! Oh my . . . I swear, as God is my judge, there was a gray Taurus parked at that corner at three o'clock this morning! When did it get moved? Where anyone would be off to at this hour, I can't imagine . . ."

"Mrs. Eihler, I swear to you, 'as God is our judge,' that we both believe you!" Kate tried to relax the rattled woman. "That someone drove away while all of this excitement was going on is the intriguing part. Mrs. Eihler, you might just be the neighborhood's 'Agatha Christie'!" Kate lauded the woman to assuage her disappointment that the car she had noticed was gone. Kate asked, "Would you mind if we told the police about that car? They'll probably want to speak with you."

"For Mimi, I'll talk to anyone she wants. Tell her I said 'who knew her delicious peach pie would have such dividends?' Thank you, girls. All the way to the door; what service! I'll go put on some water for tea and a fresh pot of coffee. How much longer do you think you'll be up there?"

"I think things are under control now." Eily guessed. "Mimi will need to speak with the fire chief, I'm sure. It might be good if our other friends could come down when they're ready, Siobhan and Annie. Actually, I'd like to encourage them to come down soon. May I impose upon you and ask for a few blankets, Mrs. Eihler? I'm worried about shock."

"I'll get them for you right now!" With that, the spry good neighbor turned and went up the stairs like she was twenty.

Chapter 81

Kate and Eily made their ways through the crowd, over hoses and around fire engines and trucks, to where their friends were gathered talking to the Chief, the Marshall, a fireman and a policeman. Eily quietly went up to each woman and removed the wet blanket she had. Kate followed, placing a dry one around each. Mimi was completely locked on to Chief Tommy McKavanagh who was explaining the situation to her. He told her that he had called the Marshall in to investigate for arson. Also, the police were now part of the operation because this fire was being treated as a crime and the scene needed to be preserved for evidence.

While McKavanagh and Mimi continued talking, the policeman had begun asking questions of the other two women, writing things in his notebook. Acknowledging the arrival of Kate and Eily, the policeman said, "Good morning, Ladies. I'm Officer Jim McGovern. I've just been talking to Miss Aroho and your friends here. How are you two doing?"

Officer McGovern had a face that was expressionless from the cheekbones down. His eyes did all the talking. They were scrutinizing every eye and facial movement, every gesture made by the women in front of him. He had a running conversation going on inside himself: "Were any of these gals bitten by the firebug? Could be, maybe not.

You never know," Then he looked at Kate and Eily's hands and continued his inner monologue, "Here we go: wallets and keys again." He couldn't help notice that all five from the burning house had keys and wallets in their hands. "Definitely weird. Who does that?"

He voiced his edited thought, "I notice that you ladies all have your purses or wallets as well as your keys with you. I was wondering how you all had the presence of mind to think that quickly given the circumstances . . ."

Annie sarcastically answered, "Practice, practice, practice."

"Not a good answer, lady," McGovern mentally noted.

Mimi stepped up and said, "Look, Officer McGovern, it might help you to know that we've all been conditioned to have the same reaction to grab the keys, grab the wallet, and get out. We were all in a very bad fire many years ago. It teaches you things."

"What fire was that?" he wanted to know.

Siobhan answered, "The Marafield fire, thirty years ago."

"You serious? The one that destroyed the Motherhouse and all those nuns got injured?"

"The very one," Eily confirmed.

"I hope you don't mind me asking, but are you ladies nuns?" McGovern was trying to get this connection straight.

"Not any more," Kate clarified.

"Holy cow! Hold on a minute, I gotta get my partner over here. Excuse me, ladies, I'll be right back."

"He thinks one of us did it!" Annie quickly whispered.

Mimi disagreed, "Nah, he thinks I did it and told you all about it in advance and that's why we all have our keys and purses."

As the Officer and his younger partner, Bernie Hogan, came back to the women, McGovern said, "See this guy? This is Officer Hogan. His aunt, Peggy Kielty Hogan, was one of the college girls who helped some of the nuns the night of that fire! We were just talking about that at a Christening party last week at his house. His aunt was there and she was telling some story about it. I don't know how it came up, though, do you Bernie?"

"I think it started with one of my cousins having to decide this school year where to go to college. Her parents want her to go to

Marafield or, at the farthest, B.C. but, naturally, she wants to go to any college a thousand miles south or west of here. So my aunt started putting it to her that she should go to Marafield, her alma mater. Then one thing led to another I guess." Officer Hogan looked around at everyone and everything the entire time he related the story of their now common reference point.

In the meantime, Siobhan was working on the name, "Peggy Kielty Hogan . . . Peggy Kielty! She was in the class behind us. Oh my God!" Turning to Mimi and the others, Siobhan said excitedly, "She was one of the girls who found us in the snow banks after we jumped! Your aunt probably saved my life that night! You tell her you met one of the people she helped that night. I always remember her in my prayer. She won't believe how we met . . ."

It was in an entirely different tone that the interrogation continued and Officer McGovern's eyes had gradually changed from piercing to their more natural twinkle state. Eily introduced the subject of the car. "Officer, an elderly neighbor of Mimi's saw a car parked in front of her house, one street over, this morning around three. She said it was exactly like her own car, but that she owns the only Taurus in the neighborhood. When we walked her home it was gone."

"What's the woman's name and address?" After he wrote the information down, Officer McGovern told them, "We have a lot more canvassing to do here." Turning to his partner he motioned to the people still milling around in the street and Officer Hogan took off toward them. He added, "Let me finish up with you ladies and then I'll go have a word with Mrs. Eihler. And, no offense, ladies, but you look pretty beat. Do you have someplace you can go after this? Do you need to call anybody?"

"The woman you're going to interview, Mrs. Eihler, offered her house to us," Mimi said. "We'll walk over there in a few minutes. I'll call my sister from there after I think she's up. We'll probably all go stay with her after that."

McGovern was glad they had a place nearby to go to right away. He resumed his questioning. "Now, back to the car. Do any of you happen to know anyone who owns a Taurus?"

They all shook their heads "no."

Eily leaned forward and whispered into Kate's ear, "Are we allowed to guess who might own a Taurus?"

He caught her, "What was that?"

"She said 'are we allowed to guess who might own a Taurus?'" Kate repeated.

"Go ahead," he breezily agreed, looking at all of them, "take a wild guess!"

Mimi seethed aloud, "This is one guess that will only be 'wild' if it's wrong . . ."

Chapter 82

Josephine was traveling east on Route 202 and was keeping exactly to the speed limit.

It was a particularly dark patch of the trip back and she unconsciously was leaning forward as if that would give her greater visibility. She was also on the lookout for deer.

As she went around the bend she could see ahead of her the unmistakable iridescent strip that runs along the length of a police car. Her heart started hammering. She gripped the steering wheel so tightly her fingers turned cold. She double-checked the speedometer.

Sure enough, sitting right in front of the big green "Quabbin Reservoir Region" sign was a patrol car.

"Now don't be a stupid ass . . . Stay calm. You're not doing anything wrong. You're not speeding. You have a right to be out here. Just keep going . . . keep going. Here we go . . . okay don't look, just keep driving. Just pass right by . . . nice and easy. There you go! See ya, doofuss!"

Josephine's eyes were focused on the dashboard, making sure she didn't speed up in her nervousness. She looked into her rearview mirror at exactly the same moment that the blue flashing lights went on and the police car pulled out onto the highway after her.

"Shit! Aw, shit!" Josephine could barely breathe. "Wait a minute, maybe he'll pass. Don't panic. Maybe he got a call. Come on, doofuss, move it over .

. . get in the next lane, go on . . . Oh my God, he wants me! Get off my tail, you jerk, I'm pulling over! Easy, Jo, easy . . . don't look frazzled. Be calm. Be polite. Be sweet . . ."

Officer Jack McGovern, bored with his detail, hoped that every car that came around the bend would be committing some kind of traffic violation, it didn't matter what kind. He had drawn such a slow, uninteresting assignment. The only thing that broke up the long midnight to eight tour was to go after cars for speeding or to pull them over for the slightest infraction. Vacation schedules, combined with two guys out, one for a bereavement leave and the other for an emergency appendectomy, found him wishing the month away so he could resume his regular detail. Before the new schedules got posted, he and his brother, Jim, were going to try and get assigned as partners.

Jack's brother, Jim, got along well with his current partner, Bernie Hogan, and they were all good friends. However Bernie's cousin had just come on the force and his arrival posed the perfect opportunity for the McGovern brothers to finally work together and for Bernie to take his cousin, Kevin, under his wing. Well respected and known for their humor and fabulous story telling, Officers Jack and Jim McGovern were referred to in the precinct as "Nice" and "Nasty," respectively, because of their patented "good cop/bad cop" routine. Even on lame assignments like tonight's, Jack knew the time would go by more quickly if his brother Jim were in the car.

The gray Taurus finally pulled off onto the shoulder. Officer Jack McGovern could see when he beamed the spotlight on the car that it was a female driver. Before getting out of the car, he called in the license plate and car make and informed the dispatcher that he was stopping a female, Caucasian, alone, and then he gave the time and location. This was a protocol he appreciated at this hour of the morning with no witnesses around, since it was meant to protect officers from accusations of misconduct for racial profiling or sexual harassment.

He got out and ambled up to the car, resting his right hand on the top of his gun butt while holding a flashlight in his left. You never knew. As he moved up to the driver, he played the light over the back seat and front. The driver already had her window rolled down and looked up at him quizzically.

"What's wrong, Officer?" Josephine asked innocently.

"May I see your license, registration and insurance card, Miss?" the imposing policeman recited.

Josephine fished out her license from her wallet with fingers that trembled and handed it to him. Next she retrieved the registration and insurance card from a zipped plastic pouch in the glove compartment. The tremor in her hands did not go unnoticed when she turned the cards over to the officer. He shone the flashlight onto the license photo then bent down close to the window to look her square in the face and at the same time scope out any hint of alcohol. What he smelled instead was gasoline.

"Miss Quarters, do you know that one of your head lights is out? I'm afraid that's a violation with a fine attached, but no points on your license. You're driving in an area that definitely needs both lights working. There are a million deer up here."

"Oh my goodness, I had no idea! It must have just happened today. I thought this road seemed darker than usual!" The relief she felt was making her giddy. She could hear it herself and, when the policeman turned back to his patrol car to write her up, she reigned herself in with the reprimand, "Knock it off, you idiot! Quit sounding so pleased to get a goddamned ticket! Just keep your stupid mouth shut!"

The policeman returned and handed her the ticket with the standard instructions that went with it. Then he practically leaned into the car as he said, "You've got a pretty heavy smell of gasoline coming from in there . . ."

"You're kidding! I can't smell a thing. Oh my goodness, I hope there's nothing wrong!" Her face finally could put on the worried look she had fought so hard to hide.

He looked toward the fuel gauge as he asked, "Did you just fill up with gas somewhere?"

"No, see? I'm down half a tank. Oh dear . . . I hope it's nothing serious."

"Could be a leak in your fuel line. Want me to take a look?" What sounded like annoying courtesy to her, felt like passing some time to him.

"Oh no, no, Officer! Thank you anyway! I don't have that much farther to go. I'll take the car to my mechanic in the afternoon. Thank you anyway, it's very kind of you. I'm just glad you noticed the smell! At least I know now to keep the windows down a little the rest of the way home. I'll have the mechanic fix that light too! I really didn't know . . . Anyway, okay if I go now?"

"Yes, M'am. Just keep a sharp watch for deer. Actually, I'd advise you to keep your high beams on while you're in this area. Just be courteous to oncoming vehicles. Drive safely." In the four hours he had been on duty, this was only McGovern's third stop. A van and an eighteen wheeler had been his previous hits for speeding. God, this was boring.

Chapter 83

"Loser! Doofuss cop! 'Maybe it's a leak in the gas line . . .' Yeah, there was a gas leak alright, Robo-Cop, but it wasn't in any gas line! Jeezus! He nearly gave me a heart attack! Oh God, I just want to get home, get out of these clothes and take a shower. I don't know if I can sleep, I'm too wound up. Maybe I'll figure out the directions to Thistle, Connecticut. Find my old altar partner from the Chapel, Miss Perfect, the former Sister Maura, darling of Marafield.

"Wonder if Siobhan would even recognize me after all these years . . . I know what she looks like though . . . the 'Master Teacher' from Yale. I saw her on 'Five O'clock Live' last year being interviewed about children and violence in school. Puke! Still doing that 'can't we all just get along?' crap. Like she would know . . . she doesn't know! She doesn't have a clue.

"How would she know what it's like for a kid to go to school and pretend everything's fine . . . to have to pick clothes out to wear according to what bruises or cigarette burns you're sporting that day? She couldn't possibly know the kind of rage that builds up in a kid when I try to tell my mother certain evil things and then get smacked to the floor for saying bad things about my stepfather. We didn't have guns then. We only had matches . . ."

Chapter 84

"Hey, 'Nice,' where's 'Nasty'?" The desk Sergeant asked brightly when he saw Jack McGovern without his brother, Jim.

"He's bringing me coffee like a good little brother!" With that, Jim and his partner, Bernie, came in and sat for a few minutes before report to have coffee and catch up with Jack. The three of them thought they'd pitch the partner thing today before they left. Give the Captain some time to think about it.

"So Jack, how was 'Car 54 Where Are You'? Any action?" Jim loved to tease his brother about his temporary assignment since he knew he hated it so much.

"I'll never be accused of quota netting, I can tell you that much," Jack answered. "I had a rousing night of three speeders, one disabled car, and another one with a headlight out. America slept safely, thanks to me. What did you guys do?"

Bernie said, "we had a Pharmacy alarm go off, a little shoving match at the bowling ally, and a house fire on Locknell Way."

"Wow . . . nice neighborhood. What kind of fire?" Jack was just being curious since they were such big homes.

"A biggie. Whole back of the house is gone," Jim recounted. "I felt bad for the owner. Nice lady. You know the Fire Chief, Tommy

McKavanagh, don't you? He called in the arson squad and they called us. That's how we got it."

"Arson? In Glendarff? What's that about?" Jack furrowed his brow as he sipped his hot coffee. "Did you get anything?"

"Yeah, we got two things: a piece of home made peach pie and one possible lead. Even if the lead doesn't pan out, the pie was great!" Jim joked.

"Well besides stuffing your faces, what did you find out?"

Bernie told him, "A neighbor saw a car, a gray Taurus, parked in front of her house around three, just before fire. She walked up to the fire when she heard all the commotion, and then when she walked back to her house the car was gone. At least we got something. The perp used gasoline, they're pretty sure. So there probably was a vehicle of some kind involved. You wouldn't lug a can of gasoline all around that neighborhood, not at that hour anyway."

"Wait a minute: gray Taurus? You guys might owe me, big time." Jack flipped quickly through his clipboard, gave a big grin and said, "No, you DO owe me, big time! I stopped a gray Taurus on State Road 202, east bound, at 4:20 this morning. Female, Caucasian, alone. Headlight was out."

"Let me see that," Jim said as he grabbed the clipboard out of Jack's hand. "Jesus, you never know . . . look at how the cops in New York collared 'Son of Sam,' remember that one?"

Jim gave Bernie a hearty slap on the back and said, "Ready for a little overtime, partner?"

Jack said, "Hey, wait a minute! Count me in! After all, it was my lightning perspicacity that helped you guys!"

Both Bernie and Jim shot Jack a look while Jim said for both, "Your lightning what?"

"'Perspicacity!'" Jim gloated, "I heard it on a BBC quiz show this morning: 'acute perception' . . . is that me or what?" Jim spoke over their laughter, "You two go tell the Captain about this. I'll go get print outs of the plate, license and address. Meet me back here."

Jim and Bernie went to look for the Captain and got halfway down the hall when Jack yelled after them to wait up. When they met he added, "Hey, I almost forgot! Wait till you hear this . . . The gray Taurus? It reeked of gasoline. I even offered to check out the gas line for her, but she said she'd have her mechanic look at it. Could be legit, you know. Or, she could have had a really bad hair day! I'll meet you up front."

Chapter 85

Josephine was showered and feeling revived. She had determined that her gas stained black shirt was unsalvageable when she took it off and examined it in the light. She tossed it in the hall to throw out when she went back downstairs. The jeans were only a little cruddy from smashing into the hedges, so they went into the hamper. Wrapped in a seersucker robe and with a towel twisted around her wet hair, Josephine picked up the shirt and went downstairs to put on some coffee and have a bowl of cereal.

On a hook on the pantry door hung one of those cloth tubular plastic bag caddies made out of gingham. Josephine pulled a bag from the grocery store out of it, rolled up her black shirt as tightly as she could, put it in the bag and then emptied yesterday's coffee grounds on top of it. She tied the looped handles together then dropped the compact bag into the bottom of the trashcan under the sink.

"Well, congratulations, Josie. Well done. You've put in a full day's work already and, look, the sun's just rising! Boy, when's the last time you saw a sunrise, huh? Why, I think this might be one of those 'Maxwell House' moments: a nice pot of fresh coffee, a bowl of 'Life' . . . HAH! . . . and a red, red sun shining through the back door. Hah! At least I have a back door for it to shine through . . . Ka-BOOM! Maybe I don't have a deck, and maybe I don't have a garden. Maybe I don't have a three car garage, and maybe I

don't have a privacy wall . . . but, baby-baby-baby, I still have a back door! Ka-BOOM, Mimi Aroho, wherever you are!"

"Which reminds me, let's see what's on the local news this morning . . ." Josephine turned on the little black and white Zenith that she kept on the kitchen table and waited for the commercials to be over. As the 6:30 'Morning Update' came on, she washed the cereal bowl and spoon she had used, poured herself another cup of coffee, sat back down and lit a cigarette. The news began with an 'Around the Nation' segment. Junior Bush was making his way to the GOP convention that would start on the 31st in Philly. She scoffed when they showed, one more time, the clip of Bush senior referring to "Dubya" as "my 'boy' and I'm so very proud 'im."

"You'll have to do better than that at the convention, Pops, if we're going to get your 'boy' elected," she advised the screen. Next was a clip of Gore popping the veins on his neck trying to rally the audience. "Clinton's cooked your goose, pal. Too bad. You're probably a decent guy." Then, when Clinton was shown promising to veto the Social Security tax repeal, Josephine blew smoke right onto the tiny t.v. screen. "Go away, will you! Ugh!" She took another puff for good measure and repeated her aimed exhalation of disdain. Then the station cut away for commercials. She nodded and winked at her own power.

When the broadcast resumed, local and regional news started. The anchorwoman, Wonita Kaye, read the teleprompter, "A pre-dawn fire swept through a private home in the exclusive village of Glendarff this morning. Occupants managed to escape without injury from the registered historic home. The Fire Marshall already has indicated that preliminary findings seem to point to arson. Let's go live now to Carol Swinton who's there at the scene in Glendarff . . ."

Josephine wasn't breathing. She didn't even feel the hot, lit nub of the cigarette melding into her finger. The towel fell off her head onto the floor but she didn't feel or hear it.

"Good morning, Wonita. Behind me are the charred ruins of a home so important in the history of home design in Northeast America that it once was featured in Architectural Digest. The owner, a prominent architect herself, and badly shaken by this morning's events, has declined to be interviewed. However, I have here with me one of the members of the arson team

investigating this crime. Sir, what can you tell us about the cause of the fire?"

A gravely serious man about mid-thirty gave a no nonsense synopsis. "We have substantial evidence that we believe will support our initial judgement that an excellorant, probably gasoline, along with other chemically treated flammable materials, was used to start this fire."

Carol Swinton did a follow up, "Can you tell me if there are any suspects in custody yet?"

The fireman was out of his area of expertise but passed on what he had learned, "It is my understanding that police have a lead on a car spotted in the area just before the time of the fire. Other than that there's nothing more to tell." He put his forefinger to the rim of his hat in a tip or salute gesture and walked off camera.

"Well, there you have it, Wonita. Arson in Glendarff . . . probably started, as the fireman just told our viewers, with gasoline. Police may have a lead in this crime: a car seen in the neighborhood around the time of the fire. This is a troubling first for Glendarff and this suspicious fire has left neighbors here both worried and watchful. I'm Carol Swinton for News 12. Back to you, Wonita."

Josephine was paralyzed. Frozen. The high color that the shower had brought to her face had drained. She sat with her jaw dropped and mouth opened, staring at the television, hearing nothing. Robotically, she slowly raised her hand and pushed the "off" button. That small motion began to bring her back and, mechanically, she got up from the table.

Taking the trashcan from under the sink, she emptied its contents into a plastic trash bag, tied it, and walked out to the garbage can at the corner of her yard. After tossing the bag into the garbage can, she moved the can to the curb for pick-up later that morning.

The more she got blood flowing again, the faster she started to move. She put her coffee mug in the sink, picked up the towel that had fallen on the floor and hurried upstairs. She changed into white slacks, a short sleeved red, white and blue scooped neck knit top, and white tennis shoes. Into a floral flight bag she folded navy blue slacks, a navy blue long sleeved tee shirt and her black Rockport walking shoes, and underwear.

For good measure, she threw in a pair of khaki shorts and a pink polo shirt. Next, her cosmetic bag was retrieved from the bathroom, along with her deodorant, toothbrush, toothpaste, hairspray and brush. She dumped the armload on top of the other stuff in the bag, zipped the bag and ran downstairs with the bottom of it hitting every other step.

She went immediately to the car to put the bag in the trunk. Mistake. Gas can. Reversing, she put the bag on the back seat. Josephine walked quickly to the house and collected a couple pairs of latex gloves from under the sink. She removed a brown lunch bag from the kitchen drawer and ran down to the basement. Heading straight for the fatwood box, she opened the bag and filled it with a bundle of sticks from it that she scooped up without being fussy. Upstairs again, she stuffed everything into her shoulder bag, including her wallet and the little notebook she kept by the phone.

Giving the kitchen one final look, she wondered if the Road Atlas she had taken to Glendarff was still in the car or had she brought it in with her when she got back this morning. She went out to the car, saw it, ran back to the kitchen, grabbed her bag, closed the door behind her and locked it. If she could just concentrate on getting down to Connecticut right now, anywhere in the vicinity of Thistle, maybe she'd calm down.

"Easy, Josie, easy . . . could be any car. Doesn't have to be your car. Go to Connecticut. Check into a hotel. Get some sleep. Look at the map. You can do this. They won't get you. You know you can do this. They haven't gotten you yet."

The boldness that began to wax in her only seconds ago, waned again when she looked at the crimson morning sun while turning on the car engine. In a familiar melody of Gregorian chant Josephine solemnly intoned, as mournfully as any bell on a channel buoy ever warned, "Red sun in morning, sailors take warning."

Chapter 86

Making a right turn out of her driveway, Josephine needed to put her visor down since she was heading directly east, facing the sun. Here and there a neighbor walked a dog, or began an early morning jog, or put a garbage can at the curb. The moist unguent of dew on the lawns and leaves glistened under the sun's rays. It was definitely a summer Saturday devoid of haste and hurry. Visually tranquilizing, these scenes briefly colluded in fooling Josephine into a complementary mode with the fresh world around her.

At first, the two cars that had turned onto the same street coming toward her, about six blocks away, prompted only mild surprise that activity was beginning to pick up so early. When the third and then fourth car turned and formed a four–vehicle motorcade slowly advancing, she took note.

In the sun's glare, the cars' colors were indistinguishable. She lingered at the stop sign straining to see. When the cortege was only two blocks away she realized with horror that the roof of each car was mounted with an activated police car lightbox, silently flashing blue and white lights as the police cars slowly bobbed in procession.

She turned left and sped four blocks away. Checking in the rearview mirror, she watched the first car to enter the intersection slow down, then stop. She thought she saw a cop jump out of the passenger side and motion to the cars behind. The two cars following the lead car turned onto the same street as the gray Taurus. Suddenly, sirens split the diurnal serenity of this modest community.

"Oh my God! Oh my God, no!" she screamed, so engulfed in panic that her hoarse cries were strangled with savage sobs. Interrupting herself, she yelled, "Highway! Keep going!" As though answering the voice that had just screamed those directions, she pathetically wailed like a tormented child, "No-ho-ho-ho-ho . . . Nooooo, no, God, no!" but kept driving.

At the next intersection Josephine twisted the car into a violent right turn and swerved wildly as she fought to bring the car under control. Two more blocks and she'd be on the main Boulevard. Even through closed windows she could hear roaring engines, screeching tires and keening sirens getting closer and closer. If she could just get to the Boulevard . . .

With only one block to go and the four lane Boulevard in sight, the gray Taurus slashed through the remaining distance, finally lunging onto the south bound lanes, oblivious of any traffic. What she heard first was like the mournful bellow of a herd of elephants roaring toward her door. The brakes of the enormous garbage truck could do little at such close range but scream under the defying combination of weight and speed.

Josephine saw the driver's bulging eyes and frantic waves and then saw his startled passenger brace both hands onto the truck's dashboard, willing the accident not to happen. Her head snapped against the door window shattering the glass that floated in slow motion arcs all around her. Launched by such terrific impact, the gray Taurus slalomed down and across the lanes, careening into the intersection where a second collision with an unsuspecting bus whammed it into the corner gas station that was about to open for the day.

The owner of the station, standing inside the glass enclosed office, looked up from the register just as the bus rammed the Taurus, flinging the hoodless wreck straight toward the first set of pumps. Reflexively, the owner dove under the counter and was not spared his forecast, "it's gonna blow!"

A spectacular mushroom cloud of flame and thick black smoke shot straight up, taking with it anything that was standing on the island. The gray Taurus had glanced off of the pumps and rolled a few feet when it hit, but had not been spared being consumed by flames. The owner of the station scrambled to his feet, stepping over broken glass and debris from the shelves in his office and ran toward the burning car. Three other men, running from their idling abandoned cars on the Boulevard, joined him. Their valiant thoughts of rescue were terminated before they could be turned into life saving deeds. It was over.

Chapter 87

Mimi's sister, Kathy Gordon, her husband, and their three kids were all busy in the kitchen making a special breakfast for their five surprise overnight guests. Kathy had gotten her clan up early and fed them on the first shift, arranging with her husband that he take them all out on the boat when Mimi and her friends finally surfaced. The children, Mary Kathleen, Daniel and Sarah Jane, generously gave up their rooms and bunked out in the den and family room, thrilled with the vicarious excitement that the fire of the day before had brought into their home.

"Well good morning!" Mimi sleepily called as she walked into the large eat-in kitchen. Behind her straggled in the others who also were recipients of the hugs and kisses with which Mimi had already been showered.

"Okay, guys, 'The S. S. Diversionary Tactics' will set sail in twenty minutes," Daniel Sr. announced to his children, giving a wink to the adults. "That means all people shorter than me should be at the back door in ten minutes sharp with suits on, towels in hand and backpacks loaded. Mush, mush!"

"That's not the name of our boat," Sarah Jane, the youngest, coyly said as she sauntered past her father.

"Now aren't you the bright little listener!" the father beamed at his tiny daughter. "It gets renamed for special occasions, sweet heart. Now hurry up!"

"Kathy and Dan, thanks so much for being so great yesterday and today. You're really a godsend to us," Eily voiced the group's appreciation. "But look, you guys don't have to clear out just because we're awake, you know."

"They know that!" Kathy interjected. "Going out on the boat isn't exactly a hardship for any of them, so don't worry about it. This way we can all talk freely and not have to edit, spell or pass notes. These kids have big ears and want to know everything about everything! Believe me, it's better this way!"

Dan Sr. came into the house from out front and said, "here's the Sunday paper, ladies. Any takers?"

Mimi took the thick bundle from him and sat down at the kitchen table while the others milled about filling their cups, taking some cut fresh fruit and deciding which kind of bagel to have. Mimi, looking for more coverage than the paper had yesterday on her house and the arson, turned first to the "Regional & Local" section and instantly exclaimed "Jesus, Mary and Joseph!"

Everyone flocked around Mimi, gawking at the large photo of the horrendous accident at some gas station in Sparrows Point. The caption above it declared, "Flames End Arson Chase." Everyone was speechless, including Mimi. The others quickly found seats to support their suddenly unreliable legs. Kathy took the paper from Mimi's hands and read the accident account aloud, pausing to add her own gasps of disbelief and horror along with everyone else's. When she finished, she put the paper on the table and stood quietly resting a hand on Mimi's shoulder.

"I feel sick," Siobhan whispered.

"So do I," Mimi seconded. "God help her . . . whatever possessed her into thinking she could outrun a police car, or four of them for that matter?"

"Happens a lot," Eily sadly attested. "The alternative of being caught makes people desperate. Thank God no one else was killed. The gas station owner was right, it's a miracle she's the only one that died." Everyone fell silent again.

"Eternal rest, grant unto her, O Lord," Eily quietly prayed in halting voice.

A somber chorus answered, "And may perpetual light shine upon her. May her soul and the souls of all the faithful departed rest in peace. Amen." With heads bowed in weighty silence, the women at the kitchen table automatically traced the sign of the cross on their bodies, signing 'mystery' onto all that was incomprehensible in each heart.

Chapter 88

"Hi Ted. This is Rob Young. Sorry to bother you on a Sunday morning like this, but is Ellen around? Great. Thanks."

Ellen Kelly picked up the phone and answered cheerily, "Hi Rob. I thought you were leaving for the Cape this morning . . . what's up?"

"I thought I'd give you a call first. I hope you don't mind me interrupting a day off. Ellen, have you been following the news yesterday and today?"

"No, not really. We were in New Hampshire Friday and Saturday for my sister's birthday. We just got back about a half an hour ago. Ted's tee time is 11:30. What did I miss?"

Robert Young rendered an abridged version of the events that had taken place in Glendarff and Sparrows Point to his astonished and appalled listener. When he finished, he wondered aloud to Ellen what her office would do now that the woman she was prosecuting for her client, Judy Mazola, was dead?

"Well, I'm sorry it's turned out so tragically," Ellen said, "but Josephine Quarters' death extinguishes criminal action. Looks like Judy Mazola's options now are to sue Josephine's estate."

Rob pressed, "and all that stuff I told you in my written and verbal reports about Josephine's pattern of alleged stalkings and fires that go back to Marafield . . . that just gets swept under the carpet again?"

Ellen was thinking on her feet. "Give me a minute . . . there is such a thing as 'cause of action,' the infliction of emotional distress that was caused by concealing Josephine's earlier activities. Maybe we should go after the deeper pockets in this case."

"I hope you're going to say what I'm thinking," Rob scrunched his eyes as he waited for her explanation.

"Well, given Marafield's pattern of concealment and deception over these many years that could have prevented injury, destruction and death, I think that they certainly have the more for which to account. I'll talk to Judy Mazola on Monday and have her come in to my office where I can explain this whole incredible saga to her."

"Think she'll be too intimidated to sue an organization of nuns or its mastermind parent company, the diocese?" Rob worried.

Ellen thought a minute then offered, "Well, Rob, maybe this time the lesser angels in this case will finally bow to the higher ones."

"Thanks, Ellen. Thanks."

Printed in the United States
1161600002B/127-132

9 781401 079468